CW00712633

Richard Thornley

THE DARK CLARINET

For Margaret —
dearest Vera Stook —
with all best wishes
Richard Thornley
September 2000.

BLOOMSBURY

First published 1988
Copyright © 1988 by Richard Thornley

Bloomsbury Publishing Ltd, 2 Soho Square, London W1V 5DE

British Library Cataloguing in Publication Data
Thornley, Richard, *1950–*
The dark clarinet.
I. Title
823′.914[F]

ISBN 0-7475-0238-2

Phototypeset by Rowland Phototypesetting Ltd
Bury St Edmunds, Suffolk

Printed in Great Britain

For George,
for N

One

It is best to start with the premise that men are devastatingly stupid.

It was nine p.m., there were few people about. We walked three abreast under the streetlights – me, my wife, and Peter.

My wife is graceful; she seems fragile somehow but she isn't the slightest bit fragile. She was telling Peter about the time she was flown in a private jet from Monterey to San Francisco to give AIDS-free blood to an unknown millionaire who was undergoing open-heart surgery. Peter had his ear cocked, rather too obviously, I thought, making clear the compliment of his attention. My wife is charmed by well-spoken, mock-naïve Englishmen. We stopped for him to light a cigarette.

I had stayed with him in London for a month, seeing people in publishing and television. My wife had joined me for the Christmas fortnight. It was a break from California for both of us. This evening, our last evening, we were going to my English publisher's party.

'Do you stock your own blood?' he asked.

'It's an intelligent thing to do.'

'I don't know if I could be bothered. You really think so?'

I laughed and he smiled, keeping the warmth of his breath behind the upturned collar of his jacket. It was January. Another January in London. He put the lighter back in his pocket, and I took my wife's arm.

I handed her coat to the attendant; Peter escaped us for the reception room upstairs. There were bits and pieces of brilliance upstairs. Writers would shine, were shining, or had shined for reasons they mostly didn't understand. I lived in California now, which had nothing to do with anything other than my love for my wife and her daughter. We lived by the ocean.

She left the self-effacing cloakroom attendant and we walked together up the stairs towards the noise of the party. The right side of her mouth lifted coyly. 'Love you.'

'Love you.'

At the top of the first flight of stairs she stopped me and without any unease or dramatisation she asked, 'Did you want to see them while you were in England?'

'No. Definitely no.'

And yet . . .

And yet it was in this same room, seven years ago, at this same annual party, that I first saw N. I think that it must have been in November. Yes. Not an exact anniversary. More than seven years ago. It had been before Christmas.

I don't think that my wife worries when I stand at the edge of a room like a simpleton. I have managed to convince her that my social ineptitude has something to do with research, that I am observing the people in the room. Perhaps this is in fact what I am doing. I'm not sure. It is as though I have just given up smoking cigarettes and my mind is searching half-heartedly for its missing ability to concentrate.

When I am interviewed, I am asked quite personal questions and have no idea whether my answers are truthful. When, in a newspaper, I read the answers through, I find that they are all unlikely. Nevertheless I take pains to remember the answers I have given, so that I can repeat them to myself at those moments when I have no idea who or what I am.

Writing. I am often told what to write. For instance –

In a car on an English motorway: 'People want something that makes them laugh. There's so much bad news nowadays, we all know that. People don't want to hear any more; write something that makes them laugh, for heaven's sake.'

In a plant for canning mackerel fillets: 'The *things* that go on here, you wouldn't believe it. Never a dull moment. You should put it on the television.'

On the High Barnet Line platform, Camden Town Underground Station: '*I could tell you* a thing or two about what goes on down those tunnels. Someone should write a book about it.'

In a sitting-room, Moreton-in-Marsh: '*She's* the one you want to write about. What a story! When she'd left him, she ran off, yes, ran off if you please, with a brain surgeon to Bournemouth.'

On the forecourt of a garage, Aix-en-Provence: '*Be* careful how you use it. When the Bildenberger was dissolved because Nixon blew it totally, they set up the Trilateral with the money the P2 Masonic Lodge pulled out of the Sniffing Planes affair. It all ties in, Thatcher, the Institute for Strategic Studies, everything. I'm telling you this because you know what I mean and you can get it down on paper.'

Women. Seven people away to my left is my sponsoring editor; in the centre of the room is my . . . I'm not sure what to call her . . . my practical editor? Against the right-hand door is my reader, and near the wall is my publisher. All of them are women. When I asked why there were so many women in publishing, I was told that it was because the wages were so bad. Strange? I am not sure. I am edited by these women, they suggest what I might change in what I write – helpfully, I feel; and tactfully and with sensitivity. I make the most appalling unfeminist slip-ups. I have grown up with these women; they have encouraged me to become a writer, they have introduced me to other people as a writer, they have put the ground underneath where I now presume to stand. On my identity.

My agent is a woman; my wife is a woman.

N did not tell me how or what to write. She didn't care, finally. I wrote.

Food; good, not elaborate. 'How's the food?' I say to Peter, who joins us with a charming attempt to conceal an effusion of wind from his digestive tract.

'Good,' he describes.

He is a little anxious, the initial attraction of his evening having

9

been so satisfactorily exhausted. Now he must decide how to plump out the rest of the occasion, and he looks around for someone to his taste.

My wife suggests that we visit the food, which is further upstairs. I must admit that I would have been inclined to research hunger but we are already on our way out of the room. I like Americans. If someone had remarked to her that there was ice-hockey in the basement, she would have suggested that we grab a puck. People glance up out of their conversations to look at her; a tall, beautiful woman, a woman who is unnervingly innocent. Our house in California faces the Pacific; we step down from the sun lounge to the sand to the ocean, while on the road behind our house television companies film action sequences. Owing to an ecological imbalance her daughter and I can no longer take starfish out of the rockpools, but occasionally we can see a car and two dummies hurtle over the cliff.

There are two hundred people here now; there were two hundred people at the party *then*. I was younger. On my way out of this same door. They all seemed to know what they were doing, seven years ago. Seven years ago the noise was extraordinary, a whole jazzy gilt of worded air; the atmosphere shivered like a thin, tasselled dress. Then, at the door, I might have glanced back in any direction at all, but I looked at a woman who wore this chaos as though it had been created for her. She turned and her eyes were rich, as though she had been making love on top of a man.

The food. Someone has stabbed his cigarette out on a slice of roast beef.

In California my wife and I walk along the beach, wearing coats against the sea mist. Here, now, she is pregnant, and I am, with reservations, overjoyed.

In fact, I am worried. Recently, the Dale Research Library from Chicago has sent me a questionnaire: what am I doing? have I any personal comment about my attitude to Art? And other important matters.

I have already replied, at some length. I said that I was researching about the Vercors, a mountain plateau in France where during the Second World War two hundred French civilians were victims of the most calculatedly sadistic reprisals by adolescent, SS-educated boys. One of them decided that it was better to bayonet a baby just below the left collar-bone; then the baby could be left hanging from a doorframe. Such is research. The Dale Research Library sent me galley proofs, just the other day. Apparently I am writing about Vercors, the little-known French romantic poet.

We must go downstairs again. The eating is impossibly business-like. I don't have a project that I want to discuss.

Seven years ago I wanted to discuss. I had a project. When I walked back down to the reception room I had fired my project with mediocre claret so that it should be irresistible. It wasn't. And all the while I was thinking about the woman who had so dissected me with her eyes.

I had no full image of her. But as I went down the stairs I heard a voice below me which I immediately knew to be hers. It cut through the warm fur of wine like a pure cold alcohol. Before I could recover to protest at this exposure there came a mocking laugh, like glass shattering on the marble floor, and the shards cascaded down the corridor to bed themselves in the soft wood of the street door, which closed, gently and respectfully, behind her.

I take my wife's arm, and we leave my publisher's party with Peter, walking through the deserted London backstreets towards his car.

Seven years ago I had stayed until the very end, sitting in a chair, drinking, attempting to obliviate myself. At two o'clock in the morning – it was piercingly cold although I didn't notice it – I found myself standing with Christopher Isherwood in Oxford Street. We stood for three-quarters of an hour, waiting to share a taxi to North London. I wasn't sure whether he was talking about being a writer or about waiting for a taxi when he said, with a wry grin, 'It must be a hard life if you're an ugly prostitute.' When, finally, two empty taxis arrived at the same moment, we each climbed into a different one by mistake.

*   *   *

In Peter's flat, comfortable and even plush, we sit in three chairs over a late-night whiskey. My wife apologises for an honest yawn and goes up to bed.

I follow her and unpack my notebooks from my case. I don't want to risk disturbing her sleep.

'You don't have to wave those notebooks around.'

'No.'

'Get her out of your system.'

The corners of her mouth are tense, and then, carefully, she is careless. 'I can see that you're dying to talk to Peter. Let me know what you want me to do tomorrow.'

Much to her annoyance I kiss her. It's a token. But as I reach the door she sticks her tongue out at me and smiles. We have complicity.

I am not dying to talk to Peter. We taste a collection of cheeses, flanked by celery. He asks me: 'Are you going to write now?'

'Yes.'

He is annoyed. 'Really?'

'Maybe.'

He exhales contentedly and ferrets for a cigarette. He goes into the kitchen and returns with a packet of Carr's Water Biscuits, a four-pack of Long Life and an unopened bottle of Single Malt.

Just to make sure.

'Well, I'm going to bed,' he says, and: 'It must be strange being back here.'

'It is.'

'See you in the morning.'

'Goodnight. And thanks.'

The first water biscuit crackles between my teeth, like the breaking of the thin ice at the edge of the sea in that coldest of winters, seven years ago.

My wife is right. I don't have to wave the notebooks around; I don't really even have to refer to them. N's letters and my notes are here, they are only possessions.

Two

I left university with a law degree. I trained for three years to become a lawyer, and then I was no longer sure of my belief. I went to work in a community law centre and there I fought with the law. I was approached by helpless people. I could do very little for them except perhaps disguise the fact that they could do nothing for themselves. I became more interested in them than in the law. When the law centre was shut down through lack of funding from the central government, I was left with their lives hanging around me like strips of peeling wallpaper. I wrote to newspapers, I took part in a demonstration and I went home knowing the futility of living in Thatcher's England.

'Thatcher's England' was a cliché. Nobody else wanted responsibility for the shambles of England. It was as though she had been elected by nobodies, from feelings which nobody wanted to recognise. There had been a delicious sensation that we would know the worst after the years of cheesecake socialism. It was in the air; people wished the worst on each other and themselves.

I sat in the parliamentary gallery and watched her make fools of the socialists, her legs usually crossed at the knee, a crowd of baying shireboys behind her; the poor socialists didn't know where to avert their eyes. She was the government and yet she was the opposition, constantly chiding the country for what it was and the hopeless way in which it behaved.

Ideas seemed meaningless. To have an idea was in itself the hallmark of impotence. The country was to have vision, or fantasy. Which required sacrifice. Not the old socialist tightening of belts, but clinical, spectacular sacrifice; the bloodletting of society so that the fantasy might become power.

I had been living in a licensed squat with a woman called Juliette. Our relationship disintegrated. She moved, I stayed. There were a lot of people in the area for whom I had been able to do nothing. I avoided them.

That is all I can remember, and now it is more of a mood. Or a colour which I can squeeze on to the end of a brush. I can choose whether or not to use it. The first things that I wrote were complaints, perhaps justifications.

I started writing about my former clients. I wanted to do something for them, that they wouldn't get lost. That their bitterness wouldn't get lost. A sociological document. 'C is a woman living in poverty as a result of the present housing policy in this borough. Despite the Housing Act of 1985, it will be seen that her circumstances fall far short of what could be deemed socially acceptable . . . '

Underneath it all I had the presentiment that I was nothing; that I had no self, and no feeling other than the fear of discovering that this presentiment was true.

I finally asked a friend about the possibility of publishing these case histories. I was given a telephone number and was then invited to meet a publisher. When I arrived with my papers there were two hundred people in the room, and the publisher asked me if I would leave the papers downstairs in a pigeon-hole. I was introduced to a man who asked me with whom I might compare my style, my outlook. I met this woman at the party – not met her – came into contact with her twice. She looked across at me, once, when I was leaving the room; and then, later on, just as she was leaving the party, she laughed. At that moment I knew that I was nothing, my presentiment was confirmed for me.

That was seven years ago, and still that moment makes me nervous. It's impossible to describe.

I disappeared for a while. Perhaps that's the best way of putting it. I disappeared, for myself, into nothing. There is no record, there is nothing written in the notebooks. I am sure that I survived absolutely normally but I have no recollection of how I did it. I wasn't with anybody. Juliette and I had split up months before. I had kept our rooms but I don't remember anyone else in the house being around. And I have never asked them for any verification.

Normal life just trickled in. Buses, tubes, pubs, reading, making tea, standing at the window smoking a cigarette and watching the pavement, listening in on other people's conversations. A melancholy. The launderette, the dole queue, the supermarket. A slight breeze and the world lifted me again.

On December the first I went to bed with a girl. Probably out of a curiosity to see her flat, to see if there was any female warmth in it. Scratching for a forlorn cliché. We tried to be comfortable sharing a bed, she had National Theatre posters on the walls of her bedroom. I said thank you to her. In the morning, everybody who was walking towards the tube station was holding a newspaper. I accompanied her. I pretended that I would queue for a ticket. She had a weekly pass and so filtered cleanly away down the escalator.

Thatcher's England. Outside in the street, at mid-morning, there was the cheap, smarting scent of redundancy. Men walked the streets because the buildings had shut them out. A sad caricature of empty dignity guided a dog past a parked Mercedes. My England.

The newsagents' windows were covered with postcards which described the view. Ms. Stern was willing to answer your enquiries. Black Marie, Swedish and French lessons. Pauline, full and big. Jean offers massage. Dozens of them. Wish you were here, we need the money. The Victorian value our nanny most admired: self-reliance.

It occurred to me that I might find a job in advertising. Then perhaps if I was successful I would write the words on one of the huge posters under whose tacky splendour the lower-class alcoholics sat, cussing and grinning inanely and holding out their hands.

Just as in the Mall the tourists' heads followed the straight-backed clip-clopping Household Cavalry, so, at dusk, the alcoholics watched from amused delirium as the hunched riot squads travelled north in a repetition of shrieking white vans.

*   *   *

I took the tube up to the scene of a riot.

There is something serene about a burnt-out car. At first I came across a whole line of them, parked along the side of a road. A half-dozen; and that was too many. They were like babies in an intensive-care unit, too many of them and too many slight differences. Strangely enough the line of burnt-out cars was open to the public, but further on there were police tapes stretched across the road. I showed my law-centre identification and was allowed to proceed. I found a burnt-out car whose isolation I could contemplate.

It was extraordinary; it was useless and peaceful.

N.

I can't use her full name because it would be dangerous. I would be justified in using her full name because she had what she wanted out of me. That is the truth.

She will remain as N. If this story was written, she would take it and lie reading it in that huge bed of hers, and she would laugh. Or she might leave this page open on one of the spotless kitchen surfaces, and the easy, mocking laughter would float across from the sitting-room. It would be giving too much away. George? He probably wouldn't read this type of story. He might just by accident flick through the first couple of pages, but he wouldn't get this far. And perhaps she is well out of his system.

'December 10th. Squatters' Meeting.'

I explained to a sullen crowd of squatters how it was that, short of the outright destruction of all town-hall records, there was little they could do to halt the sale of squatted council houses to Thatcher's new petit-bourgeois gentry.

I was aware that I had been asked to the meeting as part of a tactic by the Committee to mobilise the usually apathetic membership. At every anarchist meeting I have ever attended, I have been taken for a policeman. I was also aware that more than a few people at this meeting were quietly investigating the possibility of buying cheaply the houses which they now occupied so righteously.

I left the room. On my way to the toilet, one of the Committee passed me and smiled.

When I returned to the meeting, I saw N.

On what pretext did *this woman* come here?

Why? What could this woman possibly want here?

I sat at the back of the room, two rows behind her. All that I could see of her, now, was a black high heel hanging negligently away from a nylon-covered ankle.

The meeting was claustrophobic and yet non-existent. The voices changed. The talk was serious and passionate. The talk was full of commitment. I watched that slim ankle and the cushion of the heel in its darker nylon.

The voices changed. I had attended many such meetings at the law centre. Such talk of socialism now filled me with dread. Once, twice, a dozen times, the toes bent restlessly in their leather darkness, and the shoe slid upwards in caress of her ankle. And then the tendons stretched and the back of her shoe ran softly down the ramp of thin nylon.

It was for her own gratification. How could she know that this small area was all that I could see of her, or dared to see of her? And did she know that this play, this action of sliding her shoe on and off her ankle would simultaneously condense and banish any sense of reality that I had.

At times a vertigo of tension broke from above me in a giddy wave which slapped backward and forward from wall to wall. The small patch of floor swayed. And above it the tapered, cold stiletto hung suspended, faithfully submissive until invited once again to press itself upwards against her skin.

This was the only movement that I saw, the only sign she gave of life; this slow, intermittent conjunction of the human heel with the inhuman object which she summoned at her pleasure.

I could understand no other statement, no other image.

When the meeting finished, and the people in the room stood up, I was left looking at an empty frame, a still-life of light chair leg and worn carpet.

I looked then at the faces of all the people who were leaving the meeting, the interests and the resolution, the pleasure imparted by the meeting, a constructive meeting it appeared. She had bluish grey, reflective eyes, an air of self-containment; you would have said that her face had been stamped in a mould of flat, vulgar beauty, that her mouth had resented this, and that in return she had demanded eyes which could stare across waste-tips with equanimity.

I would have left the room and returned to the street with the image of decadence she had given me, the confusion and the stasis. But she looked across at me with the accusation that I had profited unfairly from her presence.

We stood, half facing each other. She kept her hands in the pockets of a leather jacket and it creaked quietly at her waist and shoulders, a peaceful sound, like the spots of rain pattering against the outside of the windows.

It was presumed that the rain would strengthen. The rain seeped into a general conversation and the members of the Committee started to leave so as not to get caught up in it. I was asked to close the door behind me when I left. I said that I would.

I asked her what had brought her here. I said that our seeing each other again was a coincidence. Was she a publisher?

'No. I was at that party because Deborah is an old friend of mine.'

'And are you a squatter?'

She smiled. 'I don't think so. I gather that there isn't much future in it.'

'There might be.'

'I suppose so.'

I bent forward and picked my papers off the chair. She said: 'You were introduced to Deborah, you hoped that she would publish your project.' She looked at me as though I was a ragged mutt. 'You don't think that she will?' she enquired.

'No.'

'And if she doesn't, is that the end of the world?' Her voice was even and yet edged with a fine suggestion of concern. At that moment I must have been so apparent to her. And then she let the matter drop, as though innocent speculation was nothing but a nuisance to her. 'I'm glad we managed to meet. I hoped that we would. Shall we go somewhere for lunch?'

At that moment the rain flurried and we chose to wait it out. I sat down. She lit a cigarette. I glanced at the back of her leg, at the knee where the nylon bridged and bypassed the joint, at the skin underneath this netting, at faint lines in the skin like there were in the cross-section of an apple, and a small area discoloured, a birthmark.

She moved away and went to stand at the window. She looked out at the rain.

The room thickened with sexual malaise. An unattached anxiety roamed between the wooden chairs. I wanted to ask her questions, obscene questions which she would answer objectively. 'Yes, she knew that he was watching her during the meeting, knew and felt that he was watching her foot.' 'No, she did not mind being a sexual object, as long as the humiliation was personal and not abstract.' 'Yes; she would like to watch two men making love.' 'Sometimes she had the exquisite desire to crouch and urinate over a Member of Parliament's face.'

She turned, with pale lips at the edge of her teeth. 'You are probably selfish and lazy with women,' she said; 'you've treated them lightly.'

I denied it.

As indecisively as it had come, the rain departed. The sky was still grey and greasy-thick with cloud. We walked out, closed the door behind us, and went to look for a pub on the outskirts of the local street market.

She picked her way amongst the squashed vegetables and rotten fruit discarded by the market traders. In the pub her glance skipped scornfully over the admiring stares of the men. With no word other than a polite 'thank you' she arranged for us to sit in the corner of the saloon bar while I bought our drinks. Underneath the blanket of cigarette smoke, down below, where we could still smell the staleness of yesterday's ash, she drew quick lines about herself. She had designed clothes, she said, with her first husband; she had lived in London, they had been very successful even in the early days when they had done the markets, they had soon graduated and had lived well. She had left him the business. She now lived in Portsmouth. She had two children, two boys. The elder one had been permanently in trouble for stealing cars, and now lived mostly abroad with his uncle. The younger one was at private school. She had been married twice. She part-owned and managed a restaurant.

She spoke without hesitation, concisely. At the end she asked me, 'Why did you give up practising law?'

I said that I was not sufficiently involved. I felt her eyes scan my face. Her hair, longish and dark, was drawn back over the top of her ear and held in place with a comb.

'No,' she said. 'Perhaps you were too involved. You must have wanted your freedom.'

'No, it wasn't that.'

'It must be difficult for you to make a living.' She dismissed my objection.

'It must be.'

'But you have your freedom.'

'Yes, I do.'

'And?'

'Yes, I have my freedom.'

I couldn't meet her look; for my freedom was truly a shabby freedom and her eyes were mocking. The saloon bar all at once disgusted me with its idiotic banter, the cheery end-of-the-day smugness of market folk, that whole raucous orchestration of street-life into which the thin clarinet wail of a woman's shoe had stepped so calmly.

Her maroon fingernail scratched at a strand of white cotton on her skirt; she picked up the cotton and placed it on the brown, varnished table. 'I think we should go,' she said. She stood up and moved away from the table, certain that she had not left anything of importance behind.

They had swept the streets of debris. Men with gloved hands fed boxes of bruised fruit to a steel-jawed council wagon. She lifted her head against the closing December gloom and smiled. Now that she no longer had to watch where she trod, she hailed the fetid juicy smell of the market street, her eyes darkened as if she was drugged. She asked me where I lived. I gave her my address. I saw her to a taxi. Her legs, momentarily, were slim and well shaped.

I carried home many images of her. She could not refuse me, and so I could play freely with her in my mind. She was accessible. I found her when and how I wanted her. I am sure that she expected this. She left me to be alone with her. Her eyes never wavered. She had a certain sharp coquetry about her, which was what I wanted before we took our razor blades and opened thin red lines on each other's body. She was constant. She was spoiled and desirable in the spoiling, controlled and evasive.

Right from the start it was as though I had come across something in myself that I wanted to know about and yet to accept ignorantly.

I desired her, and I was fascinated by her.

'You are selfish and lazy with women.' I don't believe that it was true, and yet it was convincing.

And yet it was almost as though she was referring to herself, to how she was with men. She knew about herself. That is what fascinated me. I wanted to know what she knew about herself.

Three

It is a business notepaper, carrying the name and address of the restaurant; there is a small commercial line-drawing at the top left of the paper, and a telephone number.

'I am coming up to London this weekend to do some Christmas shopping on Monday. Could we meet? I will come to your flat after lunch on Tuesday. I hope this will fit in with you, I would like to talk something over. I owe you lunch but can't do it this time around. Let me know if it's inconvenient. Yours . . . '

I received the letter on Monday, so there was no way of contacting her. She was already in London. Also in the post was a package containing my manuscript, with a short note of apology from the publisher.

On that Tuesday I went out at noon and returned home at three, certain that she would have come and gone. I had in fact put the room in order, I had arranged papers on the table, left two books open in mid-chapter and moved several remnants of Juliette, sentimental debris, from the bedroom into the small kitchen area where they held a cautious prominence.

I kept watch from the window. At three-thirty a white Mercedes parked against the pavement several dozen feet from the door to the house. After bending forward and changing her shoes, she stepped out of the car and locked the door. With her hands in her coat pockets, a black coat, she walked towards the house and I lost sight of her.

She had brought me a Christmas present.

I thanked her. She laid the small oblong box, store-wrapped and red-ribboned, on the table between the two piles of paper.

'Can I have a cup of coffee? Or tea will do fine.'

I apologised for not having asked her. She followed me across to the tiny kitchen. She looked at the bits and pieces of decoration – ornaments, photographs, newspaper cuttings – which crowded the shelves and cupboard doors.

'With milk?'

'Black, please. No sugar. I have a tablet instead. NutraSweet. It's probably cancerous but it's less fattening. May I use your bathroom? London is so filthy.'

I showed her the bathroom. Her eyes moved quickly, gaining information. I returned and switched on another bar of the electric fire. She used the toilet, and when she came back into the room she glanced at the fire and took off her coat. She sat on the wooden chair which usually faced my table, an uncomfortable chair unless you were working at the table. I placed her coffee on top of my returned manuscript. She took a small white plastic box out of her handbag and shook her NutraSweet into the mug. I brought her a spoon. She chatted.

'I shouldn't have taken the car but I honestly couldn't face dragging parcels back to Portsmouth on the train. I'll have to leave before the traffic builds up. It's all a bit of a rush. Do you live here on your own?'

I said that I did at the moment, with these two rooms; the house was shared. This room and the bedroom.

She stood by the door to the bedroom, holding her coffee and sipping it. Her investigation flitted from the bedside table to the chest of drawers to the closed wardrobe.

It was incongruous. The room was much too small for her elegance. The dress and the perfume were expensive. I wanted to get her out. I asked her what she wanted to talk about, she had said that she wanted to talk about something in her letter.

She asked me if I had a girlfriend and I replied that I had lived here with a girl, that we had split up months ago, nearly a year ago. Had she found someone else? Yes, I thought so, but I didn't know if they were still together.

'You don't keep in contact?'

23

'She's abroad, and there doesn't seem much point. There's nothing to talk about.'

'I had exactly the same answer from my first husband – that there wasn't much point. My second husband was more involved in bringing up the children, so we keep in touch . . . '

I didn't listen to her. The fact that she was speaking gave me the opportunity to look at her face and more specifically her mouth. I watched her speak and I imagined her maroon dress lying limp across a chair in the bedroom, her stockings hanging from the back.

'I did come here to talk about something. But I'm going to get caught up in the traffic unless I go now. I didn't want our meeting to become so personal.'

I said that I too had to go out. We stood up and I helped her on with her coat. We were out of my rooms very quickly and very easily. I noticed that we had been together for an hour, which surprised me.

I walked with her to her car. She chatted on about the traffic. She left the pavement and went round to her side of the Mercedes, unlocked it and sat inside and reached across to unlock my door. She said that she could take me to . . . where? . . . to Victoria, if that was on my way. I joined her in the car. I looked quickly at various parts of her body. She kicked off her heels and felt down to the rubber mat for her flats. She handed me the heels and asked me to drop them somewhere in the back. I did so. They were still warm inside and slightly moist. I placed them amongst the stack of multicoloured Christmas packages. I had touched her somehow. It was uneasy. It was nothing. She started the engine. I looked ahead through the windscreen.

She was smiling to herself. She turned right at the top of Bryantwood Road and went down to the lights. She let the engine idle and stretched back to arrange her dress and coat more comfortably.

'I know that you have a legal training. I want something done. Would you be willing to travel?'

'Where to?'

'Portsmouth.'

The lights changed and we followed the traffic into town.

'I think so.'

She drove fairly fast down the Caledonian Road.

'I know that Deborah sent back your book. I'm sorry. She said that you might have promise.'

We drove in silence. She watched the traffic and I felt strangely gloomy. Not about anything in particular, but about myself. And about the way she brought things into the open.

At Victoria, she stopped the car. She pulled in against white-painted pedestrian railings which came halfway up the side of my door. I thanked her for the lift. We were parked on double yellow lines. I didn't want to look at her; her body would be lit by the orange neon sign of a fast-food restaurant just in front of us, and her eyes would be watching me from the shadows of the car.

I didn't want her friendship. I looked up over the heads of the pedestrians and saw that we were parked outside a bank. A Lloyds Bank with Victorian windows, many small panes of glass and the familiar green plastic panel between the ground floor and whatever offices or flats were above it. 'I always wanted to rob a bank,' I said.

'You're not the type. I've had enough of all that, I lived with it. I wouldn't waste time trying to do things you don't do well.' She leaned forward to replace the cigarette lighter. As she sat back her face caught the glow of the neon and I saw that she was tired.

I asked her, 'What do you want me for?'

She said, 'My husband has been imprisoned. He's an innocent man, in the widest sense.'

The passing traffic shook her words. She stopped and drew on her cigarette. When the lights changed behind us, the road fell quiet and she finally spoke over the hushed, surf-like turbulence of the car heater.

'I want you to find out if there is any possibility for an appeal on his behalf.'

She stopped as the traffic once again laid its barrage around us. Momentarily her bared hand stretched into the light. She wore an engagement ring and an eternity ring. The cigarette cut a diagonal; she tapped her thumb and her little finger on the steering wheel.

25

Lowering the window, she dropped the lighted cigarette out on to the road and started the engine of the Mercedes.

'I'd better let you out,' she murmured. 'We can't talk here.'

She rolled the car forward beyond the railings.

'I'll write,' she said. 'After Christmas, when things have settled down. Have a good Christmas.'

'Thank you, I will. You too. Thank you for my present.'

I got out of the car. I walked away, past the bank, becoming one of the thronged half-people on the pavement, distracted by the different shop windows, each a part of Christmas.

I looked back. The buses and cars were bottled up behind the pedestrian crossing. The road was empty except for the white Mercedes. Without her heels she was shorter than I had expected. She stood by the side of the car, taking off her coat; which she folded and threw across to the passenger's seat. She ignored the traffic warden who was standing with his book in his hand, writing. I ran back towards her, to intercede or to use some legalistic jargon. I slowed down, unable suddenly to regulate my breath. ' . . . what you like with it, it's not my damn car.' I heard her, and the door slam; saw her immunity and the Mercedes drive off.

I was carried home on the Piccadilly Line. The electric fire was still burning and the room was a block of heavy, scented air. I didn't need to open the package to know that it was a pen. I sat up with a bottle. There was something wrong with her. She was too polished.

Her perfume wouldn't die.

The following afternoon I closed the two books and sat before the papers that I had arranged for her visit. Arrange them as I might for myself, I couldn't read them through. These case histories were hopeless, the people were hopeless; there was nothing I could do for them. Even as I remembered them they had had more hope. I had made them hopeless, I had fixed them that way.

I thought of N. I thought, that if she was kind it would break me, it would snap me into pieces. I utilised the image of the chair, of her dress and stockings. She momentarily crossed my mind.

Her letter arrived on Friday. It was brief and cold. She suggested that we should have a contract. It was her wish that both of us should be protected from any misunderstanding.

I pulled my manuscript off the shelf and over the weekend I set about regrouping the material. I would approach it from a different angle, I would draw from the different cases to illustrate a series of situations. I had been too attached to the people; they were incapable of fronting the argument. There was something irrevocably failed about them.

I missed her. Just once, but that was enough. I was in Knightsbridge and heard that fist-on-the-table thump of a bomb explosion, several streets away.

I walked quickly towards the sound. The usual Christmas crowd had thickened to immobility on the pavements, a curdled slop of consumers had spilled into the streets. The road ahead was empty and cordoned off by white police tapes.

In a sudden confusion of time and place I thought that I would see the white Mercedes, parked on its own in the naked glistening street; she would be standing by the driver's door, shedding her coat.

I moved closer.

There were simply shattered plate-glass windows and mutilated plastic mannequins with tatters of expensive garments hanging from their limbs. Bits of antique furniture and blackened mock boudoirs. Shreds of lingerie and tweed, satin and twill, splinters of tableware and the sound of the generators of the fire engines outside Harrods.

It was a wonderful sight: Harrods lit up, with scabbed bowels, Harrods bombed. And a silent crowd watching this great statuesque slut having its sores sluiced in front of everyone.

I looked around and saw several faithful souls, their eyes alight with contentment. I let myself be sucked away with the rest of the scum into the stinking mouth of the tube station. In the airless belly we were all supposed to recover our sense of gravity. And we did so. I gawped up at an advertising poster. Slim, long, exciting legs, as perfect as N's. I grasped hopelessly at the cleansing vision of destruction I had stolen from the street.

*   *   *

27

I telephoned her. I was hurried. Long after I had put the phone down the sound of her voice, making our arrangement, lingered.

I went out. There were riots across London and I was caught up in protecting people from the nervous police backlash. I was arrested on a hammed-up charge of obstruction and, once out of the area, I was quickly let go. In the pub at lunchtime it was rumoured that Stoke Newington would be next.

Disperse and go to your homes.

On Thursday I went to Portsmouth to see her.

Four

At that time I wanted, and I saw, only bits of people. I saw the angles formed by certain parts of the body, the cast of a chin, the padded geometry of juxtaposed limbs. And with clothes: I saw the point where the edge of the material touched the skin, the brutish friction between delicacies, that inflamed area between the shields and the crates of petrol bombs. The buttoned cuffs of a shirt against the wearer's wrists, a tight collar against the back of the neck, the hem of a skirt against a leg, the edge of a shoe against a foot – stimulated areas that run riot with the senses. Whole people were a fabrication.

I took a train from Waterloo. At Clapham Junction, with its multitude of lines, crosspoints and platforms, she was a child's game of tops and bottoms. Bits of her were flung as far as the eye could see; my images of N and her accoutrements were scattered back over the dull grime of the blistered city.

Farncombe and Godalming were unimportant dormitory towns. The late afternoon breathed a blue-grey mist over the countryside. Half the passengers left the train on the outskirts of London. Small groups boarded, rode for two or three stops, and got off. Housewives, college students, railway workers. Outside the window, between fence posts of dirty cream concrete, patches of green defied the dusk. There was an orange gas of sunset on the horizon.

The light bulbs in the ceiling of the coach were reproduced outside the window, the trunks of the trees lost in darkness. A man in a grey executive raincoat stood up to adjust his tie and gather his umbrella from the luggage rack. It looked as though he was preparing for suicide, so precise were his movements.

The train slowed. At Milford Station there were puddles on the tarmac platform and the platform lights hung like small shower-heads. The man stepped out, slammed the door and opened his umbrella.

In my notebook there is also the reminder that my ticket cost £12.50, to be claimed from N.

Liphook. One orange streetlamp and one smoking chimney. The silhouettes of the silent passengers crossed a wooden foot-bridge against the thin slit of smudged magenta horizon. By the time I got to Portsmouth, night had fallen.

There was only one slim, central platform, to whose sides both north- and west-bound trains climbed.

From a delicately patterned wooden roof, twin lines of cast-iron poles, freshly painted in bawdy post-office red, stretched down to clasp the concrete on which I alighted. As if to avoid offending the matronly town of Portsmouth, the whole platform and its roof were encased within an ugly open-ended screen of wood and steel, about whose dark and airy secrecy hung the fresh-scented enticement of the sea.

That wonderful, intoxicating smell! I was overwhelmed by her element, I drew deep lungfuls of the bittersweet perfume and was exhilarated.

I took a taxi. I asked the driver to stop on the promenade. I slipped over the wall and stood on a narrow band of shingled beach.

A mass of sea shifted harmlessly in its black grave. The wind complained softly across the quiet belly of the water. I dug my feet into the shingle and advanced. I tried to light a cigarette, but three or four times the phosphorus flared only briefly against the starless night.

I made my way back to the taxi and questioned the driver. He told me that her restaurant had a reputation for good food. That the town was not especially poor. It had been hit by the recession but there was a large weapons and electronics industry, and of course there were visiting American warships. In the summer there would be tourists.

I was dropped in the Old Town. Her premises were just behind the circle of the sea-wall, overlooking the narrow throat of water which funnelled Spithead into Portsmouth Harbour.

It was a large, three-storeyed building of blue painted brick, a public-house sign hanging at the corner. The blue exterior distinguished it from the row of cosy white semi-detached houses which lined the road to the sea-wall. She was at the end of this road. There was a small ill-lit carpark in the shadows of the wall, which had a half-dozen vehicles parked in it when I paid off my driver.

Someone had installed an uncharacteristic bow window on the top floor, almost certainly a bedroom window. It was lit, and I wondered if she was at that moment in the room. To my right there were some steps up to the sea-wall, but even from there it would be impossible to view this room.

The wall was built over a series of brick arches. Each arch was about ten feet deep, its outer side sealed off with concrete. Into one of these arches had been let an open window, and amongst the acid tang of stale urine this space hung like a rectangular portrait in a derelict gallery.

I was shown up to her office. She came to find me sitting among her magazines, circulars and catalogues, on the couch. She opened the door and said nothing.

Her eyes again dissected me. It was a simple statement. She ended it with a vague smile, as though feeling the effects of petty fatigue. I took the hand she offered, she welcomed me, the slight tension in her hand suggesting and searching for reassurance.

She stepped back, in fashionable, thin, black leather pumps.

I liked distance in her, the occasional surety she found in herself as an isolated object. I remembered how she had been at the squatters' meeting, in London. It was a provocation, and a pleasure in and for herself. I watched her as a blind man concentrates on the minimal changes in the soundwaves of darkness, and I saw her as the object of the desire with which she infused me.

She called me. She walked jauntily away from me, down the half-dozen stairs and across the flagstones, leaving me to turn off the light and gather bland looks from those drinkers in the public bar. She introduced me to the barman, telling him that I was doing some occasional work for her. She ordered us a Ricard. Glasses in hand we passed an open hearth in which a log fire had settled for the night. She called back to the barman, that he should keep the fire alive.

I followed her up two flights of narrow stairs, the cream curtain of her skirt swinging around her calves.

Five other tables were occupied in the small restaurant which stretched to the sea-wall. The building was like a snakes and ladders board. We sat in raised seclusion behind a balcony, on the opposite side of the room from windows which looked out on the harbour. We looked out on the other diners. It surprised me that she didn't greet them; in the few small expensive restaurants where I had eaten, the owner had acknowledged his clients. And this was a small expensive restaurant, like a club room, with good paintings and unobtrusive service.

I asked her if she would order for both of us.

I was perhaps insecure at the surroundings, but as dinner unfolded I became convinced that I wouldn't like her very much, that my being there was a mistake.

She asked me about London, and London couldn't hold her attention. I told her about the riots and the token legal work I had done. I started enthusiastically and ended up attempting a mixture of cynicism and sincerity which I thought would appeal to her. She succeeded in making me feel shabby. I asked her, coldly, if the meal was on expenses.

'Yes,' she said. 'Are you in a hurry? It's always amusing the way London people arrive, as though they're carrying the burden of the world. Don't misunderstand me, I'm sure you *are*.' She smiled disarmingly. 'The last train is at eleven-ten.'

A waiter passed. She looked angrily towards the kitchen as if to herd him on his way.

'Coffee?' she asked.

'I'd like a wash, if that's all right with you. Before we have coffee.'

'Come with me. I'll show you.'

She led me through the bar and up past the office; she unlocked a door at the top of the stairs and showed me into a large studio room. Beyond it was a bathroom. I thanked her.

'We're not so busy tonight and I wanted to let the restaurant staff go early. Friday and Saturday nights are very busy and then we're into Christmas.'

'I see.'

'That's why I had to rush you into dinner. I'm sorry to be so rude. I should have explained. If you'd like to stay overnight you can use this room.' She took a sweater and a pair of jeans off the bed and threw them into a fitted wardrobe. 'I'll be downstairs.'

'Fine. Thank you.'

She smiled briefly, wheeled, and left me. I waited until she would have reached the bar and then I went down to the office and collected my bag. I took off my watch and saw that it was only nine-thirty. I washed my hair under the shower, changed my shirt and lay down for a moment on the large bed. It must have been the wine and the sea air, for sleep instantly engulfed me.

I awoke an hour later. There was a cup of steaming black coffee on the bedside table, and a note. Her scent trailed from the door. 'If this coffee is cold I will have gone home. So will the train. Raid the kitchen for breakfast. I will be in earlyish.'

The barman's voice called time, firmly but more respectfully than would have been the case in London. He was washing glasses when I passed him. N was sitting alone at her table in the dining-room, she had some paperwork in front of her. I apologised for having slept.

'It gave me a chance to get this done. I just have to go through and check the chef's list and then I'll be finished with it.'

She came out from behind the table and walked to the kitchen. 'Or do you want to go back to bed?'

I said that I was no longer tired.

'I like this time when everything's finished. Do you want something in your coffee? Irish?'

'Please.'

She put the bottle on the hatchway. 'Cream?'

I shook my head. The coffee was good. From behind the balmy

33

screen of sleep I crossed to an even-tempered lull, listening to the intermittent sticky sound of freezers being opened and the shish of her pumps across the tiled floor. I smoked one of her cigarettes; she had left the pack behind, with her gold lighter. Smeared on the rim of her glass and on the freckled skin of two cigarette ends was the red tracery of her lips.

She returned and plucked the handset off a wall telephone. She dialled, she looked at me, she smiled and turned away. She dictated her meat order and hung up.

'*Mister Bennet.*' She mocked a deep, solemn intonation. 'He's not terribly sure of answering machines. Or of me, for that matter.' She sat and poured herself a fresh coffee. 'Right, what shall we talk about?' She raised an eyebrow.

'Why is your husband in prison?'

'For murder.'

She sipped at her coffee and I heard, and seemed to feel, its slow fall down her throat. I followed the line of her neck to the first, opaque, fastened, white button on her shirt.

'And you think he's innocent?'

'No. He's guilty. I said the last time we met that I thought he was an innocent man, in the widest sense.'

Her look softened, with compassion I thought. Though I couldn't immediately see where this compassion was directed, whether for him or for herself. 'It was four years ago and there's nothing unsolved or horrible about it. And there's nothing hidden in me which you might disturb. It's all out in the open and done with. You don't have to worry about blundering around, I'm not a secretly tormented person.'

Fine. I watched her stand up and edge out from behind the table, her hip, the pleats of her skirt brushing my elbow. She suggested that we went downstairs. Leave everything for the staff to clear. Would I see that the fire wasn't going out, and there was the same whiskey behind the bar. She would make a new pot of coffee.

'Only for yourself.' I was as awake as I wanted to be. A blurred reflection of her shirt slid across the stainless-steel surface on the other side of the hatch.

I added a log to the fire and made a fireside out of two wingbacked chairs. I tracked the sound of her footsteps and the quiet swish of her skirt towards me.

'No Jameson's?'

'I don't think I'd better.'

She walked past me and bent forward to put the coffee pot down on the table. She straightened up, and turned. I had on my lips the faint outline of a sentence but she provided for my distraction. 'I think you *had* better. I'm going to drone on at you.'

She sat in the chair; settling her legs and skirt she talked me through my way to the bar.

'I'm not the only person in this. There's George's brother, Gerald. Although I'm independent he keeps an eye on things to do with money; so he knows that I am talking to you. You'll meet him and . . . anyway you'll understand. He likes to know what's going on, and it's better to tell him rather than have him latch on to some crazy idea. That's the reason for the contract.'

She was gently turning the eternity ring round and round on her finger. Abruptly she reached for a cigarette. 'He might be useful to talk to about George.'

I didn't understand why she had gone off on this tangent. 'Where is he?'

'He's in Portugal at the moment. He divides his time between London and Portugal. My elder son is out there with him. They get on.'

I brought the whiskey over in silence. When I sat down she still didn't say anything.

'Okay.' I nodded to show that I had taken it in.

She smiled ruefully. 'I should think he would be bored to death out there, but it keeps him out of harm's way. We're not the best of friends, Paul and I. He saw me as a threat to his relationship with George . . . '

' . . . who is his father.'

'No.'

She laughed. Her eyes caught the firelight and passed it across to me, filtered in her own colours. Amusement flickered seductively, but her skin was so smooth, her face so depthless, that

35

I thought of two Mexican – stupidly – two multicoloured plastic jumping beans – her eyes – on a vendor's hardboard tray. I looked at the fire and remembered the riots, the sudden diaphanous glare of the petrol bombs, the same colour as her skirt, a contrast to the gnawing ripples of flame along the logs.

She told me that she had grown up the second sister in a family of three children, a destructive and bad-tempered girl with a brother and sister much admired by everyone for the way in which they assumed adulthood on their father's early death. She hated to be ignored. The family was reconstituted, nothing was said but it was all very definite; her mother went out to work and it was everyone for themselves. 'My mother lived off parading her grief. Other people's sympathy was more valuable to her than ration cards.'

She laughed again, this time with an edge, as though she thought she might be going a bit cranky. She ran her hand through her hair, gathering it back into a ponytail, and she tugged at it. I had an image of her causing herself a slight and not unpleasant pain. Something in her voice made me wonder if she cared a jot about her childhood.

'Ration cards?'

'I don't think they were in use even when I was a baby, but I remember them as words coming from my mother. It wasn't a very musical house.' Her expression veered between amusement and contempt. 'I started bringing boyfriends back as soon as I could, wanting her approval. When that didn't work I got married. I stole the money and dragged him up to Gretna Green. *He* was Paul's father.'

'Immediately?'

'Oh no. We were working very hard, making and designing clothes. Glorified trash really. We skimmed off a lot of easy money and put it straight back into the business. I was hard, and ambitious. When I left him I didn't take anything. That was soft. I've always been much too impatient with people. He always listened to them for exactly the right amount of time. He was an utter politician, I was the bitch.'

'Good partnership.'

'It was until I got pregnant, and then he didn't mean anything to me any more. We were childish when we started and he stuck at adolescence. "The experience that business had taught him . . ." All that rubbish and phoney sophistication at twenty-five. He adored acting as though he was middle-aged. Most of the people we came into contact with were middle-aged and wanted to be successful; he was simply successful and wanted to be middle-aged.' She held out her hand, the palm slightly cupped, as though the necessary exasperation had just trickled through her fingers. 'Three months after the baby was born I only had to suggest the divorce to him and he agreed.'

'Why?'

'I was just another example to him of what life was all about; keeping people happy and getting on in the world. The only way I tried to get through to him was by refusing any support or alimony. I should have stung him for everything he'd got. I must have been mad, looking for his love.'

I said, 'He probably didn't understand.'

'Of course he didn't understand; he didn't want to.'

'Understand what exactly?'

'That a relationship changes.'

'He might not have wanted the change.' I felt unaccountably sad at their splitting up, and more resentful than she appeared to be. Her eyes were flat now, and her expression cold.

'Life to him was a fixed progression – '

'You *both* built it up.'

'And it changed.'

'*You* changed. Women change. But you can't expect a man to throw it up and follow your changes. Why should he?'

'Women change!' She laughed and clapped her hands together. 'I hadn't thought of that. How sweet you are. Perhaps *he* should have gone to feminist meetings . . . ' She rose from her chair and walked lightly across to the bar.

'*You* didn't?'

'I took the baby and ran. Nobody needs to teach you that. You wouldn't have liked him. So you don't have to defend him. Unless brotherhood is your *pièce de résistance*. Of course it isn't, is it? I'd

37

like to think that I was good at sisterhood but I learnt very early on that I wasn't gifted that way.'

The tones in her voice, of sarcasm and sincerity, melodiously mixed, baffled and lured me. 'Damn!' she said. 'Would you go up to the restaurant and bring down a bottle of claret from the racks?'

We talked for another hour or so. We didn't touch the subject of her second husband, George, nor did she elaborate on what she expected me to do for her. Our conversation was for the most part a display of her ability to rule the passing time of night. Her tone was teasing, her intimacies arch.

She held her head high; she would look at me directly, look away and then look back, her eyes having charmingly enrolled her setting – the fire, the Persian rug, the abundance of cream silk – to complement her voice. 'This is me, here, at home' she suggested simply, and at the same time she was clever enough to intimate that her animation and her allure were my doing, were the fruits of my admiration. Perhaps so, for I felt increasingly languid before her beauty; until, suddenly, she said that we should go to bed.

'My younger son is coming home tomorrow evening, I have to pick up the car and, oh, the usual. Is there anything you need?'

'No,' I murmured, 'I don't think so. Thank you for dinner.'

As we walked away from the fireplace I took the slim cool hand she offered. 'Good,' she said, 'I'm glad you understand. I'll get my coat from the office and call a taxi.'

I waited for her at the foot of the stairs, and followed her to the door. She put on her gloves; now, in her heels, we were at the same height. The coat was cold, her eyes and neck warm. She belted the coat around her.

'Have you got far to go?'

She shook her head. 'No. Put the guard up in front of the fire before you go to bed.'

'I'm going now.'

'It's a comfortable bed. I use it occasionally when I can't be bothered to drive.' She looked at her watch and tapped her foot. 'We might as well wait by the fire.' She walked back across the room and stood with her back to the fire, letting the warmth caress her calves.

'We didn't sort anything out, did we?'

She stifled a yawn, her eyes glistened; she shivered slightly inside the coat. 'Enough, I think, for one evening. I want to get Christmas over with. Where *is* that taxi – ' She yawned fully and looked down at her shoes.

'Why don't you sleep upstairs?'

'I was asking myself the same question. But no. I want to take my make-up off, and have a shower. Anyway, I've been here all day. Comfortable as it is, it's still where I work. We'd stay up talking all night.'

She kicked off her shoes and flopped down in the chair. Her toes wriggled inside her stockings. 'I'm wary of talking with someone for hours the first time I meet them. The next morning I usually dislike them and I dislike myself.'

She raised her head and smiled. The expression in her eyes was one of disinterested consideration. 'Can you try the number again? Eight eight, three three, eight eight.'

I went to telephone from the office.

They were assuring me that a taxi should be there, outside in the carpark, when she called up the stairs. 'Sleep well.' Her heels tapped briskly across the bar floor and the door slammed shut behind her.

The guard was in front of the fire. I turned off the lights and went back upstairs.

I had one fleeting image of her; of the cream skirt, exhausted and fanned like beached surf across the stretch of bed. It was three a.m. I pulled the imaginary silk up around my shoulders and went to sleep.

In the early afternoon we walked along the top of the sea-wall, hands in pockets. Our faces were chilled by the wind coming off a crisp, tinfoil sea. She again mentioned that her brother-in-law, Gerald, was also involved, that a contract was necessary to make everything clear. It wasn't just a question of how she and I got on, it was a question of protection – that I should be protected, and that she should be protected, from any misunderstanding.

She glanced at her watch. It was two-thirty and she had to go back to pick up the car from the garage. She looked inland and pointed out various parts of the town, the shopping centre, a museum, the ghetto of hotels, a street which was full of shops selling antiques and bric-à-brac; all of this a half-mile away on the other side of a wide swath of grass, featureless but for the perpendicular war memorial which we were approaching. She said that if I came back to the restaurant she would run me to the station when she went to collect her son, at half past four.

'When will I see you again?'

'After Christmas.' She looked at me, her eyes softened. 'Trust me.'

We reached the monument. She turned her back on it and looked out at the sea as though she detested being wedged between the water and the stone. I asked her what was wrong.

'Family.'

'Why?'

'I have a son who rejects me and one who needs me, less than he used to. Public school has sealed that out fairly effectively. Neither of my sons like each other, and I don't know what to do with them. Christmas isn't an easy time.' Her mouth hard and tense, she stared at the pebble beach.

She turned back. She took my coat lapel between her thumb and forefinger as though gauging the thickness of the material. 'It isn't that serious.' She offered me the pale shell of her lips in the lightest of kisses.

She walked quickly away; she trailed her hand cursorily behind her, a pale white hand with five filed carapaces of ruddy bronze and the ring of ice-blue sapphires. We parted at right-angles; she hugged the sea-wall, I took the tarmacked path which ran in a straight line over the grass. Already, within ten paces, we were cut cleanly apart from each other by the whipping breeze and the clashing colours. She was adrift against the light and dark greys of the sea, I was absorbed by the expanse of emerald-green grass. We were the two insignificant points on this expanding triangle: our kiss remained stationary, behind us, the most endurant point, a small bright-headed pin pricking the flimsy skin of an acquaintance.

* * *

I felt very much at ease in the town. I bought her a pair of silk stockings, the shop wrapped them in Christmas paper and I left the package in her office. On our way to the station she thanked me; she would wear them over Christmas, she had people staying. I watched from a distance as the southbound train arrived. A small boy, neatly dressed in a grey school uniform, walked towards her and she embraced him. He walked away rather stiffly, beside her. Five minutes later the London train pulled in.

Five

I made myself a cup of instant coffee, stirring it with one of the spoons which my wife had used earlier in the evening, that was left out, in Peter's sink, to be washed. Round and round. Past history clinking against the side of the cup, round and round, in the bright kitchen light.

I carried my coffee from the kitchen, I opened the Scotch and poured a measure into the cup. Sipping at the coffee, I stood behind my chair, looking down on my notebook.

How had it been?

'Trust me.'

Asset-stripping had been a negative term, even amongst most Conservatives, in the 1970s. In the 1980s straightforward and shameless plunder was the governmental morality. For two decades the poor had been taxed at their place of work in order to purchase their part-ownership of the economic substructure, and this was then promptly stolen from them and sold off at a low price to those who had any money left. Who could have any trust in such a spasm of government? It didn't matter that one part of the equation was Left, and the other was Right; the net result was that only a simpleton would put any trust in Government. What people would bother to vote socialist ever again, in order to assure themselves of the privilege of having to work half a lifetime to buy back what had been stolen from them?

There was nothing to trust.

'There are ways of getting round women –

'One lets them keep one financially, and thereby one is no threat to their independence.

'One encourages them to talk about their past. One listens, with the occasional pertinent interruption. One never talks, uninvited, about one's own past except at moments of extreme tension in the relationship, and then one briefly presents an imaginary and convincing replica of the truth and immediately dismisses it as being of no importance.

'One assumes self-knowledge without mentioning it. To avoid smugness one allows them to see gaps in one's self-confidence. One presents these failings as a challenge to oneself.

'One should certainly not be ill. Nor should one join clubs or groups.

'One should occasionally be sad, which holds a certain charm.

'One should bear in mind that none of the above will work for very long. There is no way of getting round women. At best one can sidestep the onrush of their expectations, for which one is not responsible.'

I forget what happened over Christmas. I had no inclination to telephone her. It seemed wrong to attempt to make contact. I waited.

On Christmas Day I walked through a quiet city. The river oozed sluggishly past the deserted Establishment. What did they do in prison over Christmas? Religion? A film? Turkey? Paper hats? Guilt? A dismal gut-pain of separation? Memories of blue-grey eyes – vivacious, concerned, set in a pale skin.

When all the newspaper librarians and the lawyers were back at work, I waited for her to advise me. At the turning of the year I started scribbling, five or six lines at a time, short pictures of the people I had known at the law centre, colouring the London which I had found so pleasantly empty. On the morning of January the third I awoke late and saw that it had snowed insistently. It was as though someone had covered the cold metropolis with a large white dustsheet.

I telephoned her.

'Yes!' She broke in on the silent acceptance of her answering machine, an exuberant cry – again: 'Yes!'

*　　*　　*

43

It was decisively cold, like the slap of a banker's hand on a leather-topped table. Portsmouth's gaily coloured pillars hung like frozen football socks; there was no atmosphere to the station. The cold scoured my face, it dragged my breath out by the heels and sharply stocked my lungs until they felt like pin-cushions. It was a terrifying cold, unsoftened by snow.

My driver said nothing; it was enough of a privilege to be out of that cold. How slow the journey was, how safe and slow along the bare black roads, the piercing cold blackness overhead with a smattering of stars.

I walked into an empty room. She stepped from behind the door in a black dress; her eyes were brilliant, she was splendid. She held out her arms and smiled. 'It's the coldest day in Portsmouth for over twenty years. And I defy it. I challenge it!' she exulted. She stood in front of the open door, black against black with a trim of silver. She pushed the door shut. 'How are you?'

I was overwhelmed by her, by her beauty and her complete display, her richness. I was fine. I was . . . I had missed her, now. Like the plunge into scintillating, raw air.

Neither of us could manage the sudden bare predicament of joy. I gathered her and held her tightly, my hands flat against the black sequins which scaled her dress; her lips issued a warm breath against my ear.

'Well,' she said, eventually. She turned away and seemed about to search for an alibi in the silent room.

I occupied myself with my bag, eavesdropping on the sound of her footsteps. When I looked up, I saw the way in which her hair fell down her back. Her head was raised as if she was draining herself of some consumed emotion. I followed her side and her right leg, down to the ankle and the ungiving points of flagstone on which the black rubber tip of her heel trod; her deliberate removal of herself. I asked her, 'Where is everybody?'

'I don't have them in during January. There isn't much business after the New Year so we close down. Some go away and some leave for good. I work up to a full staff again in February.' She chattered on, in strange and level newsprint. 'The place is empty. Thank God. My younger son is down here for another week, bored

44

and watching videos. I said that I would be home by eleven. It was thoughtless of me to bring you down here.'

I gazed at her, similarly without thought.

'You look wonderful,' I said.

'That's how I want to feel. I don't want to explain, not tonight. Can you understand? Stay if you like.' I saw that she was nervous. She walked to the other side of the fireplace, reached for her handbag and gave me a set of keys. 'Look, these are for you. There are two locks on the outside door and this key opens the studio room. You may use it when you like. We'll work together. Once I get myself sorted out. We'll work at it regularly.'

'I won't stay tonight. I can't. I have to get back,' I said, making myself as dispensable as a travelling salesman. She would not be so frightened perhaps.

'We ought to go somewhere else to eat.'

'Yes.'

'I'll think of somewhere.'

'Only for a snack.'

'I'm not very hungry, are you?'

'Not really. And then, afterwards, why don't we go to the cinema?'

'Oh yes. I haven't been to the cinema for years. Yes.' She was pathetically eager, she was diffused and lost.

'I must have a wash.'

I went upstairs.

The atmosphere in the bedroom was dry and close. But the air in the bathroom was saturated with a perfumed humidity, there were tears on the windows. I was immediately steeped in her. Suppliant steam clustered about my clothes, unshyly transferring its attention in her body's absence.

Why was she frightened?

I opened the bathroom window and watched the sucked steam slither away over a metal rim, vanishing into cold blackness. It seemed as though the room had blinked and now stood sadly, its flat cream walls streaked with deceitful misuse.

In the angle between the boarded bathtub and the wall, on the floor, was a pair of crumpled stockings lying whorled, like black rose-heads. I shut the bathroom window and bent down to pick them up, stretching the flimsy net. One of them was laddered, the other was unscarred; I folded it and gently put it into my pocket.

We went out and ate white, plump fish. She wiped shining grease off her lips and, in the smoky light of the car, she re-covered them. We saw *Out of Africa*. An actress managed, cannily, to conjure a crescendo out of heartrending farewells to a countryside and a warmth she loved. There wasn't a dry eye in the house, out of perhaps sixty eyes, save two. N drove me to the station in her comfortable Japanese car. She was calm. I asked her if she hadn't been the slightest bit moved by the film. She said not. 'I started wondering what we were doing there, and then I just appreciated sitting there quietly in the darkness. I think that after Christmas I've simply had enough. Do you feel that I'm wasting your time?'

I looked away. Stark, lit bulbs hung around the station forecourt. She went on: 'There's a lot of things I have to get rearranged. Do you ever feel that there's something at the back of you which needs to be brought forward? I have that sort of sureness. Bear with me.'

She faced me, her eyes focused sharply. I mumbled that I hoped I would be able to help.

'You should go. Otherwise you'll miss your train.'

'Yes, I should.' In haste, suddenly into the very cold, stealing her silk. It was searingly cold, with the pavement frosted like white sandpaper. Bent with the fear of falling, I waved back at the car and she flashed the headlights. She didn't drive off until after I had gone into the station. I still didn't know whether I was supposed to stay. I thought I was being romantic.

An empty carriage. There was plenty of time for thought on the train.

During my affair with Juliette her complaining and her frustration exhausted me and drove me bananas. Quite by chance I learnt that pretending to be depressed was a way round her.

When I used to come back from walking through London as it was then – those first evenings of summer when the warm light fixed the sky over Russell Square and the girls, sitting out under blossom at the sidestreet cafés, dared the summer not to go sour on them and their new love affairs – I would arrive at our rooms with all this budding, this rapture; and Juliette hated it. In order to balance the books she made her life a misery.

I discovered that I should learn to compose my features into an expression of manful-struggle-with-gloom. A weak, strained smile, a stoical furrow on the once proud forehead, my eyes shadowed by the deeper type of pessimistic knowledge – this was a lot better.

Juliette felt more secure in dominance. I would sit at the kitchen table, apparently defenceless, making an obvious effort not to sigh, a tear seeping strenuously through a not-quite-sealed eyelid, and I would watch her through the window as she tra-la-leed and happily inserted potted flowers into our patch of garden. She would turn, brush the earth off her hands, she would catch sight of me with my soul, as it were, pinioned behind my back. And her eyes would soften into a comprehending love.

Occasionally I had to produce some totally faked emotional crisis, and then I could lay my head on her bosom and share the soft consolation of sex.

She never remembered to water the plants; I did this when she went to work.

So fastidiously did I act out my role that I was surprisingly helpless for several months after she ran off to the Algarve to seek happiness with a wealthy drug dealer.

Nothing works for very long.

Waterloo, and a taxi. On expenses.

Croft. George Croft. The trial was in the autumn of 1982. Murdered Robert Emerson.

'The climax to a career of violent, self-aggrandising crime.'

'A cleverly built empire of dubious businesses which, the judge was certain, acted as a façade for substantial, if unproven, illegal activity.'

'An organisation of unparalleled antisocial intent, which might never have been unearthed had not the true viciousness of the perpetrator been revealed in this savage crime of murder.'

'Though this could in some way be regarded as a wilful and desperate form of self-exposure, the judge was satisfied in his own mind that despite the confessions of the defendant there were more people involved – people who might be at this moment present in this court – and that the evidence laid before the court was but the tip of an iceberg.'

'"I offer no rebuke to the officers of the Metropolitan Police, but in my view the prosecution has been ill-served."'

'"George Croft, you have been found guilty of murder, the most serious crime known to society. It has been shown that you were under strain owing to your wife's involvement with the murdered man. And you have confessed freely, of your own will, that you are guilty of this brutal action. In your favour you have not attempted to evade responsibility. But I believe that you are an evil man, a man that society can well do without. I sentence you to twenty-five years in prison, with the recommendation that the sentence be fully served."'

George Croft. A strong-featured man of middle age, in his case fortified by a sense of self-discipline and personal drive. I wondered if he preserved himself in prison; if he looked as distinguished amongst the inmates as he did beside the photograph of a slob-jowled judge, who could only have ever built his empire on a costly and exclusive education, who had been bred to talk about society with the certainty that one only had to follow its rules to preserve one's natural station in life.

I closed the newspaper file and wondered, stupidly, why George Croft hadn't got someone else to kill Robert Emerson. That was stupid, because I might as well have wondered why the judge didn't keep George locked up in his own house. George Croft didn't look the type to get someone else to do his dirty work for him.

I tried to remember the face of the young boy who had walked down the platform to see his mother, but it had been dusk and I had had eyes only for her. I took the file across to the librarian's desk and asked if I might order a print of the one photograph of N. I filled out the form which the librarian handed me, and noted the names of the reporter and the barrister who had defended George. I walked out of the *Mirror* building.

*   *   *

What is there that is erotic in London?

Briefly, when the snow melts, there is an atmosphere of light-heartedness. The inhabitants are happy to rediscover routine: now we can do something, now we can get down to it. There is a feeling of self-importance. The newspapers need no longer bother with reporting the harshness of life in the provinces, frozen pensioners have had their day. All the stories which have been shelved are sifted and the best of them are brightened up. Renewed contacts suggest possibilities, the city bustles.

London delights in false starts. The promise of a promise is better than nothing at all, it is a consolation. The routine is enhanced.

The government busied itself in issuing another spate of promises. 'She Lies' was a simple graffito which was scrawled on walls and hoardings all over the city. 'She Lies.' Perhaps it was the name of a rock band. 'She Lies.'

I had a slender veil, a silk stocking, masking the chair in my bedroom.

We all lie.

That was the only erotic pastime I could find in London. All that I had before me was N. She is sitting in a chair. One leg is crossed over the other, a black dress covers her knee. One foot is contained in a black high-heeled shoe, which rests against the leg of the chair. The other shoe hangs motionlessly from her raised foot at an angle of thirty degrees. All that I have to decide is what colour stockings she wears, or whether her legs are naked. It is probably too cold for her legs to be uncovered. So I will take the silk-skinned toes between my lips. What would George have done?

I received a letter from her. Without introduction, it was a series of handwritten notes.

'I was wearing no special perfume. A light Caron behind the lobe of each ear and on the inside of each thigh. I depilated my legs the day before you came. At five o'clock I bathed and shaved under my arms. I can't remember which lingerie I chose although it is certain that I made a choice because I always do. I never wear tights, I don't like them. I wear men's knee socks with trousers or jeans, otherwise I wear stockings. The dress was black, far too elaborate, and out of date. It's a reliable dress and I wanted something I could rely on. It's a dress that makes me feel good, and I know that I am attractive in it – white, elaborate and out of date. I hope this helps you. There was talcum powder between my breasts. Johnson's Baby Powder. A scentless underarm deodorant. Horses sweat, men perspire, and women glow – at least they do if the heat is turned up or if they are nervous. You would probably have noticed this. Maroon lipstick. All rather superficial and normal. Not, I'm afraid, as ritualistic as you might imagine, nor as important. (Liar.) Anyway, before you arrived I had gone out to lunch with the man who supplies wine for the restaurant. When I got back I had to interview someone who had been sent round from the staff agency. Staff problems are the bane of my life and I need one more regular person before we reopen. We should see each other before then. We have to talk. At five o'clock I needed a hot bath and some time on my own. I was tetchy.

'I was very pleased to see you – which is too ridiculous and too formal. I lied in the car. I am not certain of myself. We must talk. Perhaps you feel the same way. I hope so. Sometimes I think that you try emotions on for size, to see if they fit. You rushed down here and you tried to make them fit, which I admire. It's honest although it's not quite the same as feeling. I wonder what we will live up to. David goes back on the tenth. Yours, N.'

I waited until the fifteenth, and then I went down to see her, unannounced, with the keys she had given me.

I arrived in the middle of a cold afternoon; a grey, raining afternoon, windless. No squalling, no drizzling; just a heavy monotonous rain, as though Portsmouth had been stored in a murky basement under a grid of leaking pipes. The few other passengers disappeared quickly into waiting cars, the town centre was deserted and smelt like a meadow. There was no penetration from the sea.

The restaurant was still closed. The studio bedroom was chilly. The bathroom was clean and appeared not to have been used for some time. I adjusted the central heating. On the bed, in the otherwise tidy room, lay a cream half-slip. I put my face to the cold nylon.

I went out to the fishbar for an early dinner. I returned through the darkened pub and lay on the bed, troubled by my own conceit in staking a claim to her property. Eventually I must have dozed, for I suddenly found myself awakened by the feeling that the room was too close and too hot.

I opened a window and saw her car in the carpark beneath me, its headlights stretching out through the thick strands of rain. I heard nothing but the continuous spatter of the rain, a series of half-noises, a trickle from a gutter, a thousand intercut eruptions of applause as each raindrop obliterated itself against the concrete sea-wall, alerting me instantly from a hundred different directions.

The sky sagged massively with water. I was tired but I had no further capacity for sleep. I looked back at the slightly disturbed bed and for the first time deliberately considered the rest of the room, its pictures and its furniture. After several minutes of preparing myself for the sound of N's footsteps on the stairs, I opened the door and went looking for her.

She was lying on a bench seat in the corner of the bar. She had kicked off her shoes and a black fur coat lay near them on the flagstones. She was spread out in a disarray of drunkenness, her right hand at her breast, an exhausted cigarette between her fingers, the fragile fillet of ash resting on the belly of a brilliant red dress. I thought that she was unconscious but as I bent to pick up her coat I saw out of the corner of my eye her fingers groping after the cigarette end which she had let fall on to her stomach. She retrieved the filter and sucked on it greedily, and then let it drop to the floor.

I brought her a fresh cigarette. At the second attempt she managed to open her eyelids, but her smeared eyes floundered helplessly with their effort to focus. Her eyelids sank down. She swallowed, heavily, several times; she dropped the lighted cigarette. I picked it up and fetched an ashtray from the bar. I moved a table close to her head. She sighed irritably, mumbled, and pushed the table away from her, struggling against it as though she felt threatened. She pulled at her hair, frustrated, resenting its touch on her cheek, or perhaps trying to hurt herself, to feel something.

51

Her attention switched. She drew up her legs, her heels stepping backwards along the cushion. She opened her eyes and gazed at her knees. She lifted her chin from a small, plump collar of fat.

I placed a cushion under her head. Her breath stank of spirits. She knew what, but not who, I was. Like some grotesquely automatic fairground mask, she pushed her lips forward into a pout and licked them with her tongue, once, twice, five or six times, trying to moisten them. And then she slurred her way precisely, asking me to look at the lights on the car, *her* car, and to take her to bed.

I ran out through the rain. I retrieved the key from the ignition and doused the lights.

On my return she had gone upstairs, guided by some enormous effort of will. I lit one of her cigarettes, and I turned off all the lights in the bar but I couldn't find the switch for the light which hung outside over the entrance. I locked the door. I sat for a moment on the bench where she had been lying, leaving her to complete whatever toilet she chose; I gathered her coat and her shoes and her personal effects and sat holding them in the darkness, listening to the insistent, numbing downpour.

I thought that I heard what might be a car engine, and I checked, in a panic, to see that I had really retrieved her car key. I had, and I wondered where I should leave it so that she would see it in the morning. I didn't want to extend my trespass, I didn't want to be there in the morning. The rain would wash everything away.

The latch jiggled, with a noise like a metallic wind-chime, there was a split second before a body thumped against the door, and then the surprised groan of that body losing its wind. The latch lifted slowly again and then dropped abruptly as the person realised that the door was locked. I sat still in the darkness, wondering what on earth I would say if this person proved to have a key.

A brutish thickset face appeared at the window and tried to look in. His steamy liquored breath fanned across the skin of glass. He swore to himself. I heard one footstep as he stepped back. He tried the door again, half-heartedly. I heard the harsh grating of shoe leather on wet gravel. He said 'You slut' with unemotional contempt; and then I heard only the undisturbed splattering of the rain as it renewed its huge disguise.

I ran upstairs with her shoes and cigarettes.

Propped on the bank of white pillows, N lay asleep, her lips and eyes tidied, a chaste fragrance of cold cream about her skin.

From the window I saw an overcoated man look quickly into her car. Then, his hair plastered to his scalp, he walked back – imperiously – to the white Mercedes. He drove off.

I wiped the bathroom clean of vomit.

Rolling her away out of her dress, I unclipped her stockings and removed them. I removed her suspender belt. I touched the weals of corrugated scarlet which ran across the blubber at her midriff. I brushed the hair away from her temples.

Her breath tensed. Her face grew mottled with pinpoints of red. She looked at me sporadically, her eyes opening and closing. Her half-focused stare emerged and retreated tortuously, like the searching flesh of a plucked limpet.

Her mouth hardened. A stream of filthy language welled from her lips. She hissed obscenities at me and at herself, plucking at the elastic of her underwear. She mumbled. She sobbed once. She cupped her right hand between her legs. She turned away on to her left side. She huddled into a foetal position. Her face collapsed, her mouth fell open. Her breathing was noisy and childish.

I turned up the level of the heating. I switched on a reading lamp, which couldn't disturb her. I took pen and paper and I sat in the wingchair across from her haunches. From this vantage point I watched and I wrote my way through the streaming night. At the first sickly blight of dawn I drew the covers over her side and turned down the heating; an hour later I left her. I travelled back to London amongst a crowd of clean-shaven businessmen, carrying with me a lock of dark pubic hair. Just before Godalming the rain stopped; London itself was dry.

Six

'Her room. I cannot believe that she has designed it for herself. Certainly not for her ease; the pictures are too striking.

'Over the chair there is a pencil drawing of a manacled prisoner. There is a calm splendour about him. There is no sense of his defeat, there is no restlessness, bitterness or self-pity. There is patience, and transcendence. Both of which would seem to have nothing to do with her, and nothing in her would suggest that she is envious of these qualities, or that she sees them as virtues.

'Above the bed is a large oil painting of an ox. The ox watches the painter. It stands firmly on a beach with the ocean in the background. It is stubborn, strongly or stupidly. Again: what does she see in this?

'Her brother and sister are both married and live averagely in the suburbs of London. Her father is dead; she sees her mother occasionally as a matter of duty, she accepts that they don't get on well. She never sees her first husband, her second husband is in prison, her eldest son is on the edges of crime – probably because in the wake of her early divorce he looked to his new father as a way of escaping a suffocating maternal embrace – and her second son is shepherded by the private school system.

'She was not born wealthy, she has accumulated wealth. Not by accident, but she has managed it and continues to do so without overmuch concern or application. It is as though she is a part of a wealthy society; her wealth is a result of some work and some coincidence.

'Which is how I find her beauty. Again, it is as though the world is beautiful and she has merely cornered a part of it. But her viewpoint is different, her knowledge is that the world is ugly and full of pain; pain rather than suffering, because suffering is only half the story and it is certain that she is aware of her capacity for inflicting pain as well as for suffering from it.

'At thirty-eight or thirty-nine she lies on the bed, naked with her bottom towards me, a woman with pale skin and long dark hair, perhaps sixty-eight inches from foot to head, small-breasted, firm-shouldered, resilient even in vulnerability.'

And that night, just the tremendous feeling of endurance, an absolute happiness, sitting with her while she was sleeping, in that warm bedroom with the rain teeming indifferently outside.

She couldn't have remembered anything. She telephoned, four or five days later. When I thanked her for her letter she laughed. She said immediately that I should plan on spending two weeks, maybe three, in Portsmouth; that she would drive up to London to introduce me to George's mother and to his brother Gerald, and then we would return south. I was to represent her.

She collected me at Victoria. She glanced at my clothes. A different tie, she thought, something expensive. The suit was right, she had meant to tell me to wear one. She produced a silk tie from the glove compartment. I put it on. She appraised me.

'What am I supposed to be?' I laughed falsely.

'A lawyer. And I will pay you for it. I *will* pay you.'

'Don't be stupid.'

'Don't *you* be stupid.'

We stared at each other, until my eyes sank under the weight of her decisiveness.

'I see.'

'You are to ascertain the grounds for my husband's appeal.'

I looked ahead of me through the windscreen.

'How much?' I said.

'Five thousand.'

Twenty minutes later she dropped me off and told me to walk several hundred yards to the address which she had given to me. She would be there.

It took me some time to find the address. The Mercedes was in a small private carpark. A man stood with N at the door to an estate agent's office. He was carrying too much weight in an expensive dark suit. I recognised his face immediately as the face I had seen at the restaurant window on the night of the rain.

N introduced me to Gerald. He was strongly built but he waited for me to decide on the force of the handshake, which he matched. He led us to his car. He gave N the keys. He sat, half facing her, as she dealt with the traffic.

'What do you think you can do?' he challenged me. 'We don't want to get George's hopes up, do we?'

'George doesn't know a thing about it,' N said.

'Are you going to tell him?'

'No,' she said.

'Well?' He looked at me sharply.

'But that doesn't mean that we shouldn't try something without his knowing,' I said; 'it's certainly not going to do him any harm. It's nothing he'll know about unless we think it could work to his advantage.'

'His and who else's?' Gerald watched, impassively, the shops at the side of the road.

'Yourself and Mrs Croft. That's my understanding. I'm not at this time representing George, and the basis of the agreement – which I presume Mrs Croft has been through with you – is that the work I do will be confidential.'

Gerald offered no comment. I went on to describe what I had learnt from the newspapers about the trial and its background. I gave the story colourlessly and avoided any innuendo such as the judge had made.

During the wine-bar lunch, N seldom spoke and Gerald was very much the authority. He wanted to find out about me. He drank steadily and did not in fact ask a difficult question. Sometimes he would drop unselfconsciously into a broader London accent and show his familiarity with the part of North London in which I lived. I felt that this was a dangerous time; he was inviting me to relax and admit that our conversation was just a game.

But he wasn't sure. I earnestly confessed to him that I didn't know what I could do until I started working, and that even then it might have an unsatisfactory result.

N went to the ladies' room. Somehow, as she walked away, she carried all the authority with her. She was a great deal more sober than Gerald, but it wasn't that. Gerald held his drink remarkably well, with only an increased blinking of the steady cornflower-blue eyes and a sporadic moistening of his lips to show for the intake. He now took me aside and spoke in a man-to-man fashion of how unhappy N had been over Christmas, how the family worried about her and about prodding her feelings back to the surface again.

'We thought,' he said, 'that it had all died down, you know what I mean?' He gazed at me blankly; the look in his eyes was like a high, unscalable, slippery wall; and then he blinked. It might have been stupidity, or else his satisfaction with making his ambivalence clear. It wasn't comfortable, and it wasn't benign.

'I'm sure it's painful for her.'

'It would be, wouldn't it, really?' He said this as though he couldn't have cared less, as though he was disgusted with her. When she came back to the table he drained his glass and stood up to button a double-breasted jacket. 'All right, love?'

'Yes,' she said, 'shall we go? I said that we'd drop in at your mother's for tea.'

'I'll have to give that a miss. I'm taking her out for dinner tonight, I wouldn't last the course. No,' he said, stopping me from picking up the bill, 'go on, I'll do it.'

'Thank you for the lunch.'

'What time is the plane?' N asked.

'Mid-morning.'

They walked ahead of me, past the bar and out of the door into the bright grey afternoon. I stood at a distance, unsure what I was supposed to do. I overheard snatches of their conversation, about her son, about Portugal, about his mother. I gathered that this was the last time N would see him before he departed. He nodded a farewell to me and took the Mercedes off in the direction of the City.

When we were sitting in the back of a taxi, and N was staring, uncheerfully, out of the window, I asked her, 'That went all right, didn't it?'

'Yes, but don't try and be friendly, not with him. You're wasting your time. He doesn't trust it. Leave well alone.'

I expected her to ask me what we had said in her absence, but she showed no interest. Instead, she again rebuked me.

'There's no reason why it shouldn't have gone smoothly. I'm the one who's paying.'

The taxi took us across Kensington and left us on the edge of a large housing estate in the shadow of the Westway. We stood in front of the Queens Park Rangers football stadium, silent and empty.

'George's mother works here,' N said; 'she's spent her life being a part of the place. George was an apprentice professional and his father played for the club for several years.'

'George didn't make the grade?'

'He never really wanted to. He had a go at it, for his father's sake, but he grew out of it. There wasn't any bad feeling. George used to call him the last of the Dunkirk defenders.'

'Is the father still alive?'

'No. He died some years ago from lung cancer. Jean keeps his memory alive on three packets a day.'

We met Jean in the promotions office, a jolly and chaotic room staffed with the same good humour and amateurish enthusiasm that you might find cramped backstage at a fringe theatre. Jean must have been close to seventy; she was thin, with a shock of dry white hair and eyes that still sparkled through a misty surface.

'Hello, darling . . .' She was very pleased to see N, and proud that we had come to the office. 'I got your message and I'm just going to empty the ashtray and then we'll go home for a nice cup of tea.' N introduced me, and Jean introduced the two other girls in the office. While she tidied her desk and washed out her tea cup, she asked N about the drive up to London. 'It's *cold*, isn't it?' she appealed to me. 'I don't know how you can live down there so near the sea. But then the air's better, isn't it?'

'Yes,' I said.

'I don't know what's happening to this city,' she puffed finally

58

at her cigarette and ground it out, 'they've got rid of the fog but the air still smells bad to me. They say it's that Westway and the traffic, but I don't know. Now then, are we all right?' N helped her on with her coat. 'Thank you, darling.'

We walked almost to the other end of the housing estate, it must have been built in the fifties, with bubble-glass windows on the stairwells, five storeys high. Jean opened the door to a flat on the third floor, and immediately went to switch on the living-room fire. The room was nearly too full of knick-knacks, some from places like Venice or Bruges, bits of china and gold-painted plastic. And photographs in cheap frames of her husband's footballing days, photographs of her sons with their wives, and photographs of her grandchildren. There was a large television set, and a video machine which she said she hardly ever used unless Gerald sometimes dropped in recordings of her favourite television programmes, an episode of *Dallas* that she had missed or the Royal Ballet.

It was a very colourful room, like a plush gypsy caravan, and, next door, a rather stark kitchen with well-wiped formica tops and a stately, round-cornered electric stove. She brought us ham and chicken sandwiches which she had made up before going to work, wrapped in plastic film, and cups of tea, and she was certain that we would be hungry. She was satisfied when I ate, and she talked with N about the children and how Gerald looked, and about how well she was although she smoked too much. She was occasionally vague and I guessed from her shortness of breath that she had emphysema of sorts, but she was, as N had said, a lovely woman, and the two of them got along better than most mothers and daughters would have done, perhaps because they had both given birth only to boys and had been surrounded by them.

N didn't tell her what we were supposed to be doing, and the only time she mentioned George was when they were both in the kitchen, washing the cups, and it was as though it was a family affair which shouldn't be talked about in front of me. Afterwards, while we waited for the rush-hour traffic to die away – the television was switched on for me to hear the early-evening news as though I wouldn't be interested in their conversation – Jean referred to her own husband's death and to missing him in a way that was heartfelt without being gloomy, and the unspoken implication was that N felt the same, that they shared an unmorbid recollection of different gatherings in the flat. Neither of them were going to give up living or let themselves be swaddled in black bandages. When the room was stifling with heat and cigarette smoke and we had drunk a small Scotch to keep out the cold, and had called a taxi, N took my arm in a casual way at the front door and her mother-in-law told me to come and see her any time if I telephoned first or if I wanted a ticket to the football games, and she knew that we hadn't talked about anything that I was involved with but there would be another chance now that we knew each other. It would be nice to have a bit of company.

'Yes, she likes men,' N said, 'her boys.'

'And she likes you,' I said.

'I want to get home.' She looked at her watch. 'We should be there by ten.'

We transferred to her car. There was no sign of the Mercedes in the office carpark. N drove us out of London, the tall lights of the motorway screening her with an orange wash.

'Yes,' she said, 'it went okay. But we must have a contract,' she cautioned. 'Will you do that?'

I said that I would. She looked tired now, underneath her eyes, but she smiled occasionally to herself as though she was overhearing an absurd conversation. The motorway ended, I lost sight of her and was filled by a lulling sureness.

When we arrived back in Portsmouth, I went upstairs to the studio room and barely opened my suitcase. I lay awake for an hour or so, listening to the sea. Later, unable to get to sleep, I switched on the light and emptied every piece of furniture in the room. I laid N's clothes out on the bed, and her shoes, and her underclothes, and a silver-grey dressing-gown which was hanging in the bathroom. Beside the bed was a crumpled tube of lubricating jelly, and there were lipsticks and face creams in the bathroom cupboard.

I could construct nothing out of it all.

*   *   *

In the morning I went to the library and I read the *Portsmouth Herald* from cover to cover. In the afternoon I walked through the picturesque Old Town, the boat-repair yards, the streets with lines of two-storey semis, the streets with individualistically designed and often whimsical middle-class houses, the shopping precincts. I walked along the esplanade and the inner-city ring road, and out to the ten-year-old housing estate which skirted the naval dockyard and the military airfield.

I saw small yachts beached by the low tide, an imperial town hall, a shuttered arcade and fairground, a casino with a lush red interior. I saw shops that sold paintings, old maribilia, freshly washed secondhand clothes, naval dress shoes, home recipe sausages, old velvet curtains, china replicas of John Wayne.

There were an unusual number of attractive girls, men with greased hair, laughing schoolchildren, eight-year-old cars, houses with small follies in the garden, shrubs, shrines, small clean cafés, idling police in cars, amiable bystanders in bus queues.

N. As an object to contemplate. An icon.

I understood that somewhere in this town she lived with her son, or by herself, but the town closeted her.

Portsmouth was a discreet town, disciplined and probably virtuous in an unbiblical way. Perhaps with a few bits of camouflage over building contracts and prostitution, but there was no vicious exploitation of anyone or anything, not even the sea. A port, a dockyard, a company that built weapon-control systems and satellites. A solid town, a catering town, middle of the road, plenty of outsiders – settled and transient – largely under the Official Secrets Act. No danger of wealth, no danger of decrepitude, no suspicion of callers. Healthy. Clean.

I understood why N was here. Here she sat on a cushion with the vast, uncomfortable bed of London behind her. She recognised that she was the same as a lot of women, she didn't want to make herself exceptional, an ostentation – but she was dismayed by replicas of herself, the woman in her spiced thirties. She wished to have unlimited access to her integrity. She didn't want to be discussed. She didn't want to be humiliated by the stale caresses of uniformity. A large provincial sea-town, with its tradition of brief settlers and absentees, suited her perfectly. She had no sense that she might be buried here.

I returned before closing-time to her premises. I went upstairs, and when I unlocked the door to the studio I knew, from a scent and a warm humidity, that she had bathed in my absence. That her naked body had lain relaxed and abandoned to the ministrations of the tap-water.

The white enamel of the bath shone brilliantly. She had left no trace of herself, not a single particle of dirt, no strand or curl of hair; there was no shallow pool of water around the drain. A smooth primrose rectangle of soap lay in the dish, its back arched, like a perfumed torso caught in agony. At once, I felt antiseptically naked, as though part of myself lay sprawled before her, demanding her touch. I felt like an obese, down-at-heel crier at the flap of a shabby circus tent, waiting for her as she came closer to explain what she wanted.

'George?'

'Yes.'

'Strong. He's a very strong man.' She answered my enquiry. She looked off into the fire. The fire didn't need another log. Everyone else had gone home. She stood up and went to the bar to fix herself a drink. Her voice was unnaturally loud, thrown high so as to be sure that I would catch everything she had decided to say.

'He's generous. He's much too generous. Vulgar people often are. George is like a bull in a china shop. He can't understand other people. He's like a child.' She came back, glanced at the fire, stepped into her shoes and looked quickly over her shoulder to check the seams at the backs of her legs. 'When he wasn't on the move, he'd fall asleep. He'd fall asleep anywhere. In taxis, in cinemas, anywhere. It's very difficult for him in prison – they don't give them very much to do. And now, when there isn't anything to do, he can't sleep. He only sleeps for three hours a night.'

She deposited her drink on the side-table, looked at her nails and sat down. She regarded me. 'Do you know that I don't actually miss him?' She sipped at her drink and set the glass back beside her. 'I came to understand that he spent his whole life avoiding people. Not just women, everybody. That was the thing which initially attracted me to him, it was an energy in him. Does that make any sense? He was sure of himself.

'I wasn't, after the divorce. It wasn't fashionable to be a single parent, my mother never forgave me. She was the type of woman who believed that you chose your bed and you lay in it. The loyal prostitute. There was no way round her. So I felt guilty about bringing the baby up on my own. Every time Paul cried it seemed as though he was blaming me.

'And then I met George. I didn't want to get involved. George couldn't care less, he didn't see any point in talking about that. If we got on, we got on; if not he'd stay around the Bush, he had a lot of family. Life was family. Life was simple. "Don't worry about the kid, darlin', it'll either die or it won't. My old mum will look after him for the evening; we'll drop him off there and we'll have some fun." That's typical George. It was genuine.

'He loved Paul in his own way, and Paul adored him. They went off to the races together before Paul could walk. George loved family.

'It took me five years to understand that that was exactly what he meant. Our child, David, had to be an accident, he would never have been born on purpose. George could understand an accident; it was something that needed a bit of caring and a bit of sorting out. He was so fixed on the right thing to do that he wouldn't hear of me having an abortion. So he married me.

'He was doing very well, he and Gerald. I never asked where it came from. Bullion, I suppose. Off on a job and then keeping very quiet for a bit, channelling it into businesses. He worked with a lot of Europeans, the police were a long way behind in those days, they never came close to him. For all I know he bribed them. I never had to lie for him. It might have been his charm. He isn't a nasty man, some of them are – Gerald can be. George was always straight and likeable. Not greedy. He shook the Christmas tree and things just fell off into his lap.

'He thought it was down to me, I was lucky for him. We were winners. We were made for each other.

'We had everything, and later on most of it was clean. Though George could never resist temptation. He was too insulted by other people's stupidity. Whenever he pulled something big, he honestly believed he was educating the people he stole from. He couldn't for the life of him understand how they let him get away with it, how he was invincible. It was part of our luck. According to him, it was because of us, it was because we were together.

'Then he discovered that I was having an affair with some-one.

'The affair was nothing, it was just small and sordid. It was something perverse in me.

'George went round to where he lived and murdered him. Then he went on a bender, hiding out in London. I tried to find him. For a week I tried to get to him. His family thought that they were protecting him; or protecting me from him, that's how Jean saw it. She somehow thought that it would all die down, as though George had been sent off in a local derby game.'

'What did Gerald do?'

'He did what he could. At the end of the week George got away from them and turned himself in at a police station. By the time a tame policeman had got hold of our lawyer, George had confessed to about half of what he had done since leaving school. When he came to trial he got twenty-five years. He refused to grass. He's served four. He asked me if in view of the sentence I would like a divorce.'

'What did you say?'

'I said no.' She got up hurriedly, and went to stand in front of the fire. 'At that time I didn't think it would be right or kind. Now I think it would have been kinder to have said yes. It would have cleared things up for him. The blame would have fallen squarely on me, which is where it probably belongs. You see?'

She collected a cigarette and lit it, and left it lying in the ashtray. She passed me on her way up to the restaurant. While she was gone I knelt and warmed my hands, and watched the firefly fragments of soot at the back of the chimney breast. She came

Seven

Her time for me was at the end of the day. We talked in the bar between midnight and two, when she was most comfortable. She was a maker of lists, my questions were a diversion. She would remember something that had to be done, which she would write on her agenda, and then she would offer me a story from her past. She was more than often nonplussed by the aberrancy of direct enquiries.

When she had nothing to add to her lists, and no response to my queries, she affected tiredness.

Desire?

She didn't refuse my appreciation of her, the way she moved, on what part of her body she rested her hand. And I, occasionally, felt the weight of her eyes on me, some light stirring of her interest.

But she had a lover; she had George.

George was a remarkable man. When she described him her eyes lit up and it was difficult not to sit spellbound before her, relishing with her the way in which he undermined the world. There was no 'why' with George. He had a way of seizing the frustrations of the timid and sailing through the foibles of the self-important without disturbing the stagnancy of the realm. People needed George. They were bored and unfulfilled, they smelt corruption and didn't know how to take advantage of the climate, and there was no dreadful risk in trusting him. Far from recruiting them, it was more as though he was propelled upwards by their own stifled expectations. He didn't attack society, he more or less dissolved it, melting its fat and revealing its brittle bones.

Of course, my own point of view was prejudiced. I had no love for established people, nor for the Establishment. My attitude was conditioned by bitterness and perhaps a crabbed envy, for the best that could be said of my own career was that I had participated in a hopeless rearguard action. I found the Establishment impenetrable, indifferent and powerful. George had simply found it ridiculous, and this was a joyful discovery for me.

We laughed together at the endless fund of hypocrisy. I was amazed by the unrestrainable and almost festive displays of corruption. But mostly I was held by the warm eagerness in N's eyes as her delight in George's perceptions rekindled their days together.

They were wonderful evenings. She was full and rich, at times shockingly beautiful. I sat opposite her, drinking it in, sharing the ironies and the contempts and the joys; and noting down what she said, the names, the places, the weaknesses.

When she fell silent, between two and three in the morning, we were both exhausted, both rather bleary from the intensity of feeling – I would say from the intensity of giving: me to her, she to George. At this time there was an artificial numbness between us, suggestive of need yet tranquillised by the acceptance of partnership. She would go home. I don't know what she thought, but every bit of life left when she closed the door behind her. I would stay up for another hour or so, adding to my notes and thinking about her.

She had placed a cassette-radio in the studio room but I had no desire to hear any sound other than that of her voice. I found it impossible to reflect clearly on my own feelings. I was tied to her love affair with another man, for whose benefit we were working.

What was there about George? In everything she had said, there was not the slightest hint of his ambition. I had no sense that he was an ambitious man. I could see no motivation behind George other than that he had lived for N's love.

Though she would always return home to sleep, she started to use the studio room more often, for changing her clothes or for bathing. I slept late in the mornings; she once told me that she too slept like the dead, as though there was some huge decomposition running its course through her. At dinner she would talk about the town or the occasional problems which the restaurant provided. When the restaurant closed she pulled the wispy night in around her and we started to talk.

I knew that I was helplessly in love with her, and that I wouldn't do anything about it. We were happy together with our routine. I felt that I was helping her, becoming close to her at her own deliberate pace. I wasn't certain what part our work played in this, but that didn't disturb me. She paid me one thousand pounds. I wasn't sure what she wanted but I had enough material to make sure that George and Gerald stayed in prison for a very long time.

We had just finished dinner and had laughed at the way George had handled her first son's precocious gangsterism, when she said: 'I have to go and see George tomorrow. To visit him. I'll be away for two nights. Would you stay at my house?'

I looked at her in surprise. She levelled a teasing glance at me. 'Or will you go back to London?'

'Of course not,' I protested, 'no. Have you got cats to feed or something?'

'Is it too much of a disruption?'

'No.'

She laughed. I asked her what was funny.

'Feeding cats. It is, in a way. It's Fiona.' She had mentioned Fiona occasionally; I hadn't met her. 'Fiona has a lover who is married. I don't know if it's sad or funny, but they don't have anywhere to sleep together unless he drives out to see her in the country. His wife doesn't seem to mind as long as he's back in the morning for breakfast, which means that he has to get up at five in the morning. So Fiona asked me about using the room upstairs. It's rather romantic, isn't it, or is it just idiotically furtive? I can't decide.'

'You want to give them the room?'

'Just for a night. If you don't mind staying at my house.' She said that they would bring their own sheets. 'Will you meet them in here tomorrow evening and give them the keys?'

She stood up with her coffee cup and I followed her into the kitchen with our plates. 'Of course,' I said, and after that the

was very much inland. It could have been in any town. A bland
paving-stone path, a little bit of grass rather than a lawn; two thin
decorative columns and mock carriage-lamp lights flanked the
white front door. I didn't understand what she would do in, or
what pleasure she would take from, this house, this 15B.

It had the feel of a functional, suburban London apartment.
Perhaps that was because she was in a hurry. She showed me
how the heating worked and then showed me her younger son's
bedroom which was where I was to sleep. She gave me a key, took
an extra packet of cigarettes out of the carton in the kitchen, and
left, reminding me to meet Fiona at nine.

'What do they look like?'

'The same as any two people having a sneaky love affair,' she
called back over the top of the car.

When she had driven off, I went into the house. I stood in the
narrow hallway, in front of me was a reproduction antique table
on which there was a telephone. I tried to remember how she was
dressed but I couldn't remember anything except for the layer of
powder on her cheeks. For some reason I dialled my number in
London and listened to it ringing, and then I left the house and
walked back to the restaurant. The town was alien, the clean
midday lounge bar was alien. I went upstairs to the studio room.

Any two people having a sneaky love affair. There was something
provocative about meeting them formally, making smalltalk and all
the while knowing that they were waiting to take their clothes off
in order to engage in sexual activity, in N's, my, bed. In N's bed.
Taking turns to use the bathroom, or perhaps rubbing their bodies
together in the steam. The bodies of a mid-forties travel agent,
thick-waisted, and a lean mid-thirties woman, Fiona. He was
Michael.

I gave them the keys as soon as I saw them, sitting by the fireside.
She was an insignificantly attractive woman who said that her
cottage in the countryside was lovely but very cold in the winter. I
don't know how to describe her but there was an air about her of
being second best, which she found necessary to override, and
so she portrayed herself in thick strokes as the determined

was very much inland. It could have been in any town. A bland paving-stone path, a little bit of grass rather than a lawn; two thin decorative columns and mock carriage-lamp lights flanked the white front door. I didn't understand what she would do in, or what pleasure she would take from, this house, this 15B.

It had the feel of a functional, suburban London apartment. Perhaps that was because she was in a hurry. She showed me how the heating worked and then showed me her younger son's bedroom which was where I was to sleep. She gave me a key, took an extra packet of cigarettes out of the carton in the kitchen, and left, reminding me to meet Fiona at nine.

'What do they look like?'

'The same as any two people having a sneaky love affair,' she called back over the top of the car.

When she had driven off, I went into the house. I stood in the narrow hallway, in front of me was a reproduction antique table on which there was a telephone. I tried to remember how she was dressed but I couldn't remember anything except for the layer of powder on her cheeks. For some reason I dialled my number in London and listened to it ringing, and then I left the house and walked back to the restaurant. The town was alien, the clean midday lounge bar was alien. I went upstairs to the studio room.

Any two people having a sneaky love affair. There was something provocative about meeting them formally, making smalltalk and all the while knowing that they were waiting to take their clothes off in order to engage in sexual activity, in N's, my, bed. In N's bed. Taking turns to use the bathroom, or perhaps rubbing their bodies together in the steam. The bodies of a mid-forties travel agent, thick-waisted, and a lean mid-thirties woman, Fiona. He was Michael.

I gave them the keys as soon as I saw them, sitting by the fireside. She was an insignificantly attractive woman who said that her cottage in the countryside was lovely but very cold in the winter. I don't know how to describe her but there was an air about her of being second best, which she found necessary to override, and so she portrayed herself in thick strokes as the determined independent, the proud householder, the serious woman; there was to be nothing negligent about her, her manner maintained. By contrast, she implied, there might be something negligent about N; which she really didn't want to know about, it was none of her business, unless, of course, I might want to let her know.

I borrowed the keys back off her and brought down all the papers which I had left in the studio room, packaged inside a large envelope. With these confidentialities by my side, I could be glad of her company. I wanted to get drunk. I absolutely did not want to be coldly sober between midnight and three, missing N.

It wasn't strange that Fiona wanted to talk about her, I suppose. N was the only person we had in common and probably the only subject we had in common although we frittered away Law, Travel, Countryside Life, Books and Astrology. I had a great deal of information about N tucked in the envelope beside me, and I had no need to give any of it away in the hope of getting something back.

I saw that Fiona wanted to establish for herself that N and I were having an affair. Perhaps because that would somehow consolidate her affair with Michael. Perhaps because that knowledge would lessen the possibility of ill-reputation she had assumed in having asked N to lend her the room. Perhaps because she was just downright inquisitive.

It was as though she wanted to keep Michael up for half the night so that she would become both his taxation and his reward. It crossed my mind that the whole evening was a kind of absurd foreplay for her. She seemed to be a persistent, shrewish woman and he pretty much your average, well-meaning bloke – what did I care? Perhaps they would have a row when they got upstairs, they would kiss each other hesitantly or perhaps with frantic wet mouths.

I left them at closing-time. I took a bottle and a taxi to N's address, with her reputation intact. Upstairs, I blundered into sleep.

High white shelves held innocent boyhood objects clear of a beige carpet. Pencils and pens were neatly arranged on the top of a small desk. The doors to the fitted cupboards were painted in off-white. They had small golden handles, and dull-black keys independent, the proud householder, the serious woman; there was to be nothing negligent about her, her manner maintained. By contrast, she implied, there might be something negligent about N; which she really didn't want to know about, it was none of her business, unless, of course, I might want to let her know.

I borrowed the keys back off her and brought down all the papers which I had left in the studio room, packaged inside a large envelope. With these confidentialities by my side, I could be glad of her company. I wanted to get drunk. I absolutely did not want to be coldly sober between midnight and three, missing N.

It wasn't strange that Fiona wanted to talk about her, I suppose. N was the only person we had in common and probably the only subject we had in common although we frittered away Law, Travel, Countryside Life, Books and Astrology. I had a great deal of information about N tucked in the envelope beside me, and I had no need to give any of it away in the hope of getting something back.

I saw that Fiona wanted to establish for herself that N and I were having an affair. Perhaps because that would somehow consolidate her affair with Michael. Perhaps because that knowledge would lessen the possibility of ill-reputation she had assumed in having asked N to lend her the room. Perhaps because she was just downright inquisitive.

It was as though she wanted to keep Michael up for half the night so that she would become both his taxation and his reward. It crossed my mind that the whole evening was a kind of absurd foreplay for her. She seemed to be a persistent, shrewish woman and he pretty much your average, well-meaning bloke – what did I care? Perhaps they would have a row when they got upstairs, they would kiss each other hesitantly or perhaps with frantic wet mouths. I left them at closing-time. I took a bottle and a taxi to N's address, with her reputation intact. Upstairs, I blundered into sleep.

High white shelves held innocent boyhood objects clear of a beige carpet. Pencils and pens were neatly arranged on the top of a small desk. The doors to the fitted cupboards were painted in off-white. They had small golden handles, and dull-black keys removed her cosmetics with thin paper towels which perched lightly like stained meringues on the polished surface of the dressing table. She anointed her face. Relaxation settled ponderously, as though summoned by the ritual; her eyes darkened and her movements became brittle, each one slightly incomplete, as if her limbs were resentful subcontractors denied access to the final blueprint. It seemed to be only a matter of time before her body abandoned her. I watched this body, she looked at me and her eyes followed mine with an impersonal wantonness. One side of her robe slipped with clumsy indiscretion across her thigh to the edge of the stool. She looked back into the mirror, watching me. She asked me if I had found her stocking. I lied, and she pursed her lips disdainfully. She drained her glass; she stood up and gathered her robe about her and walked with short, mocking, geisha steps towards the bathroom.

'Will you come downstairs afterwards?'

'Why should I? Don't you feel just as much at home in here?' She smiled a hideously polite smile. Out of sight now, she dropped the robe on the floor and I heard her step into the bath. An electric ventilator hummed.

I poured myself another glass of wine and went away downstairs. I sat for perhaps an hour, bemused by the wine burning through my empty stomach, light-headed and expansive, until a feeling of futility slowly ate into my expansiveness, tightening its control, and I sat while the little trickles of acrimony converged and set themselves into a thick, hard block. I lost all control of myself, I could feel my body tensing with the worst kind of shame and fear and impotent hatred. I imagined what I would do to her. Terrible images goaded me. Running a knife down her back-bone to her coccyx, like slitting canvas, cracking the knobbly vertebrae with a meat cutter, gathering her up by her chin and her vagina and snapping her, in the darkness of the sitting-room, with its dead television and bandage curtains.

Automatically I climbed the stairs. Her door was ajar. I turned off the hall light. It was pitch dark. I closed my eyes and felt a colossal power across the top of my shoulders and in my arms. When I opened my eyes I saw immediately the crack of light in

74

removed her cosmetics with thin paper towels which perched lightly like stained meringues on the polished surface of the dressing table. She anointed her face. Relaxation settled ponderously, as though summoned by the ritual; her eyes darkened and her movements became brittle, each one slightly incomplete, as if her limbs were resentful subcontractors denied access to the final blueprint. It seemed to be only a matter of time before her body abandoned her. I watched this body, she looked at me and her eyes followed mine with an impersonal wantonness. One side of her robe slipped with clumsy indiscretion across her thigh to the edge of the stool. She looked back into the mirror, watching me. She asked me if I had found her stocking. I lied, and she pursed her lips disdainfully. She drained her glass; she stood up and gathered her robe about her and walked with short, mocking, geisha steps towards the bathroom.

'Will you come downstairs afterwards?'

'Why should I? Don't you feel just as much at home in here?' She smiled a hideously polite smile. Out of sight now, she dropped the robe on the floor and I heard her step into the bath. An electric ventilator hummed.

I poured myself another glass of wine and went away downstairs. I sat for perhaps an hour, bemused by the wine burning through my empty stomach, light-headed and expansive, until a feeling of futility slowly ate into my expansiveness, tightening its control, and I sat while the little trickles of acrimony converged and set themselves into a thick, hard block. I lost all control of myself, I could feel my body tensing with the worst kind of shame and fear and impotent hatred. I imagined what I would do to her. Terrible images goaded me. Running a knife down her back-bone to her coccyx, like slitting canvas, cracking the knobbly vertebrae with a meat cutter, gathering her up by her chin and her vagina and snapping her; in the darkness of the sitting-room, with its dead television and bandage curtains. Automatically I climbed the stairs. Her door was ajar. I turned off the hall light. It was pitch dark. I closed my eyes and felt a colossal power across the top of my shoulders and in my arms. When I opened my eyes I saw immediately the crack of light in her doorway, a sour light, almost tangible, like a velvet mould on the skin of the street glow. With one fingertip I pushed the door open and walked silently across the carpet.

The light was a dusty soup in which her naked body floated, face downwards, the fanning pigtail of hair like a charcoal smear on her right shoulder. Her head was turned away. My eyes, in stealth, measured her fat; the voluptuous larded buttocks and the tight patty of breast which cushioned her ribcage. From her arose the smell of soap, of innocence. I stared at her in weak hatred. I reached out with my hand.

'What do you want to say?' she demanded curtly.

'Nothing.'

I touched her foot. Her body tensed and relaxed again. I knelt at the end of the bed and kissed her ankle; a hard, ridged skin, like tortoiseshell. She retracted her arms and buried her face in the pillow. I caressed her calf, wanting to quiet her, running my finger over the smooth skin at the back of her knee. I bent to kiss her foot, she pulled it away. 'Don't!' her voice cracked.

She scrambled up the bed and faced me, half her head was in shadow. The room was murky then active with a long flash of skin and I suddenly felt a sheer unusualness as she hit me, her hand sweeping in front of my eyes, the rings on her finger tearing open the side of my face; a sudden cold and wet, like a white cloth hanging over the edge of a table and a wine glass lying sideways, spilling on a sheet, which would stain. Her eyes blazed with spite.

I got to my feet, holding back my face, and I thought quickly that I should go to the kitchen. I glimpsed only a pure white calf, spattered with blood down to the ankle. I staggered to the door, pursued by a viciously prowling fury and the frenzy in her voice. 'Don't ever think you can treat me like that! Ever! Ever!'

It was calm in the pale glare of the kitchen, it was ordered around the edges of the sink. My face was bleeding profusely, which didn't seem to matter. The only thing I could think about was someone saying: ' . . . it's not important what women say, the importance lies in how they say it'; and I heard those words echoing over and over again, and I couldn't get any further, couldn't think who had said them or where, whether they were in a play or in a her doorway, a sour light, almost tangible, like a velvet mould on the skin of the sheer glow. With one fingertip I pushed the door open and walked silently across the carpet.

The light was a dusty soup in which her naked body floated, face downwards, the fanning pigtail of hair like a charcoal smear on her right shoulder. Her head was turned away. My eyes, in stealth, measured her fat, the voluptuous larded buttocks and the tight putty of breast which cushioned her ribcage. From her armpit the smell of soap, of innocence. I stared at her in weak hatred. I reached out with my hand.

'What do you want to say?' she demanded curtly.

'Nothing.'

I touched her foot. Her body tensed and relaxed again. I knelt at the end of the bed and kissed her ankle; a hard, ridged skin, like tortoiseshell. She retracted her arms and buried her face in the pillow. I caressed her calf, wanting to quiet her, running my finger over the smooth skin at the back of her knee. I bent to kiss her foot, she pulled it away. 'Don't,' her voice cracked.

She scrambled up the bed and faced me, half her head was in shadow. The room was murky then active with a long flash of skin and I suddenly felt a sheer unsunalness as she hit me, her hand sweeping in front of my eyes, the rings on her finger tearing open the side of my face; a sudden cold and wet, like a white cloth hanging over the edge of a table and a wine glass lying sideways, spilling on a sheet, which would stain. Her eyes blazed with spite. I got to my feet, holding back my face, and I thought quickly that I should go to the kitchen. I glimpsed only a pure white calf, spattered with blood down to the ankle. I staggered to the door, pursued by a viciously prowling fury and the frenzy in her voice.

'Don't ever think you can treat me like that! Ever! Ever!'.

It was calm in the pale glare of the kitchen, it was ordered around the edges of the sink. My face was bleeding profusely, which didn't seem to matter. The only thing I could think about was someone saying: ' . . . it's not important what women say, the importance lies in how they say it'; and I heard those words echoing over and over again, and I couldn't get any further, couldn't think who had said them or where, whether they were in a play or in a

Eight

I awoke, and in the bathroom mirror I saw that the healing process had begun, ugly and yellowish. I walked through the town and out along the estuary. If my thoughts didn't get me anywhere at least I could tell myself that cold, open air was good for wounds. I understood that she was a creature of formalities.

The studio room was chilly when I returned from my walk. I turned up the heating and sifted through my notes, putting them into chronological order. N came in and sat quietly in the wingchair. There was a deadness about the room which corresponded to the apparent inertia of the cloudless dusk. She sat with her legs crossed at the ankle, the heel of her right foot resting on the upholstered stool on which I had left a pile of papers. Her cream, pleated skirt hung in a modest crescent to the floor. She appeared to be meditating, her hands folded on her stomach and her eyes half closed. Finally I could stand it no longer. I asked her if the silence didn't get on her nerves.

She said not, that she was glad of the quiet. She reached into her skirt pocket and drew out a folded sheet of paper. There were, she said, several addresses on it – of the lawyers who had handled George's case, of George's old haunts in London, and some others. She handed me the paper. I said that I thought I had enough to go on from talking to her.

Attached to the paper was a cheque for a thousand pounds.

She looked at me.

'I've warned you so often,' she said quietly. 'When people love me they usually get hurt. It's not something I'm proud of. I'm not being coy or self-pitying, it's just something I've learnt.'

When her voice died, in the half-light, it seemed as though she might disappear, leaving behind the cream material, the pale skin and the dark cadence of hair.

I bent forward towards her ankle and removed the pile of history. Sitting over the desk I rustled uselessly and slowly through papers that I could hardly see, but the reassuring sound padded the atmosphere in a way that I half remembered from my childhood when someone had come into my bedroom and adjusted the stiff eiderdown on my bed while I lay precariously on the edge of a wonderful sleep.

'Gerald is coming,' she said. Her voice was low and sure.

'When?'

'Tomorrow night.'

'Does he want to stay here?'

'No. There's a whole group of them, they'll stay in a hotel.'

'Will he stay long?'

'I don't know. Someone's putting a car on the ferry for France.'

She seemed weak and defenceless, and suddenly I felt as though we were hopeless conspirators, threatened by our own ineptitude and our unsureness towards each other.

'Should I be here?'

'He'll think it strange if you're not. He knows you've been working here.'

I stood up.

'Will you go?' she asked.

'No,' I heard myself saying, 'of course not. Of course I won't.'

At dinner she was ostentatiously light-hearted. She planned what she would do tomorrow, she asked me to go shopping with her; she wanted to set the evening up as a party. She put her cigarettes and lighter in the pocket of her skirt and left to go home.

I sat in the deserted restaurant. I poured myself another drink and strangely enough, in her absence, I felt entirely unthreatened. We had done nothing. We had committed no crime. What were we to each other?

I cleared away the debris of our evening together, carried out the crockery and cleaned the ashtray. I turned out the light and stood, quietly confident that the room was ordered and faultless; as we were; and it came as an innocently rewarding sanction to see that the dining-room was now dressed in a chaste moonlight, which lay, gauze-like, across the tables. I took my glass upstairs with me, assured that I would be able to face her brother-in-law on the morrow.

She was standing, naked, in front of the face mirror in the bathroom. She put her fingers into a pot and extracted a glob of cold white cream, which she rubbed slowly over her cheek-bones and forehead.

There was a patch of yellow dead skin on the backs of her ankles, and a royal-blue vein behind her knee. Her hair was fastened. It was, from the top of her head to the mid-valley of her shoulder-blades, in the shape of an hourglass, and it trapped the bathroom light in hues of mahogany. Over her shoulders a mantle of light brown freckles, which poignantly baptised her.

We looked at each other through the mirror. Her lips were pale and drained of warmth. Only her eyes, blue-grey and distant, danced with graceful restraint, like a voice with a lilt in it, to the backdrop of white-costumed skin. She slid her rings off her finger and placed them on the bathroom shelf, where the sapphires gleamed softly back towards her.

I reached for the wisp of pubic hair which protruded from the vault of her crotch. She suffered me generously. The lips of her vagina were closed, her hair stiff and lacquered. I probed her like a clumsy criminal, seeking sanctuary, until she raised her hand and ran a questioning finger down the surface of the scar on my face.

She sipped at my glass of wine and turned back to the mirror. When I left the bathroom, she pushed the door shut.

I went to the window. The sea was black and unflustered by the touch of silver moonlight which fell like a veil from the bared stars. So calm, such a foreign stillness. Like the moment before tears, when defeat is a blissful ointment.

Reflected in the window her clothes lay lifeless on the bed. She came back into view. She looped the cream skirt over the arms of a white plastic hanger, draped the shirt around its shoulders and hung it from a cupboard door handle. I lost sight of her. She was behind me somewhere in the room, not close, nor near the bed.

Comfortable rolls of cloud were folded back above the shore.

Thick mooring posts, like minarets, punctured the skin of the sea. Across the sea a light came on in the top room of a house, a small tawny yellow mosaic amidst the moonlight. I watched this pinhead of light on the other side of the water. There were often people; people getting up, people who disliked her milk, or people with a child who had a nightmare.

'Don't worry.'

But I did. She sat in the armchair in the loose silvery robe. Her face was pale and transparent. She was as fresh as a sheet of glass. Above her head was the large, framed drawing of the prisoner; he sat, his hands unmoored in front of him, his face sublime and calm and unshaven, shadowed in grey pencil.

'Come here.'

I crossed the room and crouched before her on the floor. She leaned forward and put my forehead to her belly. The edge of her gown slid across my eyes and I smelt the tight, reedy smell of her skin. She clasped me against this small, plump belly, her fingers tracing the contours of my nose and lips. In a while she gently pushed my head away and closed her robe. 'So serious,' she murmured. 'What is it?'

She lit a cigarette.

I asked her if I might see her naked. She lifted her head and laughed at the ceiling, showing me her neck, that nervous, careless laugh. She thought that my request was ridiculous; but she sat forward on her haunches, on the floor in front of me, her arms crossed, holding the robe around her. She hugged herself and shivered, and looked down at the small patch of carpet between us. 'Oh God,' she whispered. She knelt up and the robe slipped open, hanging at her sides, framing her naked body dispassionately.

I was drunk and exhausted by her beauty. I looked at the neatly flattened pad of pubic hair, her waist and her breasts; at the large mole, like a third nipple, beneath her left breast. With her right hand she took the gown off her left shoulder and it fell with a splash of light into a pool around her calves. My senses reeled. I stared dumbly at her determined mouth and the sharp eyes which were watching me. She reached out, shadowing her breasts from the moonlight. 'Lie back.'

I did as I was told. She left her cigarette burning on the side of the ashtray. I watched the thin trail of smoke weave upwards until it shuddered uncertainly and died in dispersion. She knelt beside me and uncovered me, like a nurse carefully baring an open wound. With her hand, caringly, she released me from captivity. Gently and surely she catered for me; objectively. As through an advancing anaesthetic, I felt the pads of her fingers spread a pool of dying cells across my stomach.

When I awoke I was leaning against the side of her chair, fully clothed. A girl was vacuuming the carpet around the bed. The room was entirely clean and was hung with screens of bright sunlight. The girl left the room. I saw the fresh complacence of the bed. There was no sign that N had slept there. I remembered her breasts, borne aloft on her ribcage, nipples like long, pock-marked, sea-worn pebbles. And then I remembered that in a few hours Gerald would arrive, and that we were compromised, and that she had decisively changed the nature of our love.

I drank a cup of coffee in the bar, surrounded by the turpentine smell of furniture polish, and I found N in the office looking through her accounts. She chided me for my late rising.

I felt insecure before her efficiency, as if I would never be sure of what had happened the night before unless she verified it for me. And so I pestered her with questions about her body – was she naked every night when she removed her make-up (no), had she breastfed her children (yes) – a set of sporadic innuendoes, until she snapped: 'For God's sake don't be so innocent! If I'd have wanted to, I would have had you the first night we saw each other!'

She took her coat off the door and handed it to me to hold for her. The rings were back on her marriage finger. She said: 'If our only way through this is for me to treat you like an idiot, then I will. It lets you off the hook, doesn't it. Now shall we go upstairs and get your notes out of the way?'

A wrapped and sealed person, she stalked past me.

'Joking aside,' she said from in front of the bathroom mirror, 'our arrangement is very clear. We have the contract. It protects both of us.'

She finished her lips and firmed them appreciatively. There was an edge to the rich blue eyes. She put her lipstick in her bag and came up to me. She tapped me on the chin. 'You haven't shaved.' She pressed my bottom lip between her thumb and forefinger until I blushed with pain. She was on the point of saying something but she bent and kissed me cursorily and went over to her perfume drawer.

'You know Gerald, and it won't take you more than a couple of minutes to know his wife, Sylvie. The two other decaying sluts who are coming tonight spend their time balancing the pros and cons of their own emptiness, and they blame it on anyone other than themselves.'

I asked about the men.

'They never left nursery school, which makes them just a bit more appealing. George saw it very clearly. I was not supposed to see it.'

I could imagine George's protests and the precise measure of her disdain. I shaved cautiously around my scar.

'You'll do the bar this evening?' she called. 'It will give you something to do.'

'Yes.'

She waited for me. She took my papers down to the office and locked them in a wall-safe.

'We'll start with the shopping.'

The ground was cold, a hard sheet of particles, like the surface of an aluminium oxide belt. Each footstep cracked and vibrated, bestowing on the ugly precincts the atmosphere of a courtyard. The air was a frozen glass mask. It stuck to my face, leaving small slits for my vision of N, sumptuous in wool and maquillage. She thrived on the abrasive glance of that stern, loitering winter. I followed her, stood by her side in shops and carried her purchases back to the car, undismayed by her perfunctory changes of mind and brusque commands. She bought me a shirt and a pair of hideous beige trousers – the same colour as the carpets in her house – which I should wear in front of the company. Her eyes glittered with amusement.

Volte-face, she took me across the street to an old-fashioned gentlemen's outfitters. She studied my eyes and bought me a towelling bathrobe, full-length and cornflower blue and remarkably expensive.

'Good.' She snapped her cheque book shut. 'That will do.'

Upstairs in the studio room I caught the last stages of her preparation; I sat on the bed, considering her beauty. She stood in front of me, the hem of her dress lifted slightly as she put on her earrings.

'And now,' she said, 'you must ignore me for the rest of the evening.'

I tidied the room. I changed and strewed my own clothes about the room in case Gerald should investigate.

From the bedroom window I watched them arrive. The white Mercedes with German export plates, a red Mercedes and a Jaguar were parked away from the sea-wall.

And with the cars came the heavy gold jewellery and the suntan – the men wearing it confidently like a fawn blazer, the women crinkled about the neck and chest.

I watched from halfway down the stairs. They were formidable stereotypes, assured of their images. They homed in on the bar; the women took stools and the men stood; they drank vodka and tonic or gin and tonic, with plenty of ice so that the sound in their raised glasses matched the sound from the necklaces of the women, as they bent to gulp.

N had her hair pulled over to one side and pinned. Pale, pretending to be exhilarated at their company, she again played the perfect widow. Strikingly beautiful, she nevertheless radiated an irresistible sense of incompleteness and solitude, a slightly off-centre determination to enjoy herself. I couldn't take my eyes away from her.

I went back to the studio and wondered how I could go through with the evening.

I thought that I should meet them quickly as if I was on my way through. I would go down the stairs and be on a course for the Gents.

evening, there's the cup replay. Give me a ring.'

me buy you a drink.'

in this company.'

towards the bar with Gerald, N glared at me for

round,' Gerald brayed, 'I had to drag him away

me to the two other couples and finally to Sylvie.

carried on with their conversation. Gerald and

remarks about the journey between Portsmouth and

car, and it was probably only the incidence of

him that prompted one of the women to become

was working on a project.

to discover that it was Gerald's turn to construct

shut off any nosy investigation. 'Local history,

his drink held at chin level. His raised elbow

barrier in front of N's shoulder.

and I was immediately established as someone of

interest to them, although Gerald's wife said that

interesting and another woman said yes it was,

that the Old Town was especially interesting, with

because the matriarchy had to run things

ere away at sea.

said that it sounded familiar. A big, red-faced

toupee laid his drink on the bar and said

if not the eyes, of the company on her, N

She looked down at her glass.

she said negligently, 'this type of work all fits in

I registered his attitude and thought that it

'Wednesday evening, there's the cup replay. Give me a ring. We'll have a chat.'

'All right. Let me buy you a drink.'

'It'll cost you in this company.'

When I walked towards the bar with Gerald, N glared at me for a moment, and then she lit a cigarette and talked to the woman at her side.

'Look who I found,' Gerald brayed, 'I had to drag him away from his desk.'

He introduced me to the two other couples and finally to Sylvie. They nodded and carried on with their conversation. Gerald and I exchanged remarks about the journey between Portsmouth and London, train and car, and it was probably only the incidence of my talking with him that prompted one of the women to become inquisitive.

I said that I was working on a project.

I was intrigued to discover that it was Gerald's turn to construct a red herring, to shut off any nosy investigation. 'Local history, isn't it?' he said, his drink held at chin level. His raised elbow formed an aggressive barrier in front of N's shoulder.

'Yes,' I said, and I was immediately established as someone of absolutely no interest to them, although Gerald's wife said that local history was interesting and another woman said yes it was, wasn't it.

I told them that the Old Town was especially interesting, with its history of matriarchy; because the matriarchy had to run things while the men were away at sea.

One of 'the girls' said that it sounded familiar. A big, red-faced man with an expensive toupee laid his drink on the bar and said that that was the way it should be and had to be some of the time.

With the thoughts, if not the eyes, of the company on her, N drew on her cigarette. She looked down at her glass.

'Of course,' she said negligently, 'this type of work all fits in with the tourist board.'

'It's the Americans, isn't it? They like that kind of thing.' There was a sneer behind Gerald's words, although the tone of his voice showed no malice. I registered his attitude and thought that it

86

might give us something to talk about on Wednesday evening if he obliged me to remember his invitation. And then he showed that it was time for me to be quiet.

'I suppose that you have to make up something about anything these days, to keep them happy. I expect he could, couldn't you?' Gerald raised his head and jutted his chin; it was, I thought, his way of giving an ostentatious wink. The company laughed.

'Don't knock him, Gerald,' Sylvie flapped. 'I expect it's interesting.'

They fell to talking about the presence of American tourists. The women assumed that they would be good for N's business, and she agreed with them. Gerald summoned the barman and nodded him in my direction.

I couldn't tell with him, I could never tell, what, or whether, he thought. He had the blank, flat look of an unsportive predator. And beside him – I risked a glance – N had adopted a scratched veneer of the same world. Her cheeks were flushed; there was a strange coarseness to her features, a shallow swank which altered the tone of her beauty. I could not believe that this was the same woman who had uttered that astonished, waifish 'Oh God' as the moonlight sought her naked body.

She caught my eye and flicked me a look of such rigid censure that I swayed back on my heels. I heard Gerald laugh.

'Bit strong, is it?'

I faked a cough. 'Yes.'

'Here, get him another tonic. In there.' Gerald pointed the barman towards me. And they talked about someone they all knew who had choked to death on a fishbone. They never stopped talking and they never stopped drinking. I went to the Gents.

When I came back my space in the male group had been filled, they had shut themselves off. One of the men nodded absent-mindedly when I took my drink off the bar, and I went over to the pinball machine, in an alcove by the door, out of their way.

I didn't dare look again at N.

As they left to go upstairs to the restaurant, I overheard her voice – she out of all of them was probably the only one who knew that I was in earshot – I imagined her eyebrows raised in that might give us something to talk about on Wednesday,' hmm

Gerald raised his head and jutted his chin; it was ... nA
way of giving an ostentatious wink. The company laugh
'Don't knock him, Gerald,' Sylvie flapped. 'I expect
ing.'

They fell to talking about the presence of Americ
The women assumed that they would be good for
and she agreed with them. Gerald summoned the
nodded him in my direction.

And beside him – I risked a glance – N had adopted
veneer of the same world. Her cheeks were flushed;
strange coarseness to her features, a shallow swank
the tone of her beauty. I could not believe that this
woman who had uttered that astonished, waifish 'Oh
moonlight sought her naked body'.

that I swayed back on my heels. I heard Gerald laugh.

I faked a cough.

'Here, get him another tonic. In there,' Gerald
barman towards me. And they talked about someone
who had choked to death on a fishbone. They never sto
and they never stopped drinking. I went to the
When I came back my space in the male group
filled, they had shut themselves off. One of the
to the pinball machine, in an alcove by the door, out of

As they left to go upstairs to the restaurant, I
voice – she out of all of them was probably the only
that I was in earshot – I imagined her eyebrows ... N

that he was in control. When she had ushered them

I carried the plates into the kitchen.

back to find me amongst a pile of greasy dishes.

spensable you are,' she cooed, drunkenly. She stood

a brandy.

all right,' I said. 'He invited me to a football match on

She checked, and then brushed her annoyance aside.

like that and bitch, Sylvie? Who nags at him. It's the

knows of stopping him seeing right through her,' she

resonant derision.

herself another brandy and, noticing that I was

she stubbornly drank down half of it. 'They're not

ry soon'.

ve got a long time to last'.

she grinned mirthlessly. There was a kind of vagrant

in her, a promiscuity which frightened me. She fitted

t my side. She opened my shirt, and while the white

the surface of the dishwasher she rolled my nipple

n her thumb and forefinger, scratching it with her

I vainly murmured a weak complaint, succumbing

pain. Her bottom lip slipped out from between her

withdraw her arm, the smile frozen on her lips. 'I'll

r Gerald's like.'

be stupid.'

what? Stupid?' She laughed and walked out of the

ce as she turned to go downstairs bore an expression

ble self-contempt. I called after her, she looked up

amusing trace of her face twitched; she was alarmed, it was as

you didn't recognise me. 'Go to bed and wait',

umpwed by sickly smile.

em coffee. The women sat by the fire. They had an

dly exhibit fund of observation about their lifestyles and their

ld... they would jog each other into unanimity. The men

for the challenge of ostentatious relaxation; jackets

and our... language loosened, N sat in the corner, gazing quietly made him feel that he was in control. When she had ushered them all downstairs, I carried the plates into the kitchen.

She came back to find me amongst a pile of greasy dishes.

'How indispensable you are,' she cooed, drunkenly. She stood and swallowed a brandy.

'Gerald's all right,' I said. 'He invited me to a football match on Wednesday.'

'Did he?' She checked, and then brushed her annoyance aside. 'And do you like that arid bitch, Sylvie? Who nags at him. It's the only way she knows of stopping him seeing right through her,' she cried, with a resonant derision.

She poured herself another brandy and, noticing that I was looking at her, she stubbornly drank down half of it. 'They're not going to go very soon.'

'I know. You've got a long time to last.'

'Have I?' She grinned mirthlessly. There was a kind of vagrant madness about her, a promiscuity which frightened me. She fitted her body against my side. She opened my shirt, and while the white froth rose on the surface of the dishwasher she rolled my nipple tightly between her thumb and forefinger, scratching it with her crimson nail. I vainly murmured a weak complaint, succumbing listlessly to the pain. Her bottom lip slipped out from between her teeth, and she withdrew her arm, the smile frozen on her lips. 'I'll show you what Gerald's like.'

'No, don't be stupid.'

'Don't be what? Stupid?' She laughed and walked out of the kitchen. Her face as she turned to go downstairs bore an expression of unmanageable self-contempt. I called after her, she looked up and the right side of her face twitched; she was alarmed, it was as though she didn't recognise me. 'Go to bed. Go to bed and wait,' she said with a sickly smile.

I served them coffee. The women sat by the fire. They had an inexhaustible fund of observation about their lifestyles and their friends, and they would jog each other into unanimity. The men had regrouped for the challenge of ostentatious relaxation; jackets off, ties and language loosened. N sat in the corner, gazing quietly at the fire.

To break the kitchen drudgery I would occasionally go down to them, refilling glasses and emptying ashtrays. Whenever I served her, N would automatically flinch, she would sit a little straighter and her eyes would look anywhere except at me. Once, when I came down, I saw her looking at Gerald with a kind of pitiful, crestfallen pleading in her eyes. I said that I was going to bed, and I wished them goodnight. Gerald proclaimed that he would see me on Wednesday.

N stood up and thanked me courteously. There was a dull light in her eye and a reserved friendliness, as though she had escaped her confusion; and again I wasn't sure about her, to whom she was performing and the extent of her performance. She accompanied me to the stairs, talking inconsequentially about business matters for the next day, and when we were shielded from the fireside mob she whispered to me that I should wait up for her, that they would soon all be gone, that I should trust her. And: 'Love me.'

I did wait, loving her. It must have been an hour or so later when I heard the harsh clack of a woman's heels on the flagstones, and the firm pattering of her feet on the stair carpet. Afterwards, a heavy tread and the door of the office closing quietly. I waited.

And then I opened the studio door and tiptoed down the stairs. From the fireside came the sound of voices. They were, again, talking about N – the same indifferent speculation, the same simple equations – this time a bit more barbed; it was now all 'she this', 'she that', and 'of course she . . .' and 'well she would' and 'it was her doing, wasn't it'.

From behind the office door I heard her protestations and Gerald trying to hush her. He told her that none of them could make a go of it without George, that nothing was the same; twenty fucking years and his own wife was a useless, selfish cow.

In the bar downstairs they decided that they'd better go. One of the men called for Gerald. I got up from the stair on which I was sitting. Just as I did so, N opened the office door. I caught sight of Gerald – unmoved, smoking a cigarette, staring coldly at the wall – before her body filled the open door. She had her back to me. Gerald grunted: 'Get rid of them.' I turned and crept back up the stairs. 'No,' N drawled, *you* get rid of them.'

Nine

Portsmouth. A provincial Sunday, aimless and left to litter. A day strewn with trash that ought to blow away unrecognised, but wouldn't. Outside the window a buckled grey sea moved stiffly under a grey sky, and along the edge of the beach there was a thin ceinture of ice.

She telephoned me in the early evening, asking me to pass on a message to the barman. I didn't see her that day, or the next. On Tuesday afternoon I heard her moving about in the office, and when I reminded her that I was going up to London to meet Gerald, she offered to take me to the station.

She met me in the bar at seven. I read no change of feeling in her towards me; her eyes were lazy, untroubled pools which would have closed calmly over any animosity that I might have shown.

In the car she said that Gerald wanted to see what I had written.

'I don't have it; it's in the safe in your office.'

'I know. Don't ever give him your address in London. You're not in the telephone book, are you?'

'I might as well have it disconnected. I seem to be living down here.'

'Not yet,' she said. 'Not quite.'

Her fingers traced the long buckled scab on the side of my face as we waited at the very end of the platform. As the train approached, dragging its panoply of lighted windows, she withdrew into the darkness and left me to the windborne smell of decaying seaweed.

I still find that carpark episode erotic. I remember it perfectly well, she and Gerald crunching across the costume jewellery of that stubborn winter. I remember the minutest details and have seen them, suddenly, many times over the years. The position of her head. The taut bow of her calf muscle. The whiteness of her fingers against Gerald's coat.

And I remember very clearly the wilful, successful way in which I stood in my rooms in London that night, meticulously constructing the full image and cementing it in my mind.

Why? How could my feelings have become so malleable? So surrendered. So, somehow, relieved.

The relief perhaps at not understanding her, nor having to understand her. A simple matter of watching her screwing, carelessly. They had screwed like strangers, without any sense of loneliness. I had seen the boss, N, engaged in sex; seen her fucked, on heat. This contrast with the imponderable chaos of feelings. The spectacle of her at copulation.

My feelings were, I realised in London, too claustrophobic. She had the power of centring everything around herself. I would have to find out about her.

More truthfully, I was hurt.

The next day, I arranged to meet Len Davis, the journalist who had covered the trial for the *Mirror*, in the Fleet Street Golf Club.

Davis was a short rotund man, sag-chinned and with a worthy untidiness. He freelanced in travel blurb, was the European stringer for a combine of American industrial journals, and featured for the *Mirror* on big crime cases.

He loved crime. He had three or four books at home, half-written, which he would go back to when he retired.

He would never retire. At sixty he looked too fond of the bags under his eyes. His favourite gesture was to push his glasses wearily up to perch on the top of his head, while he thought. It was theatrical, courtroomish. Not academic. He had a brother at the Yard. Was one of his books about the Croft trial?

No. He remembered the trial, and of course he remembered George Croft; there were two of them, brothers. But there wasn't anything in it. Oh yes, he dared say that a lot didn't come out, but there was enough and it was all straightforward. Croft had had a good run. They'd been out to get him for a long time, and when they did it all fell into place.

'Wasn't it surprising that he confessed?'

'Not really. A lot of them do. They want respectability, strangely enough. The problem is that they live in a complete social vacuum and most of them can't wait to get out of it. A lot of these big boys feel that they live in a film of their own lives. They could get away with a lot more, a lot more, but they start living off their own paranoia. When they make mistakes it's like' (his American magazine style?) 'it's unconsciously wilful; they want to create a reality for themselves, they want the public to know about them. You see, there isn't any social stigma against a robber. The public love a robber. A good criminal is a hero. And he feels that. But then if you've done a successful job,' what does it mean? You've got nothing you can show for it, no applause, nothing you can talk about. You might have five lines in a newspaper, and it's not enough. They want to be recognised. They don't have the emotionless make-up of stockbrokers, totting up the next hundred thousand. In a strange way, they're more like actors, a good criminal is.'

Davis rubbed the bags under his eyes, and brought his glasses down. I had got him started on his philosophy and he liked an audience. But in this case I thought that he was barking up the wrong gum tree.

'So the confession side isn't extraordinary?'

'No, not at all. Sometimes it's done to take the heat off everyone else. Some kind of martyrdom which suits everybody, including the police. That was one of the things in the Croft trial; everybody went home happy.'

'Everybody?'

'I thought so.'

'He had a brother, didn't he?'

'Yes. A weak character. I've never heard of him again.'

'And the wife?'

'Very charming. She was younger than he was. Very striking. Good-looking. In fact, I think we tried to build something around her.'

'How?'

'The paper made her an offer, as I remember. The usual angle: the swimming-pool life, "the tempestuous marriage", the affairs, photos of her in a bikini. That kind of thing.'

'Did she have affairs?'

'You haven't done much research. He murdered one of her lovers, that's when it blew up.'

'But were there a string of them?'

Davis shrugged. Once again I suspected that he had seized on a convenient stereotype.

'Do you remember her?' I asked. I showed him the photograph his paper had printed. For a couple of seconds he looked at it intently, and then he pushed his glasses up again and held the photograph at half-arm's length, pursing his lips.

'I wonder what's become of her,' he mused. 'She would have landed on her feet, I expect.'

'Who put the offer to her?'

'I did, on behalf of the paper.'

'And she didn't take it?'

'No. Oh, she played with it while the trial was on. It kept us occupied; it kept *me* occupied. She was clever.'

'And having affairs.'

'Who doesn't? In her case, who knows?' He shook his head.

'Do you?'

'If she didn't, it wouldn't have been through a lack of suitors.' He was old-fashioned, and protective of her, charmingly so.

'She wasn't interested.'

'Oh, she was interested, in everything. That's what made her so attractive. She wasn't as shallow as most of these women can be. To be honest, I liked her. But then when the trial finished, I realised that she had taken me for a bloody ride.'

'How so?'

'Well, that's not the right word. Professionally I should have got more out of her. I didn't bugger up the negotiations, because it was crystal clear afterwards that she would never have agreed. It was against her sense of honour. If I didn't know it at the start, I should have discovered it and then gone after a different angle.

But she had a way of diverting you. She was seductive, in more ways than the obvious.'

He changed his story. He said, 'I wouldn't think she had affairs, no. Or just the one. She wasn't that kind of woman.'

'Emerson.'

'What was his name?'

'Robert Emerson.'

'Yes . . . '

Davis seemed to be reflecting about something else.

'What about him?'

'Emerson? I can't remember anything about him. That's another reason why the story didn't make it. No love interest. I never did understand the affair. As far as the prosecution went, it was just the straw that broke Croft's back. It was clear-cut and all out of the way very quickly. She was never called to testify and that was an end to it. There's nothing in the case. You reminded me that I hadn't forgotten about her, but otherwise it was due process of law. What did he get, twenty?'

'Twenty-five.'

Davis nodded. I asked, 'How did she react to that, the sentencing?'

He thought.

'As you might have gathered I was pretty sold on her.'

'But still, she was in there at the end?'

'Yes. She held herself together very well. Very well,' he remembered. He seemed to feel that he had said enough; I watched him think about her. He came back to the present. 'Go on,' he said, 'you jog my memory. I'm the only one who's doing any work.'

'Okay. What's this about her sense of honour? You said something about a sense of honour, why she would never have agreed to sell her story to the newspapers. Why a sense of honour?'

'You're right.'

'I'm not right, I want to know about the end of the trial – '

'And the two of them.'

'If you like.'

'That's one way of looking at it. They both had a great sense of discretion. It wasn't that they were covering anything up, I don't think so. Except for the usual, probably the brother and a few small fry who nobody was interested in. I don't know where she came from, but it was clear that they had different backgrounds. What was remarkable was the feeling you got of there being two very strong sets of honour. Much stronger than the business of her having an affair. They were a good match, they could have survived that. In a case like Croft's, you would expect some acrimony to come out at the trial, at least a few fireworks. But they were very cool about it. Very formal. It became apparent to everyone that they shared a . . . an attitude – '

'What kind of an attitude?'

'You would have said that crime was his job and that the company had gone bankrupt. And she would adapt to not having him.'

'That's very cold!' I exclaimed.

'It wasn't,' Davis retorted. 'Somehow there was more love in that than in all the wailing and gnashing which usually goes on. Reserved, yes; but very loyal on both sides. They must have been very close, you know.'

'I suppose she gave everyone that feeling.'

Davis was for a moment taken aback by my cynicism. After a while he shook his head, as though I had been adolescently severe.

'No,' he said, 'I wouldn't have put it that way. And I wouldn't condemn her for being attractive. Being attractive isn't a fault. She had a lot of spunk, and a lot of principle behind it.' His face showed that he doubted whether I had the same.

I would have liked to see him again, and I kicked myself for having been so careless in trivialising his memories. She must have made a deep impression on him.

'I'll tell you something for nothing,' he said. When I looked up he was regarding me kindly, as though I was a cub reporter. 'I'll never get round to writing this book of mine, but if I did Croft would get a mention.'

'Why?'

'I don't know if you're interested in the sociology of crime, but he was a big step forward from the Kray era.'

'How?'

'Well, at that time it was much more family areas, or manors;

99

East London, West London, or south of the river. So inevitably, as they expanded, the gangs would run into each other. George Croft didn't bother with any of that. I doubt if he cared very much about his hoodlum brother. He pulled people in from all over Europe to do a job. It threw the Yard into a right panic, they had no way of dealing with it; and of course he never had to keep them sweet with backhanders. Croft had a lot of vision, or someone did. And he – or they – inspired trust; otherwise he would never have been able to keep it all together given the distances involved. He didn't have to use fear, like the Krays did. He didn't have to be nasty. Mind you, he wasn't a frustrated man. Not when he was married. Now tell me,' he leant forward, butter wouldn't have melted in his mouth, 'what have you got to do with her?'

'I know her.'

Still smiling, he got to his feet and I helped him on with his coat.

'Give her my regards, will you?'

'I will. She gave me your name,' I lied.

'Did she ... did she ...' He was genuinely pleased. 'All the way from Portugal?'

'No, that's Gerald's hideout.' I stopped; he had caught me off-guard. 'Confidentially,' I said.

He nodded. 'It would be. Rotten people have rotten lifestyles, sooner or later. I didn't think she'd leave England.'

'What's the *Mirror* like these days?'

'Well,' he grinned wryly, 'it used to be a good socialist newspaper, didn't it?'

On the way out, I realised that we hadn't eaten any lunch. I apologised, but he seemed happy enough to chew on the thick London air. His farewell was cheery – 'any time, give me a ring,' he said – and the brisk life of the street swallowed him up. I went across the road to McDonald's.

It struck me that I had learnt absolutely nothing; or that the information had bounced off me because I was so involved with N. I could have talked to him for an hour about the way she sat or walked across the room. Having her described to me was lightly meaningless, like the sweep of a wind across a field of wheat.

The wheat swayed and straightened up, the patterns created had disappeared. I knew her, I knew how she was, far better than anyone else; there was no point in talking to anyone else about her.

I suddenly missed her. I missed her meaningfulness, her immediacy. I went to the door of McDonald's, hoping to catch sight of Davis, for I would have run after him and talked to him about her. But Davis was lost, somewhere in the middle of a million people.

And so, with absolutely nothing to say, I telephoned N.

'Do you want me?'

'Yes,' she said.

And she set my mind at rest. Neither of us said anything for a long time; perhaps according to British Telecom it was five seconds, but it was a very long time, a long, unheard echo, a glass case of jewels laid out side by side.

'And I want you in one piece, so be careful. Please be careful.'

She put the phone down. That was in order, perfectly in order. It was a wonderful phone call.

And then I suddenly wanted to ask her everything; and everything that Davis had said came back into my mind. 'A lot of spunk and a lot of principle.' What would Davis have made of it if he had been with me, watching Gerald and N in the carpark? Rotten lifestyles? N's principles in dealing with rotten people? 'Croft had a lot of vision, or someone did.' Someone had vision. Nothing in George convinced me that he had any vision. Davis seemed like a good judge of character, and he had rated N very highly. Everything in N suggested that she was the one with vision, but which of them was the one who inspired trust?

There remained the rotten one. The 'weak character'. The hoodlum.

'So be careful. Please be careful.'

I enjoyed football, but I didn't want to be kicking around with Gerald. Oh yes, beside N's quicksilver mind, he was slow; but he was nasty. In the sociology of crime he was a weak character, but close up it wasn't a polite matter of character.

The family club.

I bought a copy of the *Evening Standard.* London was happy.

Arsenal and Chelsea had won their cup matches on Saturday, Tottenham had an easy replay, and Queens Park Rangers were also at home tonight and would probably go through, according to the commentator, although you could never be sure with Rangers. They were the family club. Tom on the right wing, Dick on the left and Harry in the centre. Jean in the promotions office, Gerald and me in the grandstand.

I trusted N.

I ate a burger and telephoned Gerald's office from McDonald's. I said that I could meet him in West London since I was already near the Central Line.

'Well that's not going to do you any fucking good.' He was pre-match liquored, or just liquored.

'Why not? Aren't we going to Queens Park Rangers?'

He guffawed. There must have been others in the party, for I heard him roar, 'Anybody want to see bloody Queens Park Rangers?' and someone replied, 'Turn it in.'

'No,' he came back on the line, 'we're going to see Tottenham.'

'Oh. Well where shall I meet you?'

'You'll have to get down here to the office.'

The phone went dead; as if Gerald was bored and had killed the matter.

I got a cab. On the way down there I tried to act as I thought Davis would have acted, a man apparently having difficulty in remembering where to put his feet, until he felt that the ground was solid.

They were all well-oiled, a half-dozen of them in the pack, all about Gerald's age except for a thin boy in his late teens whom I seemed to recognise from somewhere. Gerald offloaded me on to him. 'Paul,' he called cheerfully, 'get this old tart a drink.'

N's first son, Paul.

The same beautiful eyes, but without depth to them.

A fashionable look, proclaiming cheap bisexuality.

George's adopted, become Gerald's protégé.

From somewhere a scum of tinny contempt, which he ladled over me. I understood why N had said that they would never get on. He was the one person I had met in my life who, for me, epitomised deceit at first hand.

When N, later, asked me about him, I couldn't bring myself to reply. I didn't want to think about him, I wanted nothing to do with him. I couldn't bring myself to describe him, nor to explain the instinctive reaction of angry disgust which seized me.

I had one quick, strong drink and then Gerald clapped me on the shoulder and decided that it was time to be off.

Paul gunned the Mercedes through London with his fingertips. I talked football in the back with Billy, a raddled and yellow-toothed publican, all the while keeping half an ear on Gerald's conversation with his nephew. They were irritable with each other. Gerald was irritable with Paul's bumptious, plain-sailing assumption that they would get everything done that they had to get done before going back to Portugal the next day. But Gerald was as drunk as usual, and Paul showed him no respect.

'And where the fucking hell are we going?' Gerald looked at his watch. Paul ignored him. He had us at White Hart Lane ten minutes before the kick-off.

'Leave the keys with the old man. Give him a couple of quid.'

Paul's face rested in the same blank insolence.

'And get back to the office by ten tomorrow,' Gerald ordered. 'I want to be at Heathrow for eleven.'

Billy and I got out of the car. Gerald buttoned his coat and was immediately the well-padded businessman, of a higher social caste than the people who thronged past us on their way into the stadium.

'Paul not coming with us?' I asked him as he turned away from the car.

'No, he's going to park the car at the filling station up the road. Last night in London, it's the clubs for him and the football for me.'

'Don't they have any in Portugal?'

Gerald snorted. 'It's not the same, is it? Over there they fall down every five minutes, they play like a bunch of bloody fairies. Anyway, we couldn't talk about his mother in front of Paul. You can talk about anything in front of Billy; can't you, Billy?'

Billy was nervous. Billy agreed with Gerald. He took his cue from Gerald and dropped back as we walked towards the ground, through a sickly smell of hot dogs and stewed onions.

'I want to see what you've got,' Gerald said, 'what you've been doing.'

'I haven't got it with me.'

'I can see that. After the game, we'll go and pick it up.'

'From Portsmouth?'

'You're fucking joking! You think I fell out of a banana tree? From where you live.'

'The papers are in Portsmouth.' I thought quickly. 'She never lets them go out of the building.'

'I gave her a message for you, didn't she tell you?'

'I haven't seen her since Saturday night. I don't see her that often. Her private life is her own affair.'

He stood still, and jutted his chin up at the stadium lights. Out of the corner of my eye I could see Billy looking for something, anything, to do. Eventually he went and bought a couple of match programmes.

'All right,' Gerald said. 'She must have forgotten.'

'I don't even know if she knew I was coming up to see you.'

He vented his annoyance elsewhere. 'Don't piss about out here, Billy; they give you a bloody programme with the seat. Pay a thousand quid a season, the least they can do is let you know what you're paying for.'

Billy smiled faintly. 'It would be,' he said, at a loss.

'Listen,' I demanded, 'even if you want to wade through a lot of illegible notes I don't think it would make any sense to you. You want me to be careful, don't you?'

Gerald grinned. 'Getting it in the neck, are you?'

From inside the stadium came the roar of the crowd. Around us latecomers broke into a trot, holding the front of their coats.

'Let's get inside,' Gerald said. 'Too concerned about herself, she is. Well, they all are, aren't they?'

But he was thinking. He walked into the ground and paced along the wide concrete corridors, deserted except for clusters of last-minute drinkers.

The crowd were massed over our heads, chanting and clapping with that slow lunge into chorus, and finishing with a quickened gunfire-beat of urgent venom which petered out and lost itself in a single-minded roar around the terraces. The noise intensified, it was like being on the crest of a towering wave as it moved inexorably towards land. Plastic cups were thrown to the ground as people scattered upstairs to see the kick-off. Billy rubbed his hands together. Gerald reached into his pocket and pulled out a key. He unlocked a door in the wall, pushed us inside and shut the door behind him.

The noise was cut off. I could even hear Gerald's footprints on the carpet as he walked past me; and the quiet thump as he threw his overcoat over the back of a chair.

'Fix us a drink, Billy. There's glasses in the cupboard, the fridge is on the left under the sink.'

There were ten seats in the box, in two rows of five.

Gerald sat in the front row, I waited for Billy to pour the drinks and then I sat beside Gerald. Billy sat behind him. We were totally sealed off from the game. The crowd murmured their enthusiasm; the players ran around outside the plate-glass window. I picked up the programme. Tottenham were playing Rotherham in a fifth-round replay of the FA Cup. Gerald watched the game, apparently unconcerned.

Tottenham scored one inside ten minutes. Billy reran the goal rhapsodically. Gerald grunted his approval. From the restart, Tottenham might have had another one; the visitors' defence looked as though they had just been introduced to each other. They were out of their depth, overawed by the crowd and paralysed by the skill of the home team. The match was as good as over.

I detected a malaise in Gerald.

'What was George like as a player?' I asked him.

'He would have done all right if they'd transferred him to Rotherham.' Gerald laughed.

'He didn't take it seriously?'

'Of course he did. Too bloody seriously. Didn't he, Billy?'

'Well, he did, he did. You would have said that he had cold feet.'

'Cold feet?' I doubted it. 'You mean he was scared?'

Billy answered.

'George was *never* scared – '

'No.' Gerald picked at his collar uncomfortably.

'George never looked as though he had warmed up before a game, that's what I mean by cold feet. He was a strong defender, but he wasn't a player, was he? It wasn't in his feet, he was never a player.'

'Too bloody arrogant,' Gerald said, keeping his eye on the game.

'He didn't trust himself with the ball. He wasn't a footballer; he did it to please his father, didn't he, Gerald?'

'If you say so, Billy.'

Billy shut up. Gerald was restless. He didn't, I saw, particularly enjoy football, or perhaps George had precluded his enjoyment. But he wanted me to know that he wasn't being unfairly dismissive of his brother.

'No,' he said, 'it didn't go right for him. The ball never ran for him.'

'That's it,' Billy agreed, 'and it either does or it doesn't.'

'It must have depressed him.'

Gerald didn't see it that way. 'He was gloomy anyhow, George, when he was younger. He was too wrapped up in himself. Too much of a trier. He was a cold bastard most of the time, he took himself bloody seriously. He thought that just because he'd decided to carry the weight of the world on his shoulders, everyone else had to snap to attention. Nobody did, so he disappeared up his own arsehole. Which is where he is now. Right back where he was. All a bit soft, isn't it?' Gerald had said enough, and he had said it with a hatred that could only be fully released away from the family. He turned back to the match. 'They might as well play without that fucking goalkeeper,' he scoffed. 'Go on, Stevie boy, bang him into the back of the net.'

There was a knock on the door. The others arrived. 'Where have you fucking been?' Gerald stood up and laughed. 'We're going to get six or seven tonight, they're playing like the bank manager's after them.'

His friends hadn't found anywhere to park their car. I took it for granted that Gerald wouldn't have told them about the filling station; that was his way of maintaining his position over the crowd. I moved back to sit next to Billy, but the pack stood around the bar for most of the match.

George in prison. And that was why neither Gerald nor Jean seemed surprised by it; he was back where he had come from. In the interval he had had N. She had brought him out of himself, and then – ?

Tottenham made heavy weather of the *coup de grâce*. The match was embarrassingly one-sided. They got another goal just before half-time, and in the second half they got four, clinically, haughtily, to the bullyboy jeers of the barside pack.

We stayed on at the end of the match so as not to get caught up in the crowd. The executive suite was supplied with a colour television and the minute the final whistle went Gerald switched it on. The Royal Wedding was being re-broadcast in an edited format. It introduced a mood of funereal nostalgia.

One of Gerald's guests lived locally and would walk home. Billy took the spare place in the other car.

Gerald locked up the box.

The two of us walked a hundred yards to the filling station and the Mercedes. We heard on the radio that Queens Park Rangers had lost.

'They would, wouldn't they.'

'So you're off tomorrow?' I said.

'All things being equal.'

'For the summer?'

'Could be. We'll have to see what comes up.'

'Do you want to stop somewhere for a drink?'

'No, I'll take you home. Have you got any plans for the summer?' His mood was flat and he was being unnervingly polite.

'I don't fancy London much.'

'It's full of bloody foreigners. All sorts.'

'Mostly Americans.'

It triggered him off. He sat upright in the driving seat; responding to a nervous tic, he stretched his neck, as though his collar was too tight.

Americans and blacks. Gerald didn't like them, never had. Right back to the fifties. When they stayed here after the war, when they were a novelty. When all the fucking women wanted a piece of black, a black dick stuck up them, everywhere. Couldn't get enough of it. That's how the blacks stayed in the country. Then they sent for their bloody wives and cousins, gave them a hatful of piccaninnies, set them all up on social security and pissed off to screw some other woman. But that was how it had started, after the war, when the white women wanted them, like animals.

I thought that his vehemence would be a convenient screen for my departure. We caught up with the football traffic in Stoke Newington and I told him that I lived nearby and he could drop me off.

For a moment he seemed completely out of control, out of his depth, blinking and inwardly raging at his frustration, jutting his chin spasmodically as though he was having some kind of seizure.

The traffic was moving at less than walking-pace. I reached for the door handle, expecting his grip on my arm. I had crossed him somehow, or got to know him, or was about to leave him; none of which he liked.

But he chose not to do anything about it. He recovered a disturbing equilibrium.

'Where d'you live?' he said.

'Just off to the right, at the lights.'

There were two lanes of traffic, he was trapped on the inside, he couldn't make the turn without giving himself away.

'Anything else you want to know?' he said.

'I don't want to know too much,' I said. 'Just how to leave the country fast if I have to.'

He expelled a snort of shallow amusement through his nose. 'Clever, you are. It's not how, it's *when* you leave. When I see what you've written. Tell her,' he snarled.

I thanked him for the football.

I turned right at the lights and from the window of a pub watched the Mercedes inch past in the line of traffic. Half an hour later I caught a bus. The upstairs was empty and I had a view out of the back and side windows, just in case the Mercedes had returned.

Ten

I told her.

'Are you scared?'

'Yes, I am.' I had been, last night, in London; and on the way down, in the train, in the morning, I had carried the fear with me.

'He's gone.' She shrugged and picked up the phone. She called Gerald's office and asked to speak to him. 'I see. Thank you.' She put the phone down. 'He's gone.'

She looked at me patiently.

'He'll be back,' I said.

'We'll be ready for him. We will, you know.'

The phone rang and she answered it. She was bored by the caller at first; her right foot played with her shoe, knocking it over and reclaiming it like a cat with a mouse. She raised an eyebrow and smiled at me affectionately, yessing at the mouthpiece of the telephone, leaning against the desk. Then she dug her foot into the shoe and walked around to her side of the desk and sat down; she reached for a pen, she flicked through her appointment book. I made to leave.

'Where are you going?' she said.

'To the studio?'

'Just a moment.' She cupped the mouthpiece of the phone in her hand and looked at me, half concerned, half amused. 'You're not still worried?'

'Yes.'

She pursed her lips. 'Don't be.' She stood up, hampered by the telephone and the caller on the end of the line. 'I thought that I wouldn't see you until this evening, and now there's the rest of the afternoon to get through. You will have forgotten about Gerald by this evening.'

She turned away and addressed the telephone. 'Yes, I'm sorry. Let's see now. Not next week, some time the week after?'

She cupped the mouthpiece again and asked me: 'What shall I wear?'

I slept through the afternoon; at one point I was disturbed by a nightmare, but my body felt like lead and it dragged me back into unconsciousness. I awoke at the touch of her lips. She was bending over me, her hand stopped her hair from falling across my face. I smelt the hot warm smell of clean bath-water from next door. A finger touched my lips.

'I'll see you at the bar. There's no hurry.'

She absorbed my worries. I don't remember much of our dinner conversation. We argued, until I saw that she was kidding me along with a steady irony in her eyes. There was nothing to worry about.

I do remember her placid contempt for Gerald when I told her about our conversation, but she didn't want to hear what he thought about George. It was now, of course, she said, all so legal for Gerald. She stayed my hand when I went to refill her glass. 'I don't want us to get drunk. Just forget about him.'

I didn't tell her about Davis. He seemed so far away and she made everything seem irrelevant. It was as though visiting London and checking up on her had simply been *my* affair; here was the centre of the world, in this room now, in front of the fire, beside the sway of the cognac around the glass which she held in the palm of her hand, in the luxuriant tumble of hair which lay in my lap as she sat in front of me with one arm carelessly resting across my knee, looking at the fire, comfortable. The surface of the world might spin for all its worth, but this part of it was calm, this centre. The cognac stilled, and she sipped at it. She asked me what I was thinking about.

I said that I had stopped thinking, which she didn't believe.

'All right,' she said, 'but perhaps I should tell you something.

III

You *are* still going to work for me, aren't you?'

'Yes.'

'I know you won't forget about everything, even though we . . .' she thought about it, but let it drop just the same, ' . . . well, we are, so that doesn't matter.'

I could feel a certain tension in her shoulders, as though she was about to shiver.

'You know,' she resumed, 'Gerald isn't the slightest bit interested in doing this for George. It's all my idea and it has been from the start.

'You shouldn't bother with him,' she exclaimed, 'you shouldn't let him get in our way.'

She fidgeted. I pushed the chair back and lay down on my side behind her, my head propped on my arm, watching her profile.

'Now that he's away, perhaps you'll understand that there's only the two of us. It's what I've wanted since Christmas.'

She gathered the coils of her hair and lifted them clear of her shoulder, depositing them behind her. She found a snippet of white cotton on the skirt of my bathrobe and picked it off; and then she looked forward at the fire, ill at ease.

She suddenly started to describe her affair with Emerson, the clandestine freedom and the sheer, intense pointlessness of it. How she had willed herself forward into that blind alley. How she had humiliated herself.

When I had listened to her before, talking about her life with George, she had spoken with the excitement of love; but now there was nothing. She was blinkered and running a course between impregnable barriers, not looking at me for support.

' – with a man who hated women,' she muttered. 'Loveless. Unpleasant. There are times when I hate myself.'

I found it hard to believe the story of their affair, but I couldn't not believe in the soundless cry of pain which came from her. I wanted to tell her that I understood her weakness, and that it didn't matter. But I couldn't catch her eyes.

'I wanted to tell you everything,' she said. 'You should know.'

She twisted on to her knees and stubbed out her cigarette in the ashtray. I took her spare hand. She shuffled nearer to me and sat on her haunches against me, running her glance over the bathrobe.

'I must look a sight,' she said.

'No.'

She looked, I thought, successful – which I didn't tell her. She opened the collar of the bathrobe and prodded a crimson nail into my breast. 'I want to hide.'

She lit a cigarette and left it on the ashtray over the mantelpiece. She reached up behind her neck and tried to unclip the top of her dress, her hand fumbled with the fastener and she became exasperated. I stood up and I held her from behind, I enclosed her within the robe.

She swayed gently. She relaxed. With her heels planted firmly apart, her thigh muscles tightened and gave as she shifted her weight from side to side against my body. She lifted her head and watched the cigarette smoke as it mushroomed against the ceiling over the fireplace.

She left the cigarette to die. I wriggled her dress up to her hips and unsilked her, drawing the flimsy briefs down her legs. The hemline of her dress followed my hands discreetly, as though the fireplace was a shop window and her nakedness was prey to the bobbing curiosity of the flames.

Before my eyes she lifted one black heel free of the blue silk and staked it back down into the rug, and with the toe of her other shoe she flicked the discarded garment away from her. She turned and gathered my head up against her hips for a moment and then she stepped out of her shoes, pushing me away to lie on the rug. She lifted the skirt of the bathrobe away from my body so that I was spread on a plateau of cornflower blue.

On all fours, without a shred of modesty, she clambered astride my thighs. She reached forward and cajoled me firmly; a smile playing about her lips. I placed my hands on her knees, my palms sliding against the nylon.

As if to say 'Look! I want you to see this, this moment', she knelt up and lifted the black dress clear of her abdomen, and while I clutched the back of her knees and looked, she slowly sank down and buried me inside her, watching herself with the unselfconscious seriousness of a child looking at a scratch on its skin.

Her hands on my hips, or hanging loosely by her sides, her lips parted, her torso undulating, she began to sift the pleasure through our bodies.

'I love you.'

I lost sight of her face. I saw her hair and the puddle of ice-blue silk between my outstretched hand and the fireplace, and then I was lost in a quickening success.

The outside door rattled and we ignored it, intent on our celebration.

It rattled again.

'No,' she insisted – 'No. No. No.'

There was a crash.

She sagged forward, her eyes gritted with frustration, the blood high in her cheeks. She panted heavily across my chin. 'Leave it.'

But there was another crash.

Someone was putting their shoulder to the door.

She placed her hands on either side of my face, shielding me. Her vaginal muscles tightened.

'Who is it?' she called throatily. She coughed. 'We're closed.'

We both listened for an eternity, motionless.

There was no response.

'I love you.' She smiled at me and kissed me.

From outside the door came the sound of some scuffling and a gruff, incoherent voice.

N stood up, arranged her dress and advanced to the edge of the rug. 'Who is it!' she demanded. 'Who!'

'It's Gerald,' I said.

She shook her head, disbelievingly.

He struck the door again. I wrapped the bathrobe around me and stood by the fire. N came to the chair and took a cigarette off the side-table. She went back to stand at the edge of the rug.

'Go away!' she ordered. 'Go home! Go away!' There was no certainty to her voice. Abruptly, she walked towards me, picked up her underwear, and pushed it under the cushion of her chair. She stared at the door. There was to be no easy dismissal. The door was struck again. And again. Persistently. Regularly.

I ran across the stone floor and leant against the door. The blows were beginning to have some effect. The bolts were slipping and the latch had strained within a fraction of coming undone. Time and time again the door shook as it was battered. There was no possibility of diverting him. He was immune to any form of entreaty. It crossed my mind that at the start we might have opened a window, called out, defused the blind anger – but neither of us would have dared to do that now, the force was too insane, too vindictive.

And we were both too scared to think. From the other side a hand scrabbled violently at the latch. N screamed obscenities at the shaking door.

The crashes changed and became ominously rhythmic, suggesting a ponderous infliction of damage, as if a slow smile had come over the features of the face on the other side, as if he smelt the pleasure of entering brutally.

N and I stared at each other across the room; the anger, the shame and the perplexity were high in her cheeks. She walked to the bar and called the police.

They sent three cars and took the intruder. He was a Scandinavian, probably a seaman. He was big and drunk and didn't give them any problem. N didn't wish to see him. When I opened the door I saw that the door-mat was strewn with crushed cigarettes.

'It's a cold night, sir, I expect he was just trying to get inside for the warmth. Probably hoping that we might pick him up. Had a few and lost his way. We'll keep him in overnight, he won't trouble you again.' The policemen stood by the bar, taking it all in; me standing at the other end of the bar in a bathrobe, N arrayed stiffly in her chair by the fire.

She shut the door behind them. She twitched slightly with repulsion and we listened to them drive away.

She looked around the room. She said, quietly, that she would go to bed.

She gathered her shoes. Dangling them by the heels she started upstairs.

I sat for a moment, confused and unhappy.

I put the fireguard in front of the fire, I turned off the lights and carried her underwear upstairs.

Her clothes were put away. She lay on her side, in a foetal position, with her back towards me. She was wearing a peach-coloured nightdress. She had been crying.

She lay still for a while; and then she asked me to turn off the bedside light, she didn't want me to see her. I approached her in darkness.

She waited until I had settled and then she turned her body in against me. Her breath fanned across the pillow.

Grudgingly, she gave me access to her skin. I tasted salt on her cheeks and the flavour of toothpaste and cognac about her lips. With her arms stretched wide she was slowly crucified, without remorse; with a jolt, and with a persistent, silent humility.

The next morning her dry lips tickled my shoulder; it was as though a fly had dropped out of nowhere, for she rolled away and stood up, wrapping her gown around her, silhouetted against the grey-skyed window.

I cannot place passion in perspective. For five days I did not spend an hour away from her. Our intentions consolidated around us, as if rushing for the huge vacuum over which we had unconsciously laboured for the last four months.

I felt every movement of her body, every mood, every aspiration. Coy or brazen, scenting of soap or reeking of old episode, I desired her; when she was clothed or swollen with nakedness, when she was painted or when she was fey, I loved her. She lay, day or night, coverless, one arm left behind her, with her hand and ringed finger gripping her hair, covering her brow. She lay, day or night, a long white back and a mass of weedish hair, glistening with creams and unguent, until, startled by herself, she arched and capsized, damp and guttered, a sensitive carcass, exhausted, seeking respite from pleasure.

And between times, she said, she was only waiting; balancing on a thin sheer cord of tension, waiting for it to tauten, at a look, at a touch, at a memory. Obvious and disarmed, and with a rich bright laziness in her eyes and a full sag in her body when she dressed, she then went about her business in the bar, fully aware of the provocation from her silks and nylons – not seeking to avoid the pressure of my eyes on those inflamed areas, but toying with the friction until she could accept it no longer and we would meet violently and quickly and exuberantly, hardly waiting for the door of bedroom, bar or office to close, some screen to drop and grant us our confessional.

I cannot place passion in perspective. It is a surrender of all perspective. It is the opening of every wound, the grasping of every straw; it is reverence, iconoclasm, recklessness, the perfect exercise of judgement and good sense.

Five days. And all the people who staffed the restaurant and the bar knew about us, and were happy for us. They appeared to us as a newly forged team of benevolent intimates, a surround of warm-hearted people in the know.

It worried N. 'I think they've all gone a bit gaga,' she complained. 'I can't seem to get through to them.'

'They're protecting us,' I said.

'Why? What from?'

'Because we're gaga.'

'*I'm* not.'

'Aren't you?'

'I've never been more certain of myself in my life. It's the others.' Her plush body draped itself across mine.

'The others are fine.'

I rubbed the small of her back with my hand. I couldn't quite believe her body, whichever part of it confronted me, its separateness, her own workaday attitude towards its beauty.

'David will be home for the school holidays in a couple of days. I don't know what to do with him.'

'What do you usually do?'

'We get on very well after the first three or four days. Children are extraordinary. You haven't ever wanted one?'

117

'No.'

'You will.'

'I don't think so.'

'You'll change.'

'No.'

'Too conservative?'

'Maybe. I suppose I wouldn't mind if I could just visit them occasionally.'

She laughed. 'You'll have to find a woman who'll agree to that, and it won't be easy.' She rolled off the bed and walked naked across to the writing desk. She bent forward and smeared a peppering of cigarette ash off her thigh. I desired her again, immediately, as she knew I would. She came back to bed without the ashtray and presented herself comfortably for my attention, instructing me towards her surrender.

I wrote about her while she slept.

At one point I looked up and she was watching me peacefully, her head resting on the crook of her arm, her hair splayed out behind her on the pillow. I was trying to describe her body, but I had lost all accuracy; there were too many adjectives and they ran together in a blur.

'Go on,' she said drowsily. 'I didn't want to disturb you. I wanted to watch you think.'

She was smiling at me, enjoying my discomfiture. I came back to her.

I slept. When I awoke she was kneeling in front of the window-seat. It was my turn to interrupt.

'What are you doing?'

'Getting back to normal,' she mumbled.

'Why?'

'I don't know. Not normal normal,' she smiled at my wariness, 'just normal. You were asleep.' She turned back to the window-seat. 'I haven't looked into this cupboard for years.'

She lifted the lid and looked inside. I watched from the bed while she pulled out all the contents and deposited them without comment on the carpet. Until she was surrounded by old china, kitchen mixers, rolls of wallpaper, a candelabra, high leather boots, glasses in tissue paper, half a dozen records, a Venetian figurine (from Jean?), a silver cigarette box, and so on, covering the space between the disarrayed bed and the window.

'My God.' She stood up stiffly and stared around her. 'Look at it all . . . '

'Treasures,' I suggested.

'Treasures, my arse. I'll get someone to get rid of it.' She stood, helplessly trapped in the middle, appealing for assistance. I thought that it wouldn't be a good idea for the staff to see and smell the state of our room, it was a wonderful smell of love but perhaps the boss –

She laughed. 'Quite right. We'll just have to put it all back.'

And we did.

'Are you going to chuck it all out?'

'Yes.' She qualified herself. 'Maybe.'

I claimed an old, walnut-veneered mantel-clock, without arms. 'This?'

'Yes. Burn it or something.'

I burnt the clock just before midnight. We were alone, at the end of that fifth day. N was ensconced in her chair, with her legs dangling over my shoulders.

At first the clock refused to take fire. It cracked in the middle and the wood ribbed underneath, but it preserved its shape. The flames skimmed its surface, unable to find a hold. It crackled, like an old wireless. Something peeled between two and five, the figure four fell off and was lost; but the clock retained its shape, perching on the logs.

I rubbed the shiny, plucked-chicken skin on N's shaved legs.

The clock caught fire between one and two, and then the fire was eager, like ants, like adults with ice-cream; and the clock toppled forward with a great sudden heat.

I scraped the burning fragments off the rug. There was no more clock-face, there was only a black mechanism, standing on the logs like the wreckage of an airship. Satisfied skeletons, occasional sharp angles.

N watched, her face at once pale and ruddy, her eyes in a trance. She blinked and looked at me directly.

She asked me to love her.

Eleven

She didn't confide in David. He had a two-week holiday, during which time N took him up to London for three days and he made a new friend in the shape of Fiona's son. N and I slept together for the two nights he stayed with Fiona and we snatched love whenever the moment afforded. She stayed at her house. It was strange never knowing what she would wear and stranger to stumble on an absolute evenness of passion, unheralded, undwelt upon, again and again the same wonderful discovery, taken like medicine.

David was a serious, interested child, quite sure of his independence. N had given him the line of my being a local historian and he treated the studio room as someone else's library, where he didn't necessarily have to be quiet. I went out with him twice to museums, and took him along to the local magistrates' court, where we listened for an hour to the case against a vagrant who was accused of theft. He thanked me for taking him. He was very polite. I asked N if I should ask him about his father.

'Of course you can talk about it if he wants to.'

'Do you say that you are divorced from George?'

'No. That would be untrue. It's never a good idea to lie to children. We trust each other completely. You'd be surprised. After George's imprisonment I didn't have anyone else to talk to, so I talked to him. I sent him away to school because I thought that otherwise he wouldn't have a childhood.'

'What about George?'

'What do most of the kids at that school know about their fathers? Very little, I should imagine. I've met one or two of his friends, and believe you me David is by no means a screwed-up child. If anything, he's more mature. Single-parent families are often a blessing to the children.'

'You don't have to be so defensive.'

'I'm not. It's true.'

'What about Paul?'

'Exactly. Who knows that it wouldn't have been better for him if George hadn't turned up?'

'That must have been your decision.'

'It was. But that doesn't stop it from being a bad one.'

She took David to see his father. When they came back they were both tired. I knew that N would want to see me. They stopped in at the restaurant for a snack. It was late and she went to the kitchen to find something to eat.

David took a pile of coins over to the pinball machine. I watched him from the bar. He looked terribly alone; at one point the machine was silent and I thought that he was crying. N brought down a plate of sandwiches and a cup of cocoa for him. I nodded across at the solitary figure, and for a moment she worried. 'Leave him,' she decided, 'he'll work it out.'

I poured her a drink. I pretended to clean up behind the bar and N told me how the bar was stocked, what they would aim to get through on a weekday or during weekends, what brands should go on the cooler.

'David,' she called, 'come and drink your cocoa before it gets cold, please.'

He put a coin in the machine and played stoically. She let him finish the game and then she summoned him angrily.

'David!'

'Sorry, Mum.' He ran across the room and sat on a bar stool. He looked at the cocoa. 'It's got skin on it.'

N picked off the milky skin and dumped it into an ashtray.

'Thanks,' he said, and he smiled mischievously at her. She returned his smile.

'Then it's straight home to bed.'

'Yes.' He drank half the cocoa. 'Dad goes to bed about this time, doesn't he?'

'Yes.'

'And reads. He reads everything. He'll probably get round to your book. But he's doing carpentry at the moment. It's a temporary craze.'

N bit back a laugh. 'Probably,' she said.

'What's so funny about that?'

'Nothing. Without a doubt your father will not turn carpentry into a temporary craze. Once he starts something, he finishes it. He doesn't have temporary crazes.'

'Well I probably get it from your side of the family.'

'You do not. What temporary crazes do you have?'

'Clothes. That's from you.'

N shrugged. 'I have to have a lot of clothes. When they come in here people don't always want to see me in the same dress.' She scowled at him and then ruffled his hair, which he didn't like.

'Anyway, you haven't asked me about my other craze.'

'What is your other craze?'

'Sniffing glue!'

She believed him immediately. Her eyes searched his face as if the skin might fall off his nose at any moment.

'Fifteen tubes a day,' he flirted, his eyes playing with the joke just as his mother's eyes did sometimes. 'Don't worry, Mum, it's not true.'

'It had better not be, mister prankster.'

'That lot are cretins.'

'Well stay away from them.'

He told us a school joke, at which we laughed. N said that she had one for him: he was going to the dentist tomorrow.

He said goodnight without being prompted. N asked me to lock up. I did so, and I went to bed. On the pillow was a note – 'I love you'.

During the last four days of his holiday, midway through the afternoon, he would knock at the door of the studio and come in to see me. He was bored and wanted to be entertained. He asked me about what I did and we soon exhausted the appeal of what little local history I knew. He liked bits of stories; the characters didn't have to be of heroic proportions, but, not surprisingly, he wasn't interested in theories. We tried manufacturing a 'once upon a time', set in the early nineteenth century, but the pile of events and characters collapsed under their own weight and he was clearly disappointed in my lack of stamina.

I told him the simple story of one of my clients who had kept a small farmyard in his London flat; and another one about a woman who had six months' treatment for obesity at a hospital before suddenly giving birth to a child one afternoon outside a news-agent's; and the story of someone who had sat for so long in an armchair that when they tried to get her out they found that her bottom had been half eaten away by worms.

And the one about the widow who spent all her pension on wooden planks, making the floors of her basement flat higher and higher, because for six months of the year there were six inches of water in the rooms. How cheerful she was at teatime, in her Wellington boots, and how she had asked the squatters next door to sell the lead off the roof of her building and give the money to the girl who was having a baby.

And how, four doors away from the widow, there was a man who wanted free electricity from the council because he was designing a tail that would plug into the neurons at the base of the human back – and this invention, he believed, would enable there to be two-tier pedestrian traffic in Oxford Street, when tourists could swing like monkeys on wires above the pavement.

N caught the last story; she had come to fetch David for dinner. She pooh-poohed David's suspension of disbelief.

'Some of it's true, though, isn't it?' he appealed to me.

'All of it is. The last one sounds the most ridiculous, but the man came to see me about giving the council his patent if they would pay his electricity bills.'

'Did you work it out?' N retorted.

'Of course not. What would I do with a reputation for being mad?'

'Tell me about the one with the farmyard. Will you write it for me tomorrow? Please. Promise.'

'All right.'

On his last day, I showed him something else. When he came up to say goodbye, he said, 'It's very nice to have met you.' I gave him a tenpenny piece with a small hole drilled in it, near the circumference.

'Now let's go and play the one-arm bandit.'

'All right,' he said, unwillingly. 'But you know it's rigged; my mother told me and that's why I don't play it. I suppose it's all right if I tell you. Don't say anything though.'

The bar was empty, it was before opening-time. I attached the coin to a length of thin fishing line.

'Now. You drop it in the slot, just far enough to tickle the insides of the machine.' We listened for the click, and then I pulled the coin back an inch. 'Let it drop, and pull it back, to and fro. Then you can play for as long as it takes to clean the machine out, without ever losing your money.'

'Let me try.'

He mastered the trick easily.

'That's great,' he said. He went on racking up the credits without ever stopping to play the machine. He finally retrieved the coin. 'Can I keep it?'

'Sure.'

'I don't expect I'll ever use it. It's the kind of thing that got my dad into trouble. But it's a good trick to show poor people. If you got a patent, you could sell it.'

N came out of the office. 'Ready?'

'Yes.' He stuffed the line into his pocket.

'What are you two up to?' she enquired.

'Nothing,' David said. 'Well, we're just thinking of a way to sell tenpenny coins for a pound.'

'Tell me about it some time,' she remarked caustically. An agile, flirtatious glance sparkled through her eyes.

He went back to school.

It was a lazy time, with love on our hands. Long, unwasted afternoons, waiting for summertime to come. Broken skies outside the studio window, an even temperature within. A clumsy, easy repletion, like a mixing of syrups.

The manacled prisoner disappeared. N removed it and hung a Mexican tapestry in its place; she didn't remark on this and I didn't notice it for some time, although I felt that the room was unaccountably lighter. When I did realise, the change hardly seemed significant beside the constantly shifting pattern of her hair against her skin.

She often slept at her house. Sometimes I would be up until dawn, writing the short stories which David had liked. She had given me the key to the house and, once or twice, if I made it through the night, I would walk through Portsmouth and make her a cup of coffee, leaving it beside her bed, enchanted by the pristine cleanliness of her room, the 15B-ishness of N, my mistress.

Events of passion are insubstantial when written about, and I am reluctant to give away the secrets of N's body.

She has that collection of writings, done at odd moments over the summer, when I was so amazed by her body – each movement, stasis, offering and cry; each swell of flesh, each hollow and brow of muscle – when I was so impressed by these fleeting images that I held them under a magnifying glass and preserved them in writing. I wrote them down for myself, and for her, that she might perhaps have some recognition of her beauty.

She has those writings. There is no copy of N. There could never be one. It would be fraudulent to have her fake a lovemaking. She has her secret.

It was strange with N. She once told me that she had changed all her friends after George had been imprisoned. 'Just like that,' as the old comic magician Tommy Cooper would say with a giggle when he made a farce out of the simplest trick.

I could imagine it of her – this severity with herself. A natural isolation which her friends would find over-dramatic at first, and then hurtful. They would have felt used, and, more truthfully, perhaps slightly at a loss when they were no longer being used.

I wondered if that was true of Fiona. N invited her and Michael to dinner; something of a gesture for Fiona's taking David off her hands during the school holidays, something of a granted favour in permitting Fiona to witness that we were together.

Fiona was nervous of N, and unsure of the terms on which they were to meet. N made no secret of being helpless with happiness, with the accent on the helplessness, as if she was shy socially and grateful for Fiona's support, as if she was in a state of emotional abandon and had missed Fiona's steadying influence. Between the two of them there was a champagne flirtation, while Michael and I supped small beer contentedly; as a couple of obedient, well-hunted dogs might lounge on a fireside rug.

I liked Michael. He didn't care much about anything, he always looked as though he'd been fucked off his feet. He wasn't smug, he was interested in the world. Fiona said that when he wasn't with her he was probably sitting in a pub somewhere talking to a tramp, or driving to another county to talk to a gamekeeper, or sleeping in his car after having been out on the estuary with mudflat fishermen. When he had first met Fiona's son in December, and had been informed that Father Christmas was for the birds, he had returned on Christmas Eve, half zonked on exhaustion and booze, and had stamped around on the roof of the cottage shouting 'Yo-ho-ho'; scaring them to death until he skidded and plunged into the hawthorn hedge.

He blushed and smiled at these stories. He was waiting, he said, for a few years, and then he'd cash it all in and buy a boat and sail around the world – which eventuality, he assumed, would always be a few years away.

I asked N later what she thought of him, and she said, 'He's slippery. She'll never get hold of him.'

At the end of the evening, Fiona and she were the best of friends; they had made all kinds of light plans for expeditions and redecorations and lunches. Fiona was a different person from the badgerish woman who had, on her first meeting with me, sought gossip about N to the neglect of Michael. She did, though, manage to suggest one firm arrangement: that she and Michael would like to occupy the studio room on Wednesday nights. He and I were standing by the bar, N and Fiona had been laughing together at the foot of the stairs.

'I should think so,' N said, and the matter was dropped tidily into our ears.

After they had left, N was pleased with herself. She wished, she said, when she had undressed and smooched and played, to be made love to, from behind, with my hands on her hips. There! Now! Swine-like.

Then we lay and talked about emotional security, and laughed.

She talked about her life in the summer. She would walk along the beach to the other side of the point, following a broken wave as it retreated and burrowing with her hands into the wet sand to dig out hermit crabs. And tennis; the people she played with in the late summer afternoons; and on Sundays she would sometimes pack a bag and drive off to stay with Fiona, or some other people she knew who had a large house in Kent. Fiona came from a wealthy aristocratic family, with a huge house and estates. But she was the third daughter and got nothing in the will. It all went to the eldest son, who kept trying to be eccentric and just ended up being wimpy. But rich. Fiona rented a cottage on the estate; cheaply, but she still had to pay. Like the two or three other women in other cottages, her brother's mistresses, whom he kept trying to fertilise.

'Why?' I asked.

But N was asleep.

There came a week when I didn't see her very often. She went home early, saying that she had a load of paperwork to get through, that there were things she had to get ready for the July–August tourist peak.

I was writing about her, trying, as it were, to polish the writing up; I wanted to give her a present of this writing, wrap it up and lay it before her.

The writing had become very serious – solemnly ornate, I suppose – and this was reflected in our lovemaking. To say that she didn't mind is not to say that she relished it, although she was at times aroused by my voyeurism. She didn't like the way in which I touched her; she said it was as though I was checking on her, more unpleasant than if she was in the stirrups in front of her doctor. 'Don't be such a lawyer,' she said once, disgustedly.

But I wrote about her, closely, pinpointing the minutiae of her body in desire. If I had any humour, it was in the absurd stories of my legal clients which gushed at imprecise moments across pieces of paper.

One morning, I awoke to the sound from the bathroom taps. There was a cup of coffee beside the bed. She came out of the bathroom in a pair of tracksuit trousers and a sweater, pale and without any make-up. She went over to the pile of post which she had brought with her from the office. She smiled at me absently, and I knew that something was wrong. It was a strange feeling; that I was distant from her and guilty of something.

She switched on the tape deck and inserted a cassette. She killed the noise of the taps, shed her clothes and lay in the bath.

I put on a sweatshirt and a pair of jeans and went into the bathroom. I bent over the tub and kissed her, my hands on each side of her face, bedraggling her hair. She reached one arm up out of the water and held me to lips bleached of passion, calm but set in determination. When she let me go I glanced at her pubic hair, waving gently in the sway of the water, like moss. A voice came from the cassette-player, and I knew that it was her husband's voice, it was George.

I faced the mirror and prepared to shave. She lay behind me, looking at the wall by my shoulder, or looking at her feet, her chin half submerged beneath the water. Her face was expressionless, its changes dictated by the ripples in the bath as she picked something off the surface or moved a leg.

George had not rehearsed. The soundtrack halted frequently and abruptly, there was no continuity. I made no sense of it because I didn't want to make sense of it. It was none of my business, none of it – even if he had said that he knew about N and me, even if he would go on to threaten us. It was not my business. Above all, it was not my business to hear his innocence.

I shaved methodically, at my usual pace, while the sound of his voice came and stood at my ears. When I turned round, N's eyes were fixed along the dead-still surface of the bath-water, and I walked away through the bedroom with that image of level water in front of me. I closed the door and went downstairs to the empty bar.

I would have appreciated male company. I would have liked to stand and exchange gratifying, irrelevant chat with a man, any man, even perhaps George, in a pub, in a bar, in the canteen of a factory, in an office break, at a railway station, anywhere. With a man, with men. Just to forget women. Just to participate in the easy, dull consensus of men who didn't care very much at the moment, who chuckled without guilt, who took pleasure in being away from women, who weren't haunted.

I went to the kitchen and made a large breakfast.

The best feeling in the world is the feeling of having got away with it; having visited a woman, having known and shared love without unearthing that complex solitude – and then to walk into an anonymous bar and strike up a conversation with a perfect stranger. About what is in the newspaper, about the local football team, government policy, life in another country, the railway service, the small shops that carry on a tradition of well-made shoes, the space programme, television. Occasionally thinking of the unmade love-bed, the woman getting dressed, going out or staying at home. But talking to a perfect stranger, with opinions but not too many, facts that are pleasantly unverifiable, a conversation which is agreeable to both parties without entailing any bonds whatsoever – both of you will get up and go at the same time and will never see each other again.

To be able to think of N as I buy twenty cigarettes, and to think joyfully: 'I've got away with it! How good it is to be alive!'

As I went back upstairs, the room was silent. I opened the door. Startled, I noticed N's face in the mirror on the dresser, smiling at me wryly.

'You look happy.' She bent forward and concentrated on applying her lipstick.

'Do I?'

'Yes.' She smacked her lips together and smiled again. 'Don't be so embarrassed about it. Otherwise I'll think you've got another mistress.'

I suddenly trusted her completely. There was a complicity. I sat on the bed. She pushed back the stool and walked past me to her wardrobe; ringless, she stood with her back to me, that fine bottom on a level with my eyes, an arm's length away.

She chose her clothes and dressed, and she stood with her hands in her pockets.

'You know, you'd better tell me what you want to do.'

There was no pretence that this was a casual enquiry, which might elicit a casual answer.

'I would like to go to London to collect a few things, and then I would like to stay with you.'

She told me afterwards why she had provoked this decision. It marked a commitment and she wanted that commitment; she didn't indulge in casual affairs. She wanted me to stop being infatuated with her, to take her for granted.

And in any case, she said, there were other things to write about. She had taken stock and she didn't intend to run any risks.

When I got back to Portsmouth she drove me straight to 15B and she led me upstairs to Paul's bedroom, very much the spare room. From the picture rail she had hung the entire contents of her wardrobe: dresses, skirts, trousers and gowns. On the bed there were piles of sweaters, shirts and underclothes; also some of my things from the studio.

'How are we going to arrange this,' I asked; 'what about David's room?'

'When he goes away, I shut the door and it stays shut. I don't know why, but that's the way it is.'

I nodded. She led me past the door and into her bedroom, one hand stuck in the back pocket of her jeans as though she might be keeping a grip on her wallet. The room was empty except for the furniture. We lay on the bed for an hour or so, quietly staring at each other until the room was lit only by the glow from the streetlamps. Then we made love.

Twelve

The plain details of our lives.

Every four weeks she took the car and was away for a night, staying in East Anglia and seeing George. It would go on until – 'until I decide to stop seeing him; soon, but not yet.'

Every fortnight she visited David at his school, to which she looked forward.

She was at the restaurant from ten to twelve in the mornings, from five to eight and eleven to midnight.

I adored her.

I did nothing. I offered to work in the restaurant during the tourist season, but she didn't want me to work. She laughed and said that my work was already defined. What work was that? Loving her, she said; she had lived long enough to understand its value.

There were private moments which we restored many times, each time to a new and considered perfection. She raised the boundaries of modesty. Outside, the trees leaned wildly back from the throes of a late-spring gale; inside her bedroom it was calm and structured. There was to be no wastage. Rain arrived at the windows like handfuls of grit thrown by a thwarted lover. I was dimly aware of her cervix and the stigmata left on my back by her pale nails.

May, and June. Love in lieu of summer, a teenage love. An innocence going quietly about its business. A debris of jeans and sweatshirts strewn across the carpet.

She looked well. Her friends, she told me, commented on how well she looked, how she had opened out. She was happy. She would have laughed if I'd asked her for confirmation. At first, wonderingly, I asked her to tell me about her every feeling. I wanted the secret of her experience. But she said that there was no secret.

I very rarely went to the studio. The place was now filling with tourists, and like most of England it whored itself gratefully. It served shoals of fish and sackfuls of crinkle-cut chips, and cream teas; and every couple of weeks there were Elizabethan pageants and feasting for those whose coaches couldn't get as far as Plymouth.

Midway through June, N told me that Fiona had approached her, looking for a job, possibly at the pageants. She had refused. She was annoyed.

'If Fiona wants money she should go to her family, and if they turn her down then she should ask me for a loan. But not this way. She could approach Michael, he would be able to find her something to do in his business.'

I argued that it would complicate their relationship. It would be like being married.

'That's exactly what it would be like,' she agreed.

But Fiona just wanted to make some money.

'Darling, don't be simple. Fiona wants someone to run her life for her. Can't you see that?'

Fiona was jealous of N.

'You've got it the wrong way round, it's you she's jealous of. I used to spend a lot more time with her. Until she got on my nerves. Coming to me for a job is so little-girlish.'

N did attract people.

'It isn't very difficult. It's what they want afterwards that's the nuisance.'

She raised her leg and stretched the foot.

So what did they want afterwards, all these people?

'I don't know. Something that I can't give them.'

Couldn't, or wouldn't?

'Both. Then they get disappointed and hurt. Or outraged, as if I was to blame.'

As if she had led them on.

'That's the way they want to feel. I'm not dishonest with them.

133

They are always dishonest with themselves. Look, I'm tired of these questions. If Fiona wants to be a servant, that's up to her. But I don't want her to serve me.'

My apologies for picking at her.

She smiled at my seriousness. No, she said, she hadn't a worry in the world about what was understood or not understood. She was happy. She was ridiculously and sublimely happy, and she hoped that Fiona was just as happy with Michael.

The sea-front at midnight.

There was no unearthly silence, no still darkness. Dogs didn't bark from afar.

Her perfume was stale; her clothes smelt of cooking fat, her hair of cigarette smoke. He breath was hot with ill-digested garlic and wine.

The pier had burnt down long ago. Weed slopped at the base of ugly concrete pillars, which supported the funfair. The waves pushed empty beercans up the shingled beach.

She stepped in dogshit and tar. Her teeth were not white. Her eyes didn't catch the light of any moon. Her pants had ridden up and she had to stop and pry them free. A speedboat bounced flashily and noisily across the water. Drunken hooligans jeered and threw a car tyre over the sea-wall. Walt's Waltzer – the fastest ride in town, light blue and candy pink – cranked itself up again and pumped out a blurring base, a scratched treble and a pulsation of garish light.

She took my arm and we walked on, grinning back our laughter.

George. Once took her out to dinner on her birthday, and when they came back and undressed she found that he had tied a red ribbon, in a bow, around his willy. 'Had it done in Selfridges, when they wrapped the fur coat,' he had told her.

The sea-front on a Sunday afternoon. N still with a sheen of late-morning sleep covering her eyes; smelling, if I got close enough, of young soap, bath-water, talcum powder. Slightly fragile, as if her mind was dislocated.

We came to a sheltered wooden bench, and sat down without

134

disturbing the conversation of two old men. We sat and looked at the light of the sun as it gilded a flickering sea. The light was soporific, beckoning us into a trance.

Beside us, the two old men talked. They were correctly dressed, one of them had an umbrella with him. They were obviously on a day out, had sat next to each other on the coach, had stepped down and found themselves again in each other's company, without wives. The one without the umbrella had suffered a stroke. His speech was slurred.

For twenty minutes they grumbled about death and the paraphernalia surrounding funerals, of which both of them disapproved. The strokeless man did most of the talking, making his point, and the other man agreed.

They reminisced briefly about the jobs they had had and the people they had worked for in London. The stroked man brought up the questionable morals of professional men, how people were corrupt and only sheltered by the apparent respectability of their profession.

The strokeless man agreed, and proceeded to hold up undertakers as an example.

I felt N begin to giggle. She buried her face in my shoulder, and I felt her stomach shake with laughter. She crossed her legs and strained against the coils of mirth which threatened to spring out and undo her. Finally she had to stand up, and I led her off, coughing and with tears in her eyes. She waved me away. She walked ahead of me for fifty yards, struggling to restore her composure. She stopped, and when I caught up with her she begged me not to say anything; she looked at me and started laughing again, protesting at the pain.

'I'm sorry, I'm sorry . . . ' She wiped her eyes on the edge of my sweatshirt. ' . . . oh . . . oh . . . I hope we didn't offend them. Are they still sitting there? I can't look.'

I said that they had probably just gone to call an ambulance.

'Don't.' She started laughing again.

I never managed to go out with Michael. Some evenings I wanted to get out of the house; N was working and I was at a loose end. I

135

would have met him for a drink. But he always 'had something on'. He was friendly enough and said that we should get together, later in the week, next week; but he never fixed a time.

One thing about N. She never wore any of my clothes, as she might have done. I was too big to fit into any of hers. She wasn't affectionate about clothes.

She sometimes had a triangular shadow of tiredness under her eyes, a sort of oily, moist bruise which looked as though it would quickly evaporate.

Moods of laughter; ridiculousness; and humour used almost as a weapon, to disarm ourselves. And then suddenly the quick blatant look in the eye, the stabbed suggestion of sexual availability, and conversation as a slowly paid ransom.

The chasing of the sun, from room to room. Wherever we could lie naked and warmed on a carpet or a bed, with the smell of body, skin and sweat and seepage like a humus around us.

Around the residential area a multitude of plants and shrubs lunged immodestly outwards, petals splayed in the hope of attracting attention. On warm days the shopowners in Portsmouth displayed their wares on the pavements and watched from behind their counters. Outside my favourite corner shop the rails of antique petticoats purled and rippled in a salty breeze while in the dark interior a girl jogged the pram in which her baby lay.

With my help, N sometimes braided her hair tightly so that it hung down her back like glossy rope.

Just before, and during the first two days of her period there were heavy lines running from the sides of her nose down to her chin, like tense cables, which withdrew her mouth as though she had discovered some utterly contemptible secret about someone she disliked.

This *was* ridiculous.

The radio-cassette disappeared from the studio. We noticed its disappearance on June the twenty-second. N was sure that she hadn't taken it down to the office; and even if she had, it was still missing. Had I brought it back to the house? No.

She was angry with herself. Half because it didn't really matter, half because she resented the way in which our love affair had brought about this state of nothing really mattering.

She was caught off-balance. She couldn't be sure that she hadn't taken the cassette-player out somewhere in the car, or that she hadn't lent it to somebody.

She wanted to know where it was.

We spent an afternoon searching through the house, and when the staff had gone home we searched the studio, the office, the kitchen, and the bar, until three in the morning.

'I know it's here somewhere. If I just turn round I'll see it.'

I sat in the bar. I waited for her as she enacted a purposeless normality, turning round every few minutes as though she was trying to catch sight of someone who was tailing her.

It was late and she was tired. She became angry with me for not helping her, and then she thought that I might have hidden it as a game, and finally she felt grossly deceived by everyone, including me. She knew that she was being absurd, but she was overworked and fed up and irritated and it was just typical the way something cropped up which showed that you couldn't just be happy and take things for granted.

Yes, it would have to be one of the staff, she said, or someone had left the door to the studio open and a tourist had wandered around. She wanted to forget about it.

David came home from school for a long weekend, with a friend. I had to move back into the studio and we had to tidy up the house. She complained.

'I don't want to be deprived of you.'

It was only for three days.

'You sound as if you'll be glad to get away.'

No matter how fervently I denied this, she refused to be mollified. And then she was angry because she felt guilty – or because she didn't feel guilty enough – about disregarding David's interests.

When she had fetched David, he was quite insistent that he and his friend should be dropped off at a cinema to see the new Clint Eastwood. She was hurt and wouldn't be relaxed by all the

137

rigmarole of illicit passion which we contrived to warm the studio bedroom.

She telephoned me during the night, wanting words of love.

I didn't know what to do in the studio, and when David brought his friend round the next day he was disappointed that I didn't have a sheaf of amusing stories with which to entertain them. He seemed to feel that there was something not quite right about the room. I felt the same way. I promised that I would send him a story at school; but he said I didn't have to, there were probably more important things that I had to do. He himself was busy with cricket and swimming, and in fact there was the test match on television at his mother's house if I wanted to watch it with them. His mother didn't like them being in the house on their own.

So we watched the test match, and in the evening I took them to the funfair with N.

At eleven-thirty we stopped off at the restaurant. While the boys played pinball on their last reserves of energy, N collected the day's takings and locked them in the wall-safe.

'Shall I get these out?' She tapped her fingernail on the packet of papers. 'No,' she answered herself, 'there's plenty of time. Have you any idea what you're going to do?'

I knew, more or less.

'I thought you would. We've never really talked about it, have we? We should do, I suppose.' She dithered around with the safe for longer than was necessary. 'But we will do, some time or other.'

I missed her, that night. It seemed very, very quiet when she had gone home with the boys and I was left to extinguish the lights and lie alone on the bed in the studio.

I tried to think of what I would do if she ever left me. I sat down and could only write about my feelings. I was forced, or I manoeuvred myself, into writing these to George – a strange, emotional letter, as though I was a lover whom he had left. It was a dark, unhappy letter, full of confusion and the desire for some becalmed identity, some surety of independence.

When I say that I wrote to George, I mean that I wrote from myself to N. But this was ridiculous because N and I were very much in love with each other and very secure in our happiness. So

I suppose that I was caught up by a mood and, three-quarters of the way through, this mood made its melancholy absurdity apparent. It was like writing your will at the age of twenty when you are lonely. And so I saw that the writing could be better utilised as N's testament to George.

I missed her; and with a sharp edge of resentment.

What had she said about George, on one of our first meetings?

Yes. 'The funny thing about George is that I don't miss him at all.'

The studio was empty without her. The room was bleak. Dawn was tinkering around, dismantling the cone of light from the carpark lamp. I suddenly thought of Fiona and Michael, meeting here in this room, and I felt sorry for them – indulging myself in any old direction whatsoever. Indulging myself, finally, with the image of N's naked body, laid out, face down. Bringing desire, indulgence and sleep.

I saw her before lunch. She was pale and tired. I glanced at her sharply. She had missed me.

David and his friend left on Monday afternoon. She took Tuesday off and we watched the test match as we would have liked to have watched it; bathed and dozing nude on the sun-paned carpet.

'I love cricket,' she said. 'Mmm. I don't want to understand it. I like the voices of the commentators. They're so gentlemanly and secure. It's like a bedtime story. Football commentators are so full of their own vulgar excitement. Talking of which,' she laughed and reached for a strawberry, 'Fiona and Michael are back in the studio tomorrow. You haven't left anything lying around?'

'Like what?'

'Like a cassette-player.'

She lay down with her chin on her hands, looking away from me as though she had behaved badly and was waiting with confidence for the provoked argument.

'That's insane.'

'I wouldn't put it past her.'

I didn't want to be angry, not at N. But I *was* angry. Having vented her capriciousness, N could no longer be bothered with the subject.

She suggested that we had a bottle of wine with the strawberries.

Unsatisfied by strawberries, cricket, wine or slander, N turned her head and considered me, a smoulder of demand in carious eyes. She watched me make myself ready, her bottom lip heavy with encouragement. She turned away. Her hair fell forward on either side of her face, like a hood. A middle-aged foal, ungainly, she struggled to her knees and reached one hand between her legs to secure our coupling.

We went to bed early. It was delightful to be back in our bedroom. I told her how bleak the studio room was now in comparison with 15B.

'Only because I wasn't there with you,' she said. 'Don't feel so sorry for Fiona and Michael. Not everybody is as romantic as you are. They probably can't be bothered. Anyway, it's good for her, it makes the nature of their relationship very clear.'

'When I was between men.'

When was that?

'Oh, a couple of years after Paul was born. A year after the divorce. When I wanted a man again. It was difficult. I wasn't used to going out with men and I just felt completely out of practice. I was shy, I didn't know how to dress or make conversation. It's such an effort sometimes. You have no idea what it's like to start all over again, wondering if you're attractive or if you can really be bothered to pander to some idiot. Trying to find out what he wants you to say. Especially when most of your life is centred around looking after a child.'

She looked back in bewilderment, shaking her head at how she had been. The smile returned. 'Well I was introduced to this man at a friend's dinner party, and he called me up to go out for a meal. God I was so serious. He really wasn't anything special. But I wanted him to know that I had a child so that he realised what he was letting himself in for. All kinds of ludicrous planning on my part. Wanting to be honest. I was nervous, I suppose. So I asked him round to my flat for a drink beforehand. Actually I quite fancied him.

'I planned it all out. I would leave him with Paul for a moment, with a drink, while I finished getting ready, and then when the babysitter arrived we would sweep out to dinner.

'Paul was four. He was quite shy but he could be charming, very blustery and talkative. Anyhow, the babysitter was half an hour late and by the time she arrived Paul had told him that I was divorced, that we didn't have a daddy really, only someone who lived a long way away, and we both needed someone else to live with who would take care of things like the rubbish bin and the dirty plates. And that I had dressed up specially, because usually the flat was a mess.' She laughed. 'That's where honesty gets you.'

Where did it get her?

'Oh, he hung around, and he did occasionally empty the rubbish bin. He felt sorry for me. It just petered out. He kept worrying that I didn't have an orgasm. He irritated me in the end. I had to get rid of him.'

A Wednesday evening. I was to collect her from the restaurant. I brought a bottle of champagne for Michael and Fiona.

When I arrived at eight the three of them were having a drink at the bar. N was sober and taut, with an icy control. Aloof and desirable. I could have laughed. I begged to be excused from the severity of the gathering.

I added two champagne glasses to the bottle in the polythene bag and left it at the foot of the stairs. I went back to the bar. N looked at me with a faint note of warning in her eyes, as though she wasn't sure what I was up to but she was certain that, whatever it was, it wasn't a good idea. I drank a pint with them while they talked aimlessly. Fiona invited us to spend a long weekend at her cottage, next weekend; it was so unavoidable that N had to swallow whatever reservations she had, and we accepted.

'I'll get my jacket,' she said, 'and then we should be off.'

I accompanied her to the office. She cast an eye over a pile of open ledgers and took her jacket off the hanger. 'No, I won't put it on. Right,' she said, impatiently applying a faint smile to the corners of her mouth.

'They seem all right.'

'Fiona and Michael? Yes. Shall we go?'

'They make you uncomfortable?'

'Well?'

'What is it?' I asked.

She frowned and leant back against the desk. 'I don't know why we have to stand here talking about it. If I am annoyed it's because I've missed you and I want to take a bath. Because not only are they here – ' she smirked at herself ' – which I don't mind, having arranged it with them. But they get on my nerves when they present themselves to me as if they want me to condone them, as if I was responsible for their relationship. Which I couldn't care less about. As if *we* were somehow the same. Any day I expect her to ask me how *we* arrange it. Neither of them can be bothered to take any responsibility, so they want to make it easy on themselves by involving me. But then I have what I want, so perhaps I should be more gracious. After all, she is a friend.'

The same old subject. I thought that by now even she was getting tired of it, and her reactions to Fiona. She couldn't really care, surely. It was a silly grumble. It was almost a diversion for herself, a puff of smoke, something to cover our exit.

'I want a bath,' she said. 'Can we get out of here?'

'You love that room upstairs because of us,' I erupted. 'So do I. And that's wonderful. And it should be the same for them. We can give that to them.'

Clutching the bag of glasses and champagne, I reached for her hand. 'Come on! We'll put this upstairs for them.'

'No!'

But I was already ahead of her. Opening the office door, I ran upstairs. She called my name and started after me. I threw open the door to the studio.

The curtains were drawn. I switched on the light. Gerald lay on his back, naked except for a pair of boxer shorts.

'Turn the light off,' N said.

142

She came upstairs, reached round me and turned off the light. 'Close the door.'

I did so.

'Not that he'd notice. He's drunk.' She went back to the office.

I came down the stairs and looked in through the office door. With her back to me, she smoothed her dress. 'Shall we go? Quietly and without any fuss. Fiona and Michael will see themselves out.' Her words fluttered down like a shower of slippery, glossy, unwanted advertising circulars. Her heels dug into the swollen carpet as she turned and walked towards me.

I stopped her in the carpark and held her tightly.

'Are you and Gerald lovers?'

'You're being absurd. Gerald wouldn't dare try it on with me, unless I asked him. Don't go looking for trouble. It would make things very difficult for us both. I've told him that you are away on holiday.'

'Well I'm not.'

'Well it wouldn't be a bad idea if you were!' she snapped. 'Then you could leave me alone to sort this out. I'm very capable of handling it.'

'I can imagine,' I said, staring at her.

'Can you.'

She met my stare with unsmiling, impenetrable eyes. A mask-like, set face. Like a wall with only one side to it.

I turned and walked away. I climbed the steps to the top of the groyne. Behind me, the door of her car slammed and she drove off.

I lugged the champagne along the sea-front. I returned home, to 15B, shortly after eleven and put the champagne in the fridge.

She came in at four-thirty, just before dawn, weaving drunkenly past the telephone table. She had been crying. She sat on the stairs, I sat on the carpet in front of her, clasping her legs.

' . . . such a shit . . . that man is such a shit . . . and every now and then, whenever he wants to, he makes me feel like a shit. I don't want to feel that way. Why do I want to feel that way?'

She stared not at me but at the carpet. 'Can you get me some cigarettes?'

143

While I was in the kitchen, she climbed upstairs. David's bed-room door was ajar, but she wasn't in there. The main light was on in our bedroom and she was being sick in the bathroom. I left the packet of cigarettes beside the bed and slept on the sofa in the sitting-room.

I don't know where Gerald found his stamina. When, at eleven the next morning, I cautiously approached the end of the sea-wall, the curtains to the studio were still drawn but the Mercedes wasn't in the carpark. He had disappeared.

Thirteen

'Do you *want* to explain?'

'Not really. There's nothing to explain. He has, or thinks he has, some kind of hold on me. Which he doesn't have any longer. It's to do with the family, or George, or I don't know what.'

'Don't gloss him over.'

'Do you know,' she said brightly, 'that he once found me drunk in the bar after we had been out to dinner? I couldn't get back home to bed. And he made sure that I was all right. He even undressed me and put me to bed in the studio without taking advantage of the situation.'

I didn't tell her the truth. She looked too fragile, sipping at champagne.

'But no,' she said. 'He wants what he wants, and we're going to have to come up with something, otherwise he'll have an excuse to come back.'

'Why did you get me involved with this?'

'Because I wanted you to love me.'

We were sitting in the back garden, there was an air of wan chastity about her in the rich afternoon light.

'There are other ways.'

'What do you know about love, or life?' She raised an eyebrow. 'I'm not being unselfish in this. I need help. You know that I want to be free of them. I know I'm right. They must understand that. George will understand, but I can't let myself hurt him. If Gerald should choose to be silly about me removing myself from the family, then I must have enough details about his involvement to send him to prison. If that's the only way of making him understand.

I have loved George.' She hesitated. 'But it's become impossible.'
She was embarrassed.

'Thank you,' she said, 'for the champagne, and everything.' She
wet her finger and ran it round the edge of the glass. As soon as
it started singing, she winced at the noise and stopped. 'I hate
people who do that. God, we're being maudlin.' She laughed
edgily.

She was bitter about something. She said that it was self-pity;
she didn't like herself when she was in this mood.

The long, slow dusk fended off nightfall. I watched television,
she washed and ironed some clothes and tidied the bedroom. She
didn't want to go for a walk. 'You go,' she said, 'I'll just mess
around in here. I have to decide what to take to Fiona's.'

'We don't have to take anything much, do we?'

'You don't want me to look like a tramp, do you? I know that
you care what I wear. Go on, go for your walk.'

When I returned, the light was on in her bedroom, and she was
sitting, writing, at the escritoire. She smiled absently at me. The
room was infused with a calm solitude. I kissed her goodnight and
lay in the spare room, reading, surrounded by the light material of
her ironed dresses.

Fiona lived in a very picturesque cottage. There was a bank of
newly mown and neatly clipped lawn between the road and the
black, wooden door; climbing roses, stocks and lupins bloomed
along the façade, giving off a heavy scent. 'Like lavatory cleaner,'
N remarked.

Fiona wasn't there when we arrived, but the door was unlocked.
In the tiny entrance way, there were large flagstones, old rugs, two
wingback chairs on either side of a big open fireplace, and a church
pew on which I dumped our bags and N laid a dress and a
skirt. 'It's chilly,' she claimed. It was in fact warmer outside the
house.

She left the front door open and walked into the sitting-room.
It had another, smaller fireplace. A large, well-used sofa with
William Morris covers was pushed against the opposite wall and
again there were two easy-chairs drawn up beside the hearth.

Goodish Victorian watercolours, a couple of oils on the walls, lightweight side-lamps and a standard lamp. There were built-in bookcases with a line of paperbacks and a surprising number of dense-looking tomes. There were ornaments which were obviously family heirlooms of limited value; and the cassette-player, prominent in its twentieth-century silver-grey functionality – in an alcove, at a convenient height.

'You see?' N said, mildly. She smiled at her vindication.

'You would have thought that she might at least have hidden it.'

'Oh no,' she retorted; 'I wouldn't have thought that at all. She wants us to see it.'

'Well, let's steal it back.'

'No.' N relished the opportunity. 'We'll just ignore it.'

She went on into a small bathroom, which had probably been a sixteenth-century broom closet until someone had felt that the labourers might need to wash off their sense of victory after the Second World War. She applied a middle shade of lipstick, and blotted the tart out of it with a Kleenex. She looked naturally stunning, the result of just the right amount of effort; a loose skirt, nonchalantly rolled-up shirtsleeves and a little mascara.

A car pulled up outside. N led me back into the entrance hall. I left the sitting-room door slightly ajar.

'N!'

'Fiona! How nice to see you.' They embraced on the lawn. Fiona had good legs, and the exertion of sport had coloured her face attractively.

'I'm sorry. We've just been playing tennis.' She glanced at her watch. 'Oh, we *are* late, Michael.'

'We've only just arrived ourselves. How beautiful everything looks. I do envy you.'

They sprayed each other with compliments on their way inside. Michael watched them go with, I thought, an inward sigh of relief; although, as usual, nothing showed on his face.

'Good game?'

'Yes. Just long enough to need a lager.'

He went inside and reappeared with two tins. We sat on the

grass and enjoyed the sun. Michael yawned. We picked up the sound of female voices.

' . . . when he doesn't really try,' Fiona was saying. 'That annoys me. Of course when he does try, he beats me easily.'

'Always let them win,' N said, and they laughed. 'That was the first thing my mother told me.'

'Oh, I know. Mine too.' Fiona's voice dropped and suddenly became terribly confidential. 'But I have to be careful. I do worry in case he might have a heart attack or something.'

'Surely not. With Michael? You wouldn't think so. He's so young.' N was suitably gifted in the art of dramatic conspiratorial hush.

'He is, isn't he? And he's terribly fit. It's the best age for a man. He's so mature about things.'

'Ah,' Michael grunted. 'Dear God, thank you for the maturity. For a minute there I thought that I was about to croak.'

'And of course,' Fiona warbled on, 'because of that, he understands me so well.'

'I'm very happy for you, Fiona.' Above our heads a window opened, and N called: 'Come up and see our room, darling. It's so pretty, and the bed is wonderful. Will you bring the bag, and my dress?'

I turned; and she was there, beautifully, half sitting on the window sill, smoking a cigarette, her hand held up to cup the chance of falling ash. She was smiling quietly to herself, and when she saw me grinning at her she stuck out her tongue, and laughed.

'*Is* there an ashtray, Fiona?' she called.

'Downstairs.'

'I'll get it,' I said.

Fiona came out of the door. 'Don't let her bully you. Make yourself at home.'

'I will,' I said. She went and plumped herself down on Michael's lap. He grunted disapprovingly but let her have her way.

The bed wasn't at all wonderful; unless you liked sleeping on a hillside, N decided. And so we stayed up as late as possible. N lay along the sofa. Fiona and I played backgammon with Michael, who held the board because he was by far the better player. The luckier player, I thought, but N said that he was simply more skilful. He was also very entertaining in a self-deprecating way, which amused us. N didn't like him, but she didn't let it show. It wasn't a strong dislike.

'I think I might go to bed,' N said finally, 'so that I can bag the comfortable spot.'

'If you can find it,' Fiona laughed. 'It won't be too bad, will it? It's only had Jeremy to make the dent in the middle, and the school holidays were ages ago.'

'It will be fine. I'm so tired, I won't even notice.'

She waited for me in bed, in her nightdress, securely occupying the valley in the mattress. She rolled to one side, I climbed in, and we rolled back together.

'How *are* we going to do this?' She had become exasperated.

'Well it's either me on top of you or you on top of me.'

'It's me on top of you.'

'Not with the nightdress as well.'

'Oh, all right.'

She scrambled out of bed and pulled the nightdress over her head. I always noticed her body, I was never unstruck by its beauty. I noticed an ugly bruise on the inside of her thigh.

'How did you do that?'

'What? That? Oh, I don't know, I banged my leg on the furniture.'

'When?'

'Hush, they're only on the other side of the wall.'

Michael walked along the corridor and the light went out.

'Go to sleep now. I'm tired.' She snuggled down for the definitive sleep.

I desired her, completely and irritatingly.

She chastised me maternally. 'Hush now. Go to sleep.'

She pretended to do so, one arm across my chest.

Next door, Fiona and Michael talked, though I couldn't hear what they said. Then that stopped, and the house seemed to settle.

I listened to an owl and tried to imagine a comfortable mattress. I envied N's easy flight into sleep.

I wasn't particularly disturbed when the sound of lovemaking began on the other side of the wall. I fitted it into the sound of darkness. But I was suddenly grounded by an awareness that N was wide-awake. I could feel her eyes moving, quickly; like the eyes of a night rodent, picking out insects in the darkness, concentrating and searching to establish their movements.

I feigned sleep. The intensity increased beyond the wall. A small panting, presumably from Fiona. I honestly couldn't have cared less.

I sighed, as through a dream, and moved very slightly. N took advantage of my apparent dormancy to take her hand off my shoulder. She put the end of her thumb into her mouth. I felt her listening. Her body tensed. I felt a tremendous attentiveness around her eyes, at the back of her eyes, in her mind. As a spring, coiling tighter and tighter, very quickly now; and then for a moment I lost track of her in the noise of Fiona's orgasm.

'Oh oh oh oh oh,' and a long, almost tearful, moan.

And silence.

N moved.

I let her know that I was awake. Her body unwound. She now pretended that she had just woken up.

'Was that Fiona?' I whispered.

'I think so. I think she's got a splinter.'

It felt as though she was smiling, as though she was drily amused, as an adult should be. I dutifully grinned. 'All done for us, I expect,' N whispered sarcastically, 'and probably a fake.'

I reached between her legs and she was very wet, like a burst oyster beneath an easily opened shell. I pushed her on to her back. No game, not now.

'Quietly,' she hissed. I pushed back the covers. Her knees rose around my torso. The bed had no springs to complain. She closed her eyes and her teeth fastened on her wrist as I entered her. I possessed her body, which jettisoned an orgasm, quickly.

*   *   *

I was the last to get up in the morning. When N left the bed, I awoke; but I only rolled gratefully into the unoccupied valley and dozed to the sound of the birds outside the window. When I left the room, just after eleven, I was still lumbered with torpor.

I made a cup of tea. Through the small kitchen window I saw Fiona and N, lying side by side on the lawn in the back garden, creamed and sunbathing in bikinis. I took the tea into the sitting-room and read the headlines in a copy of the *Guardian* which lay on the sofa. I looked at Fiona's bookcases. She had two rows of novels, several books about children and a large library of occult works – standard 1960s and 1970s astrology; and heavy, old cloth-and leather-bound tomes, serious stuff.

I ventured outside. N raised an arm in vague greeting and took my hand for a moment. Fiona asked me if I wanted any breakfast; but I lay on the lawn in the sun until the cosy wit of the question-and-answer programme on Radio Four got on my nerves.

'Where's Michael?'

'He took the car,' N murmured.

'Has he gone home?'

'No, he's here for the weekend,' Fiona announced. 'He's gone over to watch some dog trials, somewhere near Frome.'

'That's miles away.'

'He likes driving.'

'Have you come to disturb us?' N smiled, without opening her eyes. 'There is an agenda for today. We have sun worship for another hour, bacon and avocado sandwiches for lunch, and then Fiona wants to do your astrological chart. I've put her off playing tennis. There are cocktails with big brother at six and we're going out to dinner. There's nothing left to think about.'

'Where would you like the sandwiches?'

'How lovely. Where do you think, Fiona?'

'Out here?'

'Yes. In an hour.'

They laughed. I left them to their luxury.

The lunch was a matter of licked-finger laziness, the astrology was weightier. We adjourned to the sitting-room. Fiona questioned me as to the time, date and place of my birth. N sat on the

151

back of the sofa, looking over her shoulder, smoking. It was a strange ritual, not at all of the mystic, but of diagrams and charts and reference books, geometrical shapes and ruled lines; all of which contrasted strongly with the abundance of uncovered female skin. The two women were mostly naked, with their smells of hair shampoo, perspiration and sun cream. Their bodies were casual and undisguised.

I found that I wasn't capable of accepting my own irrelevance; I was too uncomposed, I was uneasy with maleness and the desire to interfere, to touch. Fiona muttered that the chart would take some time. N laid a hand on her shoulder and said that there was plenty of time. I went into the garden to weed and listen to the peaceful voices of the cricket commentators.

At five I was called inside to dress for our cocktails at the house.

'What about the astrology?' I said to N.

'It's good,' she said. 'You're well balanced. So far. Fiona hasn't finished yet.'

'You don't *believe* in it!'

'Of course not. I don't believe in anything. It's a lot of hocus-pocus, but then so is going to see a lawyer. And lawyers can work out quite well sometimes, wouldn't you say?'

Michael arrived at the last moment and Fiona didn't seem to mind that a quick wash left his hair dripping and bedraggled on our drive up to the house. It was, I thought, rather a self-conscious gesture, as though he wasn't happy about the obligation.

Our visit was part of a peculiar formality. Every Saturday, those brothers and sisters in residence on the estate were expected to attend drinks at the big house in order to greet the weekend guests with a sense of family. Most of her relatives, Fiona said, either went away for the weekend or found some excuse not to show up. None of them absolutely refused; it would have been pathetic to strike such a defiant posture, as her younger brother had found out.

'He doesn't *mean* to be condescending,' Fiona spoke of the head of the family, 'he just *is*. I used to laugh at him when we were younger, now there's just nothing – apart from these dreadful Saturday evenings.'

'Oh, it's not that bad,' N said, 'the house is extraordinary.'

From half a mile away, at the rise of the driveway, the house was beautiful, even with the dozens of tourist coaches squared off at a short distance. Close up, it was gigantic, implacable, and an awesome blot.

We parked at the side, on a piece of newish tarmac. There were no other cars there.

'Who owns it?' I whispered to Michael.

'God,' he said. 'And he serves weak drinks. It would take you half your lifetime to find out where he keeps the bottles, and by then you'd be round the bend from listening to his half-cock theories. He's as mad as a hatter and as tight as a shark's arse.'

Michael and I walked behind our respective lovers, in through a side door, up some stairs and along a corridor.

N inhaled the atmosphere of wealth and loved it. She checked her clothes. She was stimulated and aroused for a gracious display.

Fiona opened a door, and we entered a room with perhaps twenty people in it, most of them sitting. We were introduced to the head of the family and one or two people in his vicinity. Her brother was tall and rather withered, in his forties; he gracefully took Fiona away to discuss something. 'Probably the rent,' Michael observed.

N mixed easily and quietly, passing from the weather to children in conversation with a woman who had just come from Paris. We were offered sherry.

Michael had visited before and explained what part of the house we were in. The head of the family came over and recognised him; he asked me one or two questions and then we went across to his bureau and he said: 'Perhaps you'd care to read some of my pamphlets.' I said that I would, and he drifted away.

He talked to Michael and me again at some point about the place of alcohol within the digestive microcosm. Our glasses were empty, his own was half full of orange juice. From that he passed to smoking, and N, and a dame sitting beside her who ticked him off for being so bossy. This rather relaxed him. He took N across to show her some pictures which were hanging on the wall by the door. 'It is *so* beautiful here,' N said. Their voices carried.

153

'Yes, it is,' he agreed. 'I try to gather people around me who think in the same way that I do about life. They enhance the place. Because, after all, it is only a building. There are several cottages on the estate which I leave unoccupied for such people. Of course, at a purely nominal rent.'

'I have an aunt . . . ' N suggested.

'Not exactly that type of person. Someone more understanding of a libertarian way of life.'

'Yes, I see.' N's eyes were doe-like with understanding, a little sparkle, fetchingly, in the centre. 'Christopher, I thought you'd been through most of Fiona's friends.'

'I suppose one or two. I have known them. I'm afraid we've rather lost touch, Fiona and I.' He relapsed into an assumed dither.

'She only lives four miles away.'

'I know. Somehow it's easier to get to London. I do walk around the town, often.'

'Well I'm sure you'll find what you're looking for.'

N turned towards Michael and me, including us in their group. The Marquis of Christopher, unabashed by his failure at procuring, assumed an interest in someone on the other side of the room.

'Well, Lady Fiona,' N addressed her when she had finished her tour of the house guests, 'shall we leave?'

N took my arm on the way out. 'Don't talk about him in front of Fiona,' she said; 'she's very touchy.'

We had a huge, simple dinner at a pub some distance away. We were the last people in the restaurant, and no one talked about the family until Fiona left the table. Michael asked me what I thought of the pamphlets. They were revamped feudalism. They were too calm to be messianic, but their author's political revolution certainly wouldn't leave him as a mere cog in the community he advocated.

'Well I rather admire him,' said N. 'At least he does something with his time. With all his millions, he doesn't have to do anything. Most of the other people I've met who have his kind of inherited wealth and standing just allow themselves and their parasites to become buried in cocaine. They talk a lot of hypocritical rubbish. At least he says what he believes in.'

'Like asking you to become a mistress?' I queried.

'Why not become his mistress? It wouldn't be a bad life. Once you had the male child, you could get what you wanted off him. You'd be well set up. Plenty of women have been forced to prostitute themselves on worse terms than that.'

Michael gave a nod of agreement.

'He simply doesn't believe in marriage. I don't either,' she added.

'Ah yes,' Michael interrupted, 'but that's for a different reason. He's too scared of having to share the family fortune.'

'All I see,' N snapped, 'is a man who's had two daughters and feels driven to reproduce a son. It may be pathetic, but it's sadly pathetic. Fiona and I have three sons between us. If the family adheres to the rules then one day Fiona will have an extremely wealthy son, in spite of all her sour grapes at the moment.'

'Why wouldn't you become the mother of his son?' I asked her.

'Because I don't love him.'

'Good for you,' Michael said.

'Anyway,' N laughed, 'I might have a daughter, and I'd be out with the milk bottles.'

Fiona and she went to bed early, feeling the after-effects of the sunbathing.

Michael woke me at five in the morning. He had coats, boots and a thermos of hot coffee in the car. We drove through the dawn, back towards the big house. He parked at the end of the driveway. We walked for miles through the grounds, watching the whole gamut of early-morning wildlife. He took me to a ruin, where we sat behind a wall and watched a vixen playing with her cubs. Just when the coffee was finished, and I felt the dampness of the jewels on the spiders' webs as a cold shiver at the back of my neck, the sun sidled lackadaisically round a distant copse, warmly distilling tiredness. Michael leant back against the wall and went to sleep. I stretched out along a rotten beam.

Michael was the first to leave the cottage. N and I stayed for the late Sunday lunch, and then we drove back to Portsmouth.

'What does he tell his wife?' I asked N.

'Presumably,' she said, 'he tells her that he'll be back for Sunday lunch. Of them all, I'd far prefer to be us.'

'Gerald,' she said. 'Go to work on Gerald.'

She closed the wall-safe and handed me the package of papers.

Fourteen

'Let me get this quite clear. What Gerald wants to hear is that George was completely responsible for his actions, even down to turning himself in after the murder. That George was a melancholy loser until he met you, that he then opened out and enjoyed several years of success; that after your adultery he relapsed into his previous state which the whole family now finds either convenient or suitable. That there are no grounds for legal mitigation, nor even for very much sympathy.'

'That's not true!' she shouted.

'It doesn't matter whether or not it's true. I know that it's not entirely true because Gerald is quite happy for some reason that you should carry the weight of sympathy for George.'

'Yes.'

'Why?'

'Because Gerald is a bastard!'

'Does that go in here too; that you don't want to have anything more to do with him?'

'It doesn't need to. I will make it clear to him.'

'I thought you had already.'

'I have.'

'You feel guilty about George, don't you?'

'I am not guilty! I've had enough of feeling guilty. That is what I want to say to Gerald.'

'And to conclude that there are no grounds for George's appeal.'

'Yes.'

'That George is guilty.'

'Yes, yes, yes, yes!' She looked away helplessly, and then her eyes flashed. 'You don't care.'

'Not about Gerald, I don't. Why does it make you so uncomfortable?'

The project for Gerald became very simple. His brother George was completely responsible for his own actions, and there was no possibility of any mitigation.

After I had examined her on the angle of our approach N was quiet for several days, perhaps uneasy that she had committed herself. I had always been aware that sooner or later the work would have to be done, but I was stupid in assuming that she was similarly prepared. She seemed to feel that we had suddenly been thrown backwards by several months and she was unsure where this left us. She offered an unselfish, almost docile, lovemaking. Perhaps because I had started working I simply didn't see so much of her; perhaps to keep me working she subsumed her own gratification. She claimed that she wanted my pleasure. 'Don't worry about me,' she said, 'I just want to have you inside me.'

Fiona appeared on Wednesdays. I tidied the papers away and, more often than not, had dinner with her and Michael. N decided that she would stop lending them the studio as she didn't want them to disturb me.

I said that they didn't disturb me. It was like having a deadline. I could see how much progress I had made in a week.

'All right,' she said. She laughed. 'It's strange how I draw lines between them and us. It's almost as though we were married. I'm not being over-virtuous, am I?'

Over the period while I was working on our submission to Gerald, she went to London twice. She was certain that I wouldn't want to go with her for she knew that I was afraid of London.

She didn't enjoy her visits. Each time, she returned depressed. After one of these outings I found a bill from a Harley Street doctor, plain and undetailed. When I worried about her, she laughed and said that she sometimes had a pain in her back, not surprising considering the amount of exercise she had been getting recently. It was nothing. The doctor had advised her not to wear high-heeled shoes; not, anyway, to walk in. Darling.

She didn't ask me again about the writing for Gerald. We had embarked on the necessary blackmail and I presumed that she didn't want to be reminded of the twists and turns.

In any case – or in *this* case – it was my job; and I entrenched myself in the studio room and worked on it, confident of my ability and pleased that I was sparing her feelings. I knew that I was working for her, and for us. For myself.

She was very happy when David came home for the summer holidays, although she worried that there would be even less opportunity for us to be together. I asked her whether she thought that it would be the end of the world if I slept with her while David was there. She replied that she didn't consider this to be the right time to be open with David.

She came to the studio to make love, as though for a light meal. And sometimes she had one of the girls from the staff stay at her house while she spent the night with me. When David went to stay at Fiona's for a week, we reoccupied the bed that was rightfully ours. 'I miss sleeping with you,' she said, 'I miss the usualness of it all. But I know that you're not far away.'

She took David to see his father. This time, she said, they would stay for two or three days, they wouldn't do it all in a blind rush. She had obtained special permission to see George on a double visit. I asked her if that wouldn't be too much for David.

'Probably,' she said. 'And that wouldn't be a bad thing. It would be good for David to see that there are times when the two of them wouldn't get on. I don't want him to glorify his father. It's too easy for David to claim that things would be different if Dad was here; just because he's bored with hanging around at home. I don't want him to have that excuse. He should realise that it's up to him to do something constructive.'

'I could do more.'

'Darling, you have your own work to do for us. I don't want to complicate everything. The closer he gets to you, the more inquisitive he's going to be about what you're doing. I'll know when to tell him about us.' She paused in front of the mirror and checked her make-up. 'You could fob him off with some of your stories, if you like. He enjoys those. They're very good, you know. They're funny. You're more tolerant than I am. I like the way you see people. When all this is over, we should try to get a publisher.'

I laughed; I was embarrassed.

'Goodbye then,' she said. 'I'll see you in three days.'

I took a break from the case against Gerald. I had worked for five weeks.

The sweater she gave me on her return had been bought in London. I had a couple more stories for David, and for the first time I saw clearly that I hadn't much further to go on cementing Gerald's future.

'God, it's mayhem in August!' This was her first reaction to coming back.

She was withdrawn. I tried to find out what was wrong. Her back?

Back? Oh that. No.

Seeing George?

Maybe. She simply hadn't wanted to see him, she realised, when she had got there. The fact that there was absolutely nothing between them any more was like a rebuke. She didn't know why she bothered. She had felt insincere and tired of the whole business. He had told her that she should marry again.

Was he angry with her?

No, there was just nothing. George was quite cheerful. He was polite, and interested. He was doing a course on drug counselling. 'No, it's not George that's got me down. I don't know what it is. It'll go away.'

A couple of days later she came to me and said that she was sick and tired of the tourists, that the business was set up to run quite well enough without her, and that David was restless. She would raise the staff wages by half for the rest of the season and she was taking David off on holiday to the West Country.

'Good idea,' I agreed.

'I think so,' she said dubiously. 'I need a change, and I can't think of anything to do besides hang around you. I'm getting on my own nerves even if I'm not getting on yours.'

She asked me to water the garden at the house, and to look in there occasionally.

She came three or four times to say goodbye, distracted and rather pained at her own confusion. Her period was about due, she felt heavy and bloated and didn't know now whether she wanted to go or not. Then, suddenly, she was gone.

She telephoned me late at night, when David was in bed. The weather was wonderful, there were one or two nice people in the hotel, she was swimming or lying flat on her back in the sun.

I anchored myself to finishing off Gerald. I spent two days in the office, annoyed by the sultry weather, typing up the affidavit. I slept at N's. I bumped into Fiona on the usual Wednesday. 'You look exhausted,' she said, full of a knowing grin.

'With hard work,' I told her.

'I'll bet,' she teased. I told her that N was away and she was taken aback. 'On holiday?'

I was a bit curt, taxed both by the humidity in a static August air and by the gloating silliness of her sexual innuendo. I missed N. 'Yes, she's on holiday; why not?'

'Oh, nothing. It's not in her stars. Don't mind me, it's only my Wednesday thrill-attack.'

I sat outside in the 15B garden, listening to the dull drones of suburbia and the happier, frenetic dusk-babble of the birds. The weather wasn't particularly wonderful. The night brought only a slight slump in the tense atmosphere.

The next evening, the telephone didn't ring. I walked back to the studio, hoping that the thunderstorm whose hunger pains rumbled in the distance would reach out to satisfy its appetite over Portsmouth. The studio was tidy, as it always was after Fiona and Michael had used it.

As the late darkness fell and the carpark lamp came on, I imagined again Gerald's hands on N's body, the cold winter and the white skin, her own carmined nails.

I didn't want to drink, I didn't want to sleep. I wanted N. I was unable to let the matter drop. At one o'clock in the morning I went to the office and pulled out the stack of notes made during the past six months, and I went, once again, through the details of all the crimes which Gerald had committed. I was satisfied that there was more than enough evidence for a prosecution.

161

At six o'clock in the morning, I wrote to Gerald. Firstly, a letter as though from N, recounting her own feelings of guilt about George and how she had outgrown these feelings; how she had outgrown her vulnerability towards Gerald's exploitation of those feelings. How she no longer wished to see him on any terms other than those demanded by business. And how, should he be stupid enough to consider otherwise, she had had drawn up a complete account of his criminal activities, to which she was prepared to testify.

Secondly, a letter from myself to Gerald. I said that I had prepared, in accordance with instructions, the aforementioned account of his criminal activities, one copy of which I was sending to him, one signed copy of which I was secreting with a reliable agent in London. N would have the original. I trusted that I had not openly betrayed the terms of our understanding, but I had left instructions which would do so in the event of any harm befalling either N or myself.

At ten o'clock in the morning I called Len Davis and he agreed to receive, in confidence, whatever instructions and whatever documents I sent him.

I had everything photocopied three times. Later, that same morning, I stood in N's bathroom, wearily urinating, and I saw Gerald's face in the bowl. At noon, I dozed in front of the television while the English openers settled in on a difficult Edgbaston wicket.

At six in the evening, N phoned. She had had too much sun yesterday, she had gone to bed early. She was bored and miserable and wanted to see me. Would I come on the train?

I would. I certainly would – with tremendous joy – but I couldn't leave until the next day.

I went upstairs to pack.

In the drawer of N's escritoire I came across a letter to George, written just before her departure. It was mostly about her plans for David. The letter was unsigned and ended in mid-sentence.

There were two crumpled sheets of paper in the wastebin – one the reply to an invitation for a function at Fiona's brother's house, refused; and the other seemed to be part of the same letter to

George, although it didn't run on from the previous, unrejected pages:

'by the time you will be out, the child will be twelve, or, God forbid, older. I don't know what there will be between us. I have done this on my own. It is nobody else's responsibility. Gerald and the family will have had nothing to do with the child's upbringing.

'In fact, I have settled with Gerald. There is no reason for me to have anything more to do with him. ~~I hate him.~~ He is a loathsome man. ~~If only you knew the~~'

I wondered what she meant. How would George be out when David was twelve, in two years' time? Why?

I packed the note with the other papers. I went to sleep easily; if I had any qualms they were only on the question of how far to poke fun at the level of N's sanity. She had no reason to worry, not now. I couldn't wait to tell her. I couldn't wait to see her again.

Fifteen

A series of trains pulled me through the English countryside, all of them going a few dozen miles in the right direction. I got off at junctions, and the trains went on to more important places than Sidmouth. I felt like an important telephone message on a line clogged with thick, guttural verdure. Summer had burst luxuriantly and was waiting to go to seed.

N was stained with sun. She smelt of fresh, oily perspiration and chlorine, her toenails were chipped and the sides of her feet were dusty. It was wonderful to see her and to discover in her the same excitement that I was feeling. We walked down the station platform, stopping every twenty yards or so to look at each other and to embrace, gauche with happiness and incapable of unburdening our feelings.

She talked, as she drove, divesting herself of gabble about David and the swimming pool and the hotel.

'Is that where I'm staying?'

'Not on your life. Everybody there is just itching for an interesting situation to turn up. The main topic of conversation is either road routes or if the good-looking forty-year-old man is married to the blowsy blonde, and whether or not he's a spy. You're staying down the road at Mrs Lloyd's. She's very sweet and doesn't care less what happens as long as you don't have a pet or clutter the hallway with your rubber flippers. It's a lovely room. It has a feeling about it, a history of decorum in the conduct of secret affairs.' Her lips spread mockingly.

'Like the studio?'

'Oh no,' she cried, 'this room is romantic.'

While I got my case out of the car boot, she leant against the roof, tasting the amber plastic arm of her sunglasses. I asked her what she was smiling at.

'Nothing. Just you. Was I smiling? I knew that I couldn't do without you for very long.'

Mrs Lloyd greeted us, dressed to the hilt even though the afternoon was hot. I couldn't think what she reminded me of as she tottered ahead of us, on her high heels, down the corridor of the guest-house. A thin, parlour chair?

She was friendly, and welcomed us without being intrusive. 'It's very quiet in the back here,' she told us; 'you are well away from the rest of the house.'

'She's lovely,' N said, when we were left alone. 'She must be going on seventy. She probably has to let out rooms to keep the house going.'

Our room had a high ceiling; solid pieces of furniture hugged the walls and tall French windows looked out on to a garden jostling with blooms. There was a large, solemn bed. It was perfect.

'It seems like ages since we were together,' N sighed.

'It does. It was difficult before you left. I started missing you then.'

'I know. It was impossible.'

'And when will I see you now?' I laughed.

'As often as possible, without interfering with your work.'

I smiled smugly. 'It's finished,' I said. 'I've finished with Gerald.'

'Finished finished?' she hazarded.

'In the bag.'

'With you?'

'Yes.'

It hadn't quite clicked with her. I reached for her hand and pulled her on to the bed.

'That's wonderful,' she said. She rolled me on to my back and sat astride my thighs, looking down at me, and then looking out at the garden. 'That's wonderful,' she murmured.

'You don't seem very pleased.'

'I didn't realise.'

'What?'

'I didn't think that you would have finished so quickly.'

'Nor did I.'

'You haven't rushed it?' she accused.

'No.'

She bowed forward and kissed me, laying her cheek next to mine. 'Thank God for your confidence.' I hugged her.

She sat up. 'God,' she said, 'then you'll be bored. Oh I wish I'd known. I suppose that it wouldn't have made any difference. But damn!' She looked askance. 'What can I do?'

'You can read through it some time.'

'No, not that, silly!'

Her eyes flitted quickly, accompanying her thoughts. I smiled, half vacant with having her near me, on holiday with ourselves.

'But how good,' she murmured, turning back to me. 'What a piece of luck.' She clasped my hands. 'I'm so glad! What a nuisance.'

'Why?'

'I have to go now. The hotel is very good at organising things for the kids to do but there's a gap, about now, when we're all expected to be changing and having a drink before dinner.'

She climbed off me and stood by the bed with her hands clasped behind her neck. 'I am sorry.'

'Don't be.'

'What will you do?'

I told her that I would be buying a bucket and spade. She made some weak, disappointed, dirty remark; and then, as if she was embarrassed at her own crude sense of humour, she buried her face in my shoulder before leaving. 'I'll see you about ten.'

I bought one bottle of champagne, she brought another. She arrived in our room looking acutely Riviera-ish, having dressed for dinner at the hotel. Over the Victorian fireplace were two framed photographs – of an elegant, strong-featured woman and a handsome man, *circa* 1900. We undressed each other. Her skin was sensitive from the sun. I was stunned at her beauty.

She stayed until dawn.

For three nights we followed this pattern, until she looked exhausted. It was easy for me, I could sleep during the day. But I noticed that there were blisters on her back and she confessed that she had fallen asleep in the sun during the afternoon.

I suggested to her that we had celebrated enough. We should calm down.

She was angry with me. She accused me of not understanding what it was like to be in love, what it was like to need someone so much that it ached. But, the following day, Mrs Lloyd woke me with a telephone call at noon, and N said I was right, she would go to bed early that night; she would, unhappily, stay at the hotel.

I hadn't had time to do much around the town. I'd kept away from the sea-front so as not to run the risk of meeting David. I had only been out a couple of times and then I had chosen to walk uphill; I found some quiet council gardens with a good view of the sea, a pensioners' haunt. N seemed to have much more energy than I did, in bed or out of it. I suppose that I was waiting for the right time to show her the work I had done, which needed her signature.

I walked up to her hotel late that night. It was an imposing building, a hundred yards from the sea, with a miniature golf course at the front. There was an old-fashioned dance in progress on a veranda overlooking the putting greens. One or two dinner jackets, but mostly short dresses and dark suits. N didn't seem to be amongst them. I sealed the envelope and left it with the hall porter.

'Yes. Yes, it's exactly what I want. It's much more than I expected. I . . . I never realised what you could do.' She smiled sheepishly.

She had telephoned at lunchtime and had walked over to see me in the middle of the afternoon, still puffy with the release of accumulated fatigue. Now she looked merely and honestly tired.

'I've got a present for you. I hope it's a present.' She hesitated. 'I've offered to pay for Fiona and her son to stay at the hotel for the next week. You must need a holiday as much as I do.'

'You needn't have done that.'

'Well I *have* done that.'

'I could have taken on David as well, you know. I've brought him a couple of stories, if nothing else.' I handed them to her.

167

There seemed to be some conflict showing in her eyes, which she scattered by smiling mischievously.

'Thank you,' she said. 'But then we'd have even less time together, do you see? With Fiona here, we'll be free. David will be much happier not feeling that he has to stick to me. The boys will go off together. And Fiona's just dying to get away from Michael. Now that the blowsy old tart has gone, the spy is kicking his heels. He's a sitting duck for Fiona. Gemini with Scorpio rising, I shouldn't wonder.'

'You didn't ask him?'

She laughed. 'Of course not. That's just what I told Fiona on the phone. I haven't even talked to him. He fancies himself as a womaniser.'

'But Fiona – '

'Fiona's no slouch, believe you me.'

N returned, late at night, beautifully made-up but in jeans and a sweatshirt, discarding her wealth, a relaxed lover. I walked her back to the hotel, where she glowed amongst the dullish persistence of revellers without revelry. We had one drink in the closing bar.

'They think you're a bit of rough I picked up in the town,' she laughed. 'The middle class are so funny.'

Fiona arrived; and N and I had our holiday together. Mrs Lloyd was quite happy with whatever went on, she was happy at having lovers in the house. But more often we went to the beach, or took the car off to places which N knew. We swam and read and played cards, and ate large meals; and went to the cinema when we were sick of the sun, and loved, and made love. That week – kiss me slow; kiss me quick because out of the blue it came to an end.

'Shouldn't I at least see Fiona?'

'Hell no.' N, smelling of sun, that deep rich smell of open pores; a thigh papered with light golden sand. Shots of her in a bikini, affairs, that sort of thing. Sand on Mrs Lloyd's sheets, salt and the compact aroma of fecundity. N, full, seeping and drowsy. 'What do you miss?'

'Nothing.'

'Nothing at all? What do you do when I'm not with you?'

'Wait for you.'

'And?'

'Nothing.'

'Be honest.'

'Sometimes I somehow miss writing.'

'That's good. You should write then.'

'I'd rather do nothing. I like waiting for you. This room is sloppy with love. It's not a writing room.'

'I suppose it isn't. I can't think why I ever thought that it would be, before you arrived.'

'You didn't ever think it would be, did you?'

'Yes.'

'Be honest.'

'Maybe.' She smiled at herself.

Friday.

In the morning, she collected me early and we went back to our favourite beach. It was a long beach, but you could climb over rocks and claim an underpopulated cove. Today, however, as we drove along behind it, the beach itself showed no sign of becoming occupied. I wondered why.

'They all go home on Friday. They've had their fortnight. They pack up their cars and off they go,' she explained blithely. 'The staff come in and do out the bedrooms and another lot arrive tomorrow. The town is full of vacuum cleaners and laundry-doers.'

'Why haven't we gone?'

'Because Fiona coughed up some money and the family name. The hotel has packed us all into the bridal suite for tonight. I must admit that I balked slightly at the idea of sharing a bridal suite with Fiona. It was kind of her to give us the extra day.'

'Did she get her spy?'

'I think so. I don't think the earth moved. She said that she suspected that he worked for the wrong side.' N laughed. 'That's not bad for Fiona. She's getting witty in her old age.'

'N, what *is* this?' I handed her the crumpled page of her letter to George.

169

She slowed the car and read it quickly. She blenched. 'Do you go through everything when I'm out of the way?'

'Yes,' I said, and added a lie, 'of course I do. You asked me once to be careful about leaving papers lying around, whether because of Fiona or Gerald. So I make sure that nothing's left lying around.'

'Yes, I'm sorry,' she said quickly.

'I just couldn't help reading it and I didn't understand it.' I had meant to tease her for her muddleheadedness, but the tease had fallen strangely flat and there was nothing left but for me to work my way out of the embarrassment. 'I mean, George isn't going to be out of prison in two years. There was never any hope of that, and now we're making sure that he won't be. That is what we've made clear to Gerald. That's what you wanted me to do, isn't it?'

'Yes.'

'Even down to more or less telling George the same thing.'

'Yes.'

There was a pause.

'So I didn't understand. It suddenly worried me that I hadn't got something right, and I wanted to make – '

She interrupted me. 'I don't really understand it either. I was a bit crazy before we came away. Seeing George, being bound up with George and David. I suppose that it was just some sort of idea of how I might write to him. That's the next thing we've got to do when we get back. If I didn't have you, it would all be so confused. Maybe not; that week was just chaos. It has been wonderful here.' Her voice dropped. 'It couldn't have been better. I know that we have to come back to George. Half the mess is over and I know we'll do as well for the other half. It will be easy, won't it?' she pleaded.

She had taken off her glasses, and as she gazed at me I saw that she was looking for her confidence.

'Probably not easy,' I advised her, 'but we'll do it.'

Her smile wavered.

'Don't worry,' I said, 'we're home and dry.'

She took her foot off the brake and the car rolled forward.

'Don't think about it,' I asked her. 'I shouldn't have spoiled the week.'

'Nothing could spoil this week.'

We came to the carpark. Although there were very few people on the beach, the snack-shack and a seaside-paraphernalia booth had both been unshuttered in the hope of offering service. One man sat, bored, reading the paper; another stood with a tin of green paint in his hand, touching up the corners of his cabin. N put her sunglasses back on. It was necessary to purchase a carpark ticket and listen seriously to a third man, who advised us to park on the end of a line of perhaps a dozen cars. The two-hundred-place carpark was otherwise empty, but it might fill up suddenly and we might forget where we had put our car; it did happen.

'What a wonderful man,' said N; and the man lifted her mood completely. Our final outing became as charming as our previous visits to the beach had been.

She found a spot. She wriggled the sand into suitable shape. She paraded with a dripping ice-cream cone. She paddled through the cold, exhausted ripples of sea. She stood flatfooted on the corrugated strand. She shielded her eyes to watch an indefatigable windsurfer. All childish, with the pleasure of reshuffled years. Most of the time I lay and watched her, and wondered what she was thinking, untroubled as she had been all week.

She wandered off round the point. I went to buy a roll of film, ·wanting to capture her; but as I stood in front of the booth I knew that there was something in her that I would always look for and always miss. The man with the green paint put down his brush and sold me a postcard.

He told me to fetch my lady back round the point before too long, in an hour, because the tide came across the sand very fast and there was no way up those cliffs.

I thanked him and walked along the beach in N's wake.

She was admiring stones.

She had collected three. She was gently picking her way, barefooted, across an enormous dump of stone and rock which the ocean had rolled up to the northern side of the point. She smiled at me balmily, flushed with the sun.

'Can we carry them?'

'As long as there's not too many.'

'They're very different. Look.' She handed me the three and climbed away over the rocks. 'There's an amazing number of different colours,' she called.

Her enthusiasm was wonderful, and correct. The stones were beautifully mottled, in reds and blues and ambers.

I joined her search. Often I paused to watch the lines of her body as she clambered and bent, an utterly known and tasted and adored beauty. I was in a simple dream.

I looked past N and I saw a body, to the right of her, about forty yards in front.

Just the head, and the shoulders leaning peculiarly against a rock. But I knew that the body was dead; it was too posed, like a doll on a child's top shelf.

I started walking over the rocks to have a look.

The girl was folded into a sitting position between two boulders. The water had drained away. One arm was snapped behind her back. She was very thin, with gangly legs and half-formed breasts. An attractive girl perhaps. An adolescent. Clean. With pale lips. Some parts of her skin were white and dead. Lank, oily hair hid her eyes. There was nothing serene about her. Her thighs ran up the sides of the rock, her unfleshed bottom fitted into the snug, water-sculpted pool.

'Oh no,' N whispered at my shoulder. 'Please. Why do these things happen to me?'

I reported the body. I collected the car and dropped N off at the hotel. She walked around, madly, looking for David. She found Fiona first and learnt that David was playing tennis. Fiona took care of her, and I took care of the police.

She came back to spend the night with me; to be held, to be persuaded that guilt shouldn't exist.

In the morning, she rose from the bed and Mrs Lloyd cooked us a large breakfast. Mrs Lloyd said that it was a joy to have two people who were so fond of each other staying in her bedroom. There was a vase of sunrise-cut garden roses on the table. She had heard about the young girl, a suicide; silly things like that were best put under your pillow and forgotten about, she said, severely, to N. She wouldn't accept any payment for the extra night.

In the confusion, I asked N for one of the copies of the deposition against Gerald. Before leaving, she handed it back to me. I presumed that she had signed it. Before catching the train, I mailed this copy off to Davis.

Sixteen

This was a mad, bad time. Whether it slowly caught up with us and drew us apart, or whether both of us saw it coming and marched off in our different directions, I still don't know how to account for the period between the tragic end of that holiday and Christmas.

I like the autumn, the smells and the dilatory stroll towards winter, the retreat and the ensuing crystalline starkness.

But for N it was as if she fell hurriedly in step with the shortening days and abandoned herself to the increased tempo of the dark.

When we came back to Portsmouth, and David had returned to school, she showed an absurd insistence on making love. Often, as far as I could tell, in defiance of her lack of desire.

When I tried to understand her, she complained sadly that I no longer desired her. But this tone of complaint didn't ring true. I adored N when she was demanding, when she challenged to be loved; but at this time she didn't wish to be loved.

I asked Fiona if she had noticed any change in N. The conversation dropped through three stages. I told you, said Fiona, that you would both enjoy yourselves during this time, I wouldn't be surprised if both of you felt a bit blistered.

No, that's not it. What about the dead girl? I said; I think that it affected her deeply.

Fiona agreed. N would want, any woman would want convincing now about the life force of love; N would need to push the opposing death force out of her mind.

But not, I thought, in an automatic way; that kind of functional loving wouldn't have any value, would it?

Stay with her, Fiona advised, it's important to her. She needs you.

'Is Gerald in England?'

My question startled her. She was in the middle of undressing.

'I think so. I haven't heard from him. I could ring Jean and find out, if you want to know.'

'Did you send him the papers?'

'Obviously. Otherwise he'd be down here checking up on what you were doing. You're quite safe, you have all the exits covered. You can slip away any time you like.' She walked to the bathroom.

I knew what would happen next. She would come out and slide into bed, look into my eyes apologetically and say that she loved me.

When she came out, I asked her: 'N, what is it?'

'What's what, darling?' She was sealed. My concern was unwarranted.

I asked her if the business was doing all right. Yes, it was. Was she worried about David? Not at all. Or Gerald? No, she was only interested in how Gerald would react, and since Gerald had chosen not to react that was fine. Fiona and Michael? They would split up soon, she couldn't care less about them. The girl at the beach? What girl? – oh, that; no, that had nothing to do with her, and in fact it had made her glad to get home, otherwise she would have been sad at the end of the holiday.

'Me?'

'What about you?'

'Is there anything wrong between us?'

'Of course there isn't. Now, please, just stop pestering me. Go to sleep.'

But during the following afternoon, I engineered a row. She accused me of oppressing her. She had, she said, even had nightmares about me in which I always loomed up, wearing the same blue jacket, not saying anything, but restricting her and threatening her. I was always on at her. She couldn't think clearly for herself. She no longer looked forward to coming home and she felt nervous the minute she put the key in the lock. At the same time, I hadn't touched her for weeks. Even having sex was all up to her, she had to make all the effort, she had to start everything. She didn't know what had happened. And meanwhile I kept poking at her, asking her questions, making her feel guilty that she didn't know the answers; trying to understand her as though she was a sort of disease, when there was nothing there to understand – God knows she had looked hard enough, trying to find something wrong with herself. She loved me and trusted me but perhaps, she had to realise, she might not be capable of giving me what I wanted. Whatever that was; she no longer knew. And she was sorry if I was upset but then so was she. She felt stuck. She felt that she was halfway out there and vulnerable. She didn't know what to do about it. Worse than that; for the first time in her life she felt that she could do *nothing* about it.

Eight months later I reminded N of this moment, her words and her dexterity in concealing herself. She laughed and then she was embarrassed. We were in Cornwall. I asked her to marry me.

She had no idea how to approach George – this was to be the most painful part of the process of freeing herself. She handed me a box of half-finished letters which she had written over the last two years. 'I don't like them,' she said. 'They're not what I meant to say. They're gloomy and full of self-pity. Whenever I start writing to him I end up writing about myself. They make life seem so miserable. I don't want any of that to reach him. Burn them when you've finished with them.'

I took them away, and I judged from her lack of indication to the contrary that I should take myself away also. I thought of going back to London, but N was dismayed by the hint of such a proposal. It was only a bad joke, I assured her.

She was depressed at having mislaid her sense of humour. She was edgy and worried about worrying about herself. I could do nothing to alleviate her state of mind.

I read through N's letters. There was an enormous number of them; fifty or sixty, I would think. They were nearly all of the same

176

pattern. They started off very newsy, very gossipy, very enthusiastic about the people she had met and the plans for the business – and then, with a strange feeling of fatalism about the writing, they descended into sadness. She was humorous about herself; she knew herself very well, or thought that she did, and she was ironic about herself. Then the cracks began to appear – firstly as though she the writer was bored with herself as a subject, and then as though she had simply lost herself. A dull, sad pessimism unfolded. A hopelessness, a clear blackness which made me wince for her at its severity.

There are people who wank on into the blackness, drawing it around them like a warm and comforting blanket, manipulating themselves for external sympathy. With such people there is always the give-away scent of strong selfishness. With N, there was no such relief. In reading her letters I feared for her. They weren't an invitation for someone's attention, they weren't a complaint to God; they were a precise and cold indictment of the way things were and the way she was.

A dozen of them were finished and signed and they ended on an up note. It was as though she was reaching out, at last, to offer comfort – to George, or more likely to herself. But it was clear that she felt this to be dishonest. Therefore, presumably, she hadn't sent the letters.

I discovered a bit more about her. There were no letters written during the post-Christmas winter months. Spring, middle summer and late autumn were her times of writing.

I was being pernickety. I was looking for something to explain 'us'. Drawing any conclusions from these letters would be as disloyal and as worthless as going to Fiona for advice. These letters were N, in her relationship with George; a pained and painful N, stalked by guilt.

For a week or so I thought of simply sending them off to George, the whole box of them. Let *him* know how she felt! Let him sense that void in which she faltered. He was strong enough either to reach out and forgive her or to slap her hard enough to bring her to her senses. 'Don't be daft!' he might say. He could let her off the hook. Why shouldn't he? He had nothing to lose.

177

Except her. And he'd lost her already; which she wanted me to make known, in the best possible way, to him.

At least, having read her letters, I knew her style; and I thought that I could do a better job than she had done.

Our own love was held in trust. It had to be. There was a gulf between us.

She didn't want to know what I was doing. That much I could easily understand. She had to wait.

Waiting didn't suit her. If I had to describe how she behaved, I would say that she maintained herself. Without our deciding, the decision was that we should not be close to each other. We should not be intimate.

I started working and I remembered the evenings we had spent together after we had first met, when she described George and told me about their life together. I remembered those evenings very well. I remembered the bright enthusiasm in her eyes and her delight in George's grasp of life – her love, aroused perhaps dubiously but unchannelled by calculation. I recalled those moments and I found that with the aid of my notes I could re-create her admiration for George, the way in which she loved him and the qualities she loved him for.

It wasn't a bad place to start.

George's first career as a footballer.

His difficulty with his father. N's admiration for his courage in making the split – she had always admired that.

George's resolve in creating something new for himself, and, of course, this same resolve which touched her when they first fell for each other. His saving her from the hurt pride and arrogance of her own preoccupation with herself after the divorce.

His energy, which had dragged her out, however unwilling she had been, into the world again.

His native intelligence, his protection of Gerald, his insistence on the 'soft' methods of crime, the little ribbon tied round his prick. (Check with N, later, the correct or nice word she, or they, used for 'prick'.)

His . . . and how she . . . and what it meant to her.

178

Her love for George, hauled out of sepia confinement and coloured with the aid of the best terminology I could find.

Her birthday was at the end of October. We shared a difficult, candlelit dinner, harried by melancholy. She got very drunk. She wrote me a cheque which I tore up, and basically we fucked to hissed obscenities.

I handed it all to George, every last bit of her love and mine. We lost touch with each other. I remember being with her on Guy Fawkes Night, walking through crowds of people towards a huge bonfire after having watched a display of fireworks which spattered showers of lights over our heads; and I felt sad. Beside me, I felt her restlessness, a coldly contained energy.

In the middle of November she started to come to the studio, in the early afternoon or late at night, and she would seduce me. She sat in the wingchair, one leg folded under her, her red lips as smooth and shiny as satin-covered cushions.

If I asked her about George, she was cynically dismissive. She joked about him. There was no form of debasement which we didn't embrace. Gorged on her, I went back to the desk and wrote about her love for George.

My position became untenable. I could not support the cynicism. I yearned for the peace of love. I was sick of the way I carried on writing, from myself, about the way she missed George and about the loneliness without love. I could no longer stay with her. I was sick of the way in which everything had to be used.

I stopped, and I went back to London.

There was a cold, uninhabited silence in my rooms. I waited for several days.

And then came a tremendous exhilaration, an outpouring of affection for the people I had been dealing with before N had dealt me herself, the grotesque humour in their predicaments, the farce, the little bits of trying that went on. Things you don't notice until later.

Like the fact that I had become a writer, not a lawyer.

*   *   *

179

We made contact after a fortnight of silence; and we discovered cheerfulness to be a way around referring to ourselves. It wasn't as though we had been presented with the final blank account of our relationship. I realised that her apparent lack of concern was how she resolved to feel rather than how she felt.

And, being in London, I realised that I had a straightforward obligation towards her that had nothing at all to do with our relationship. She sent me a letter, with a cheque enclosed, and a note which said that she hadn't kept any accounts but she worried that I wouldn't have enough money to live on. 'Please don't worry about me, just let's get this thing finished. I don't want it to keep us apart.'

I went back to her on December the fifteenth. It was a stupid time to visit her, with the holiday arriving. I knew that we would not spend Christmas together. She would have the full weight of the family once again on her shoulders, and David would arrive home in a few days' time.

I hadn't progressed with the work on George. I told her as much, and she agreed that it was probably better for everything to stay in limbo over the Christmas period. She had set herself up, she was prepared for Gerald, and she didn't want to consider any new development at this time.

The three days of my visit fell over a weekend. We were invited to Fiona's for a party on the Saturday. N was bored with entertaining festive groups at the restaurant until all hours of the night, she wanted to get away from Portsmouth if I didn't mind.

On the Friday night she worked late, and she crawled into bed at three in the morning. I fetched her breakfast seven hours later. She read the newspaper, discouraging communication. I played pinball downstairs. She appeared at eleven-thirty. She had one or two things to pick up at home and then we should go to Fiona's.

Once at home, she decided that she would take a bath, and then she dozed in front of the fire while I watched rugby on television. I asked her if she thought that we would get to Fiona's.

'I suppose that we should. She's on her own. She doesn't see Michael any more. We should go. But we won't stay the night there.'

She made herself up, picking beauty out of the bag. She asked me to drive.

She didn't enjoy the party. The cottage was not sufficiently crowded for everybody to have to talk to each other and the various disparate elements chatted amongst themselves. Nobody felt like meeting new people. There was a brief flurry of mingling when the pubs closed and offloaded their beery loudness, but this died within the hour and the more precious talkers used it as an excuse to leave early. Michael arrived at this time. I found myself with him. We kept ourselves amused as outsiders.

Fiona joined us and he asked her if everything was all right. She was fine; she was a bit tired, she said, and it looked as though one group of people was going to settle in for the night, or for as long as the drink lasted.

Michael smiled at her displeasure. She attempted to kill him with a flat look, and walked away. He watched her go.

Twenty minutes later he announced that everybody was expected to walk down the road to ring the church bells. Fiona protested. The general opinion was that if Fiona protested it was probably the right thing to do.

We lost several people on the way. The church was cold, like an empty meat store. We managed a couple of clangs on the bells and that seemed to be enough to satisfy everyone's interest. We walked back down the lane to the cottage. The curtains were drawn and the upstairs lights were on. We grouped in the middle of the road, and then everybody dispersed to their cars.

'Once round the block and back again,' Michael said. 'They'll have gone by then.'

When we parked again, in exactly the same place, the other cars had disappeared. We went back into the cottage. There was no sign of N. Fiona was clearing away glasses.

'She's gone upstairs.'

'Are we staying?'

'Oh yes, I think so. She was going to bed.'

181

Michael poured me a drink and I took one out to the kitchen for Fiona. I asked her if I might help with the washing-up.

'I'm not going to do it now. I'm sorry that I haven't really had a chance to talk to you. How's it going?'

'Oh, fine,' I said.

'It's not really N's time of the year.'

'And how are you?'

'Me? The same as usual.'

'You look well.'

'Thank you. I am well. Are you in London now?'

'On and off.'

'That seems to be the way it is for everybody.' She was amused. For the first time I thought of her as a friend.

'Have you seen anything of N recently?'

'Not really. We both get caught up in our own surroundings at this time of year. Christmas is very family whether you like it or not, especially for her. What will you do?'

'I'll work.'

'Duty?'

'No. Preference.'

'You shouldn't be so severe on yourself. Most people manage to enjoy themselves somehow over Christmas.'

'Aren't *you*? Severe with yourself?'

'Not in the slightest. I've never had to be. I was a very spoilt child. I'd better go and talk to Michael and thank him for getting rid of all those people.'

N was asleep. When I came to bed we clasped each other for a moment, made ourselves as comfortable as we could, and slept.

N was alert in the morning. The cottage was cold. Half-eaten logs slumbered on beds of ash. She had already had her coffee and had borrowed jeans and a sweater from Fiona's room. She wanted to go. I took a mug of tea with me for the drive.

The car was soon warm, and outside the windows the countryside lay deserted and stiff from the touch of frost. Leafless trees poked up like radio masts at a derelict airfield, forlornly waiting for a signal across empty airwaves.

N muttered something about Michael.

'Did he stay with her?' I asked, taking up the slack.

'Yes. So much for her decision-making,' she crowed.

'Well it was a bit late for him to drive the whole way back.'

'That, of course, makes all the difference.'

'So they slept together, so what?'

'Fiona couldn't keep hold of a decision if it was only Mickey Mouse pulling on the other end.'

'Maybe she didn't want to.'

N was contemptuous. 'At least,' she said, 'now I don't have to take her complaining seriously; all this new Fiona nonsense, the new leaf, all that prattle about her determination to get what she wants. I've got the lowdown on her.'

'Why do you have to have something on her? Why not enjoy them? Why do you have to have something on everybody?'

She didn't answer. A moment later, I said: 'It's as though you're running a fucking protection racket.'

She didn't reply. I fumed in silence for a mile or two, and then she switched on the radio. I fumed silently for as long as I could. My insistence became speckled with worries about losing her, with nervousness about having offended her. I listened to the music on the radio and stared out at the dumb countryside. I thought that, yes, running a protection racket was exactly what she was doing, was what she had to do, was what she had asked me to help her do, to help her protect herself.

She turned the radio down and apologised. I apologised to her. She turned the radio up again.

We hardly got back together. When we returned to 15B, we both wandered upstairs to the bedroom. There was a huge pile of presents for David at the foot of the bed, an enormous pile. I was too amazed, she was too dismissive. She ran a bath. I showered. We exhibited a willingness to make love. We didn't manage it. Neither of us were grateful for the result.

She had one or two things to do around the house; I had one or two things to do in the studio. She had a Christmas present for me, and I one for her. We agreed that we would open them on Christmas Day. We agreed that we would telephone often. We told each other that we loved each other.

By the time that I had finished clearing out the studio, there was one train left to catch. I didn't want to leave her. It would have been like leaving myself.

The bar closed for the night and I sat up by the fire, wondering what was wrong and why we were wrong.

At eleven-thirty she put her key into the lock and pushed open the door. She had been drinking, as I had. She took my presence for granted, although she would probably also have taken my absence for granted. She carried her drink very well, almost imperially. I suppose that the weight of sadness was more imposing. It seemed to shield her. She asked me to pour her a brandy and she sat opposite me, with that same gesture of picking an imaginary piece of cotton off her skirt at knee-level.

I collected the bottle and sat on the rug in front of her. She talked about David, as a way of talking. She was very analytical about herself, very cold. She blamed herself for sending him away to school as a way of sending him away from her. She drank. She blamed herself for the way she felt that she could no longer get through to him, and for buying him Christmas presents as a way of trying to buy him back. Perhaps it was the only way she knew of having an impact on people any more; she didn't know; she was no longer sure of her own honesty. Her responses were cold, she felt that she was retreating, everything had its own equation which she had started and was responsible for –

I tried to calm her. I collected her and embraced her. I kissed her. I stroked her foot.

But she wanted to talk, she wanted to drink.

'N ... N ...'

'Stop smothering me with your weakness.'

Her eyes blazed for a second and then she regarded me with a fixed indifference.

'Go away,' she murmured.

'N ...'

'Don't plead.'

A little smile played down from her nostrils and hovered about her lips. 'Gerald will be here,' she crooned. She watched me to see what I thought of this.

'Are you scared?'

The question surprised her.

'No,' she said finally. 'No.'

She smiled at me. 'You're good at what you do. Let's go to bed. I'm much too drunk.'

I helped her upstairs. She was exhausted. She lay on the bed while I undressed her. She laughed like a slob, almost hysterically. When I unfastened her suspender belt she cried – big, hot tears – and then she restrained herself. I finished undressing her and crept into bed beside her. She turned and lay her body against mine; we touched at the knee, the belly, the breast and the forehead. I stroked her back.

'What is it?' I asked her.

'It's just the innocence.'

She cried again.

Henry Miller said that there is no better fuck than a woman in tears. I read that somewhere. I still can't decide what it means. Tears are maybe the sincerest form of flattery. Rents in the fabric of N – what sort of flattery was that?

'Will you be all right?'

'Yes, I will be all right. Go now.'

'What will you do?'

'I'll get up in about an hour. I'll have a bath and I'll go and fetch David.'

Seventeen

I spent Christmas writing about George. I thought that I knew what N wanted to say to him. I presumed that in any case she would rewrite it in her own way. At times I thought that she was wrong in the whole undertaking, that she simply wanted to leave him with a flourish – one last gesture towards a man who had long accepted the good sense of an end to their relationship. It was she, rather than George, who needed a testament to their love. She needed to have the feeling that she was giving him something.

I covered George with esteem in the same way that one would place a cloth over the cage of a tired budgerigar. That was what she wanted, that was what was fitting, that was what would relieve her of her guilt.

I thought that it was right, but I didn't like it. It would be good for her, and it wouldn't do any harm to George – she had already made her decision to leave him and I was merely helping her to do so. It was dishonesty in the service of honesty, and my allegiance was to her.

And so I wrote about why she wanted to end their marriage.

I could not understand, for the life of me, why she had had the affair with Emerson.

She telephoned me frequently – she was to telephone me and not vice versa – but this was not the time to ask about her past. She was depressed. She was, at times, accusatory. She was in the front line with Gerald. I wanted, when I picked up the phone, to be close to her; but there were desperate silences. She rang once and asked me to come down to Portsmouth as soon as possible; but five minutes later she called again to assure me that she was fine and that on no account was I to move from London.

She rang on New Year's Day. David was with her.

'And Gerald?'

'Here and there,' she said guardedly. She seemed lighter of heart, but not willing to communicate the reasons.

'Around, in other words.'

'Yes.'

'Has it gone all right?'

'Yes. It looks as though it might rain, perhaps we can do something later on.'

'Fine.' Rain was the codeword for a dampening presence. She couldn't talk. 'I love you.'

She paused, and then she said: 'Thank you. Goodbye.'

I didn't worry. Somehow, when Gerald was simply 'around', it wasn't as much of a threat as the shock of his arrival. Gerald, I understood, was a boring man. Like the sleek black front of a submarine which had crashed by mistake through the sea-wall, he looked powerful at first; but after a couple of weeks, if the obstacle was stranded there, it could be made to look ridiculous by placing a vase of flowers on its nose.

I thought about George, and how, when N had first approached me, it was with the appeal for his innocence. I wondered if I hadn't abandoned him. But, finally, I didn't care.

I had my own loneliness.

Fiona telephoned out of the blue to say that she was running Jeremy up to London to stay with his father for a few days before he went back to school. She was taking him to the hologram show in the afternoon. Why didn't we meet for a drink in the evening?

It seemed as though every moment I had spent with N returned to warm me. The arch of her body, the moods behind her smile, and her seriousness. My room was silent, and the seriousness was oppressive.

Oh, I changed the sheets. I tidied the room, oh oh. I wanted the compromise, the lack of seriousness, the carelessness. I liked Fiona. She was fun. I wanted to hear her moan. I was lonely.

I met her at a wine-bar, and she was fun. Fun at the club. And back at the flat, leaning against the door, she was fun, with her laughingly uncoy 'I'm going to stay, aren't I?' Fun with large breasts, hanging-baskets swaying over the balcony of the chair arm. All fun, I am sure.

I was not fun. Or I was, until a certain point in the night. Fiona didn't lose her sense of humour; she held nothing against me other than a momentary dismay at discovering that her diaphragm had got pounced upon by downstairs's cat when both of them had found themselves shut, unwanted, in the bathroom.

We talked; confidentially, I think. Without, I think, malice or intrigue. I don't remember much. The hangover next day was very great. I remember Fiona as madonna-ish. I remember her sitting back against the base of the uncomfortable chair, her breasts hanging forward, her look heavy with sympathy, asking me if my affair with N was making me unhappy.

Asking me if I knew that Gerald was down there.

But I had disposed of Gerald. I said that I worried more about George, about N's love for George. If that was over, *we* might be together.

I remember something which survived the hangover, which surfaced the next evening when Fiona had gone. Words of hers.

–'George! She doesn't feel a thing for George. She's a very clever, selfish woman sometimes. She rode George ragged. I've seen her use more people than you could imagine.'

– 'She's very close to you. Closer than I've seen her with anybody. She loves you. You're good for her.'

– 'She can make you unhappy. That's all I'm saying.'

I think that I cried on Fiona's shoulder. I know that the next day she was too hungover to drive and my expedition to buy aspirin would have been accomplished more efficiently with Buster Keaton taking my role.

It did me good to see her. It made me anxious to return to N. It peeled the bitterness off solitude, and once the hangover had disappeared it put me back to work on George. I wanted to clear him out of the way. I was tired of being sympathetic towards him.

I gave him one more chance.

I found the list of names which N had written down for me, months ago, and I made an appointment to see the lawyer who had defended George during his trial.

It was a strange experience, approaching the bastion of the law. I realised why I had ignored it in the first place. The law was a tremendously comforting edifice. I couldn't doubt the intelligence of the people who were lawyers, nor the hard work involved, nor the boredom. Nor, in Peter Dwyer's case, the evidence of rich reward. For once, the complacency was a relief rather than an irritation. His milieu was utterly unappealing.

Peter Dwyer, in his chambers, explained to me briefly and effectively why George Croft stood no chance of having his case reopened. And should I be interested – he didn't know for what reason I had approached him, he presumed that I was a journalist or a redeemer of criminals – but should I be interested, he had told Mrs Croft exactly the same thing two years ago. There was no new evidence. Did I have any new evidence?

I could, I believed, show that Croft's criminal culpability would more rightly be shared amongst other members of his family – his brother Gerald and perhaps one other member of the family.

No doubt. But they hadn't testified at the trial, and it had been Croft's wish that they shouldn't testify. Why should they change their minds?

I didn't know.

'And of course there is the murder.' Peter Dwyer turned his palms to the heavens. 'He would have had more of a case if someone had been hurting his wife, rather than if that someone had been making her happy. But she knew exactly what she was doing. A man of Croft's background and connections had plenty of other ways of scaring Emerson off, and he could have used them. He undoubtedly over-reacted against the innocent man.'

'What about Emerson?'

189

'He's rather dead.' Peter Dwyer smiled graciously. 'There's nothing to defend in his case.'

'What was he like?'

'He was an Australian, he had no family over here. A bit of a playboy. His money came from Australia and it went back there with his ashes. He was undoubtedly the sort of man with whom to have a casual fling, from her point of view.'

Peter Dwyer exasperated me with his 'undoubtedly's. But he was right. Two years ago, N had come to ascertain that *she* was right.

I only had to go to the authority to find out that what I was doing was right.

It was hardly dishonest, and there was nothing dark.

Three days later I had done with George. I had done more than George Croft merited. I had given him her love, and it wasn't the cold 'Dear John . . . ' I had a slight conscience but I knew that the pangs were misdirected. I had spent an age telling that to N, even when I didn't quite believe it.

She telephoned me to say that Gerald had gone. She was optimistic about the New Year.

I should have been overjoyed, but for some reason I wasn't. I felt that I had gone through the whole deck looking for one particular card, and I hadn't been able to find it. I had wanted to know her; now it seemed that I had known her all along. There was nothing suspicious about her. She was as she was, as she presented herself. She loved me and in return I had only a feeling of emptiness.

I delayed seeing her. I don't know why I did this. It was as though I was trying to create a pain out of an uncertainty. I felt inadequate and unable to imagine us being together, and at the same time I suffered at the thought of being apart from her.

She telephoned every evening. Our conversation was mannered. We talked politely about things that were confidential. I have never had such an ambiguous attitude towards the telephone, wanting and hating the near distance of the voice on the other end.

When I finally said to her that I thought I should perhaps come down to Portsmouth, she hesitated.

'Yes,' she said, 'that would be nice. You can stay at the studio. Not tomorrow night, I have to go out tomorrow night. What about the day after?'

I could think of nothing to do in London on my last evening. I looked at N's list of addresses and it seemed suitable to spend the evening in a pub which presumably had something to do with George. Maybe she and he used to drink there.

So I went there, to drink.

It was a sink-pit of a place, which had probably never seen better days. The lounge bar was loosely connected to the saloon bar, and the wallpaper was loosely connected to the wall. It was a cheap, over-decorated, end-of-the-world pub.

In the saloon bar there were two pairs of middle-aged drunks, an arrogant fivesome from the lower echelons of the recording industry and a mish-mash of squatters and punks who sat watching a soundless television set which was on a shelf over the bar.

The jukebox played Ella Fitzgerald. I bought a drink from a dumpy, friendly, London barmaid and took it through to the lounge bar. A group of four were talking with a barman whom I couldn't see. There was a flash, leggy showgirl type and a bespectacled chartered accountant cum weight-trainer. There was a woman covered in make-up who might have been the showgirl's mother and a man standing beside her who might have been her husband or her lover. Their glasses chinked. There was plenty of familiar effing and blinding and same old story-telling.

Every so often, the showgirl's mother would break off her conversation and join Ella Fitzgerald for the chorus. Two of the squatters put money into the jukebox and pressed buttons, but nothing interfered with Ella Fitzgerald. They complained, and were given their money back by the barmaid. Someone else wanted to hear the ten o'clock news on the television, and he was told that the sound didn't work. When I went up to the bar for another drink, the weight-trainer stepped out for the Gents and I saw that Billy was behind the bar. I recognised him immediately from the football match, and smiled, but he didn't show any signs of recognition. He disappeared into the back of the building.

That should have been enough. I should have gone then.

But I liked Ella Fitzgerald singing 'Every Time We Say Good-bye'. It seemed to fit the place. And I had a drink which I'd paid for. And a certain fatalism sapped me.

It was a dingy neighbourhood, the kind of area where you notice the tone of slam that an expensive car door makes, outside the window behind your back. A heavy, muffled tone. Three times. Gerald and two others.

They walked right past, without noticing me. They ordered drinks and mixed with the group at the bar. Then Gerald turned to me and nodded. He drank and blinked and listened to the argy-bargy. Ella sang on her own.

I went to the bar and ordered another drink. I was served. Gerald nodded at Billy. I wasn't charged.

'Cheers,' I said.

Gerald nodded and turned away. There were four suited backs in the semicircle. I took my drink to my table and sat down.

Gerald waited and then he joined me. He sat down.

'All right?'

'Yes. And you?'

He blinked, and tapped his cigarette ash on to the carpet.

'Finished?' he asked.

'Let me buy you one.'

'Nah. Keep your hand in your pocket.' The blue eyes considered me. 'Take it as a Christmas present.' He watched me. 'You know, it doesn't mean a bloody thing, does it?'

'No,' I said, restraining myself from asking him what didn't mean a bloody thing – in case I should be perceived as being clever.

'Storm in a teacup,' he said.

'Yes.'

'I thought you'd understand. She told me you weren't stupid.'

'What else did she tell you?'

'I never listen to her. Finished?' he asked again.

'You tell me.'

We might as well have it out here; I wouldn't get far down the road.

I looked at him, and to my slow surprise his eyes seemed to indicate that the balance of power was not tilted in his favour. I don't know why, but there was a weak query in his eyes, hidden yet genuine, a chink in the threat.

It was true that there was a stalemate. He couldn't destroy me without destroying himself. He knew that there was the set of evidence with someone else; he had no way of knowing that it was with Davis. So it was a stalemate. I hadn't thought that common sense was his strong point; and I still didn't think so, sitting opposite him. But I could pretend that I did.

'Yes,' I said, 'I've finished what she asked me to do. I've done it. I've finished.'

He blinked. We stood up. He walked back to the bar. Billy refilled his glass. I was uncertain whether to be exhilarated or confused. His blank, dead stare had followed me to the door, and it followed me as I walked down cold and empty streets to the tube station.

I didn't sleep well that night. If I closed my eyes the image of Gerald dogged me. I felt him blink. With my eyes open, I thought of N. I thought about seeing her again. It was nearly a month since we had been together. I had finished. I had completed what N had asked me to do. I was part of a very formal dance, which lasted until dawn.

I stayed in my rooms until the last moment. In the morning and afternoon I read through what I had written to George, searching perversely for some angle which might enable me to carry on. There wasn't one. She had said everything that she might possibly say to George, and she was no longer attached to him.

At six o'clock there was no longer the rush hour. She would be waiting.

It was cold. It was January again, and Portsmouth Station. I was nervous.

I took a taxi to 15B. There were no lights on, but the house was warm. I walked through the rooms. I saw our bedroom, with a few articles of her clothing on the carpet and on the bed. I was filled with a strange anguish of nostalgia, I wanted to go back and hide in that love for her.

I watched ten minutes of a television programme, downstairs in the sitting-room, and then I went out and stood on the front doorstep. I closed the door behind me.

I walked quickly through the backstreets of the residential area, huddled against the cold. Stiff, frozen shrubs rustled like plastic bin-liners. There was an unremitting hardness to all physical objects. A streetlight. A plate-glass window. A line of kerbstones. That long stretch of crisp grass in front of the war monument. The edge of the sea as it licked the shingles was like spittle around regurgitated, broken teeth.

I hardly knew her. She was thin, with few cosmetics. She was dressed in a floppy two-piece suit, trousers and jacket, and an open-necked shirt. She had had her hair cut short. She looked like an undernourished bird of prey; with piercing, sunken eyes she seemed dwarfed by the roaring fire in the hearth behind her.

Every day of our separation returned to haunt us, like a state occasion which we had tried unsuccessfully to avoid. For half an hour we searched for a way across the distance between us, but we had no sense of our footing. I was frightened of her and of our deadened response to each other. I asked her if she would mind if I went to bed.

'Of course not,' she said. She reached for a cigarette. I opened my case and took out the papers, which I left with her.

I lay awake upstairs in the darkness, waiting without any expectation whatsoever. I watched thin streaks of cloud in an otherwise open sky, and I tried to sleep. Several hours later she came quietly into the studio and sat on the bed beside me.

'I won't come to bed,' she said. 'I want to sit up.'

I had that dream, a split second of it, the image of my mother's bedside. I visited that dream and then quickly shut the door on it by waking up. It was a dream that I had had before.

It was six in the morning. The room was warm, the sky outside the window was thick black. I lay in the bed in the studio.

For the first time in several years I thought back over my mother's slow suicide. Her indifference towards my two elder sisters and me. How she had quietly refused to see any doctor. How ridiculously inadequate I had been amongst that huge burst of maturity which caught my sisters and flung them forward, until they were no more than two other shapes on the screen which I had erected around my mother and me. I was a late child, who failed to bring love. Harmless, but a spectator.

I had a feeling that N would not return. And then I was afraid that she would return, and she would have thought about us, and she would have decided against us.

I got out of bed, and went to the desk and tried to write to her.

At eight she came, in a nightdress and a coat. I tried to explain what I was doing but she took me back to bed. She made me hold her and she fell asleep in my arms.

'No,' she said, 'I don't want to talk about anything until we've had something to eat.'

I waited in the office for her to get dressed. We read newspapers during our sojourn at the Greasy Spoon. Then we went back and sat in the office with a pot of coffee.

'I didn't want to lose George,' she said. 'All these years I didn't have the courage. And I suppose that I liked the idea of having power over him, which I couldn't admit to myself. I thought about that a lot over Christmas. I don't know what you make of me.'

There was an iconoclastic clink as the spout of the coffee pot ducked against the rim of a cup. Her lip twitched irregularly. She was drawn from lack of sleep, bathed in what seemed to be a pale resolution, underneath the bob of boyish hair.

'What will you do now?' I asked her.

'I'll decide when to send the thing to George, or if I should go down and give it to him.'

'I wouldn't do that.'

'How would you do it?'

'See him, then send it to him, then see him again.'

'I'll have to think about it. Is that the best way of signing someone off?' She didn't glance at me.

'There probably isn't a good way.'

'No.'

'How about a walk?'

She agreed.

At the top of the sea-wall I turned and looked down at the very empty carpark. 'What *will* you do now?'

'January and February – there isn't very much to do.'

We walked on for a few yards. 'Don't you think that we've got everything out of the way?' I asked, blindly.

'Yes.'

She said nothing else. I asked her if she wanted to go back inside, out of the cold. She shook her head. 'I want to walk, not for very long. I don't care about the cold.'

We went on.

'Before we go back – ' she suddenly started, 'I want you to know something. I'm free now, which is different. Things are not as clear as they were before.'

'I know.'

'Did you see Fiona?' she asked suddenly.

I blushed. 'Yes.'

'Did you sleep with her?'

'Yes. Literally speaking.'

She nodded. 'It was to be expected.'

'Nothing happened.'

'No. I wouldn't care if it had. What a waste of time it all is; most of it. What did you talk about?'

'Fiona likes you, you know.'

'Yes, we're friends.'

'She said that you loved me.'

'And you believed her?'

'Yes. I wanted to believe her. Shouldn't I have?'

I saw that behind her stare her mind was picking through me. The stare was the same as Gerald's, for a moment, but the mind was very different.

'What else did Fiona say?'

196

'Not much.'

'Silly cow.'

'Did you screw Gerald over Christmas?'

'Would you have cared?'

'Yes, I would. I would have cared for *you*.'

The cold had begun to sting her eyes and mine. We walked back. She explained to me what Christmas had meant to her, and to her self-respect. She talked about her freedom. We were both frightened, at first, of nakedness and warmth; and then we weren't frightened at all. We were shy, and thin and undernourished, and we started again with freedom.

Eighteen

We were happy then. Through the winter, through January and February, we lived together and we were happy. The past had had its own design, which might even have served us at the time; but now it was shed, it was severed and we were buoyant.

In due course the restaurant opened and we made our way back to 15B. Love became her. She filled out, she became more voluptuous. She stopped smoking cigarettes; so undramatically that I didn't notice it at first. She sought to touch and to be touched. She changed her mind about small things, and then couldn't really be bothered with them. She guided me back to work on my stories, although she wasn't above interrupting me. I had ten stories, wasn't that enough? Fifteen, she commanded me. Why? Why not, she said, you don't want to be a lover all your life, do you?

Yes, I did.

I had no more stories. I wanted to write about her. I asked her to tell me again about her life. She laughed, and refused.

She went to London and stayed overnight. When she returned she had that same calmness. With absolute imperturbability she bestowed love, at her leisure, as if it were once again part and parcel of a source with which she was intimate.

There were only two bits of news – her friend in publishing wanted to read my stories, and Gerald was coming down to go through the accounts.

'I don't want to be here.'

'Well, don't be here then,' she agreed, 'if Gerald upsets you. He really isn't worth it. But if you're in that kind of mood, just stay clear of him. Don't rock the boat.'

She was to see Gerald on a Saturday evening. She was in no hurry. She sat downstairs in 15B and watched the early-evening news. Quite calmly she ate a plate of ice-cream. I looked for some tension in her but there was none; she wasn't the slightest bit enclosed. If anything she was lethargic. She stretched and went upstairs to change.

She said that she would be back about ten-thirty, and she was. She was fresh and complacent and unmoved by her meeting with Gerald.

I asked about Gerald, and I asked if she had told him about us.

'Yes,' she said. 'I don't know why I did. It's none of his business. But I think that he knew.'

'And did you tell him that you were going to divorce George?'

'No.' She thought about this. 'I shall tell George first. Don't worry.'

'How are you?' I could only wonder at her.

'I'm fine. Shouldn't I be?'

She smiled. I looked at a warm, completed circle. My insecurities touched her only at a tangent.

It was a bit like we had been during our stay in Sidmouth, only this time the innocence was no top-heavy bloom.

There was the feeling that we would stay together because there was no reason for us to do so. There was only our sense of repose from the world. For me, it was the feeling of sharing a soul without its many costumes.

David obliged us by receiving an invitation to spend the Easter holidays with a friend's family in Switzerland, and N encouraged him to go, without a murmur of complaint.

In the afternoons, she sat in her bedroom and typed out the stories I had written. I went to the studio and tried to write.

There was nothing I wanted to write about. I loved her and she returned my love.

When she had finished her work as a typist, she mailed the stories off to London. I still wanted to write about her, there were holes that I had to fill in. I asked her about Gerald, and about Emerson.

'Why?' She was genuinely perplexed. 'Let all that go. It's over and done with. It's got nothing to do with us.'

I asked her to marry me. She looked at me severely.

'That's not something to joke about.'

'It's not a joke.'

She shook her head as though I was crazy.

We waited for a month. I asked her again. This time, she put her foot down. 'You're getting worried,' she said. 'It's time we went to London.'

She sat in the uncomfortable chair in my rooms, telephoning around London. She had made, I realised, six copies of the manuscript, and had sent one to each of six publishers. Now she played them off, one against the other, bluffing each of them with another's interest.

Was this ethical?

Her contempt was sharp. She had no concern for ethics. 'There's nothing that's going to make them act faster than knowing that one of their competitors is interested. You're not pleading, you're looking for a contract. And if you can't get what you want by being honest then you must lie, whitely. You must fabricate. If you can't do it for yourself, you must get someone else to do it for you.'

By Friday afternoon, she believed that she had a final offer, from Deborah. They would meet for dinner on Saturday evening.

N and I went out on Friday night, but our celebration was private. On Saturday she left early in the afternoon; taking a taxi because, she said, she wanted to shop before dining with Deborah. She wouldn't let me go with her.

'I want you to do something for me.'

From the bottom of her suitcase, she pulled out a large envelope addressed to George.

'Please post this. I would like you to post it for me.' She looked away. She collected a few belongings and came back to stand in front of me. I held her tightly. 'Well,' she smiled, 'that seems to clear everything up. How do I look?'

'You look confident.'

'Good.'

She telephoned at midnight. She said that she was still at Deborah's. She was tipsy, her speech was slightly slurred. She was too tired to wait for a taxi. She said that Deborah had offered her a bed. I told her to take it. 'It's all worked out,' she said. She sounded tired. I told her to sleep well and I thanked her.

I awoke on Sunday morning feeling wonderful, with the thought in my mind that we would walk through a park together and then we would drive out of London. I would take her home and lie beside her and love her.

I opened her suitcase and saw her address book lying on top of her clothes. I knew Deborah's surname and there was a home number. I dialled.

I introduced myself, and I was congratulated. She was enthusiastic about my stories, and wry about N's method of blackmail in sorting the contract out. I was told that I should get a more professional agent. No, N wasn't with her. They had drafted the agreement yesterday afternoon. N had left at about five-thirty.

I drove to Portsmouth and parked N's car near the monument. A swampy green sea licked tamely at the weed-encrusted concrete beneath the funfair. There was a forbidding bareness about the sea-front, a senselessness of shingle and water.

I walked towards the brick arches and the restaurant. There was something about that one arch, the concrete streaked with stains, as if it had rusted, and the opening in the back which hung like an ever-changing picture of the harbour channel. Above the roof of the Mercedes.

I looked up at the bedroom window. The curtains were drawn. We had loved here, with a passion, through the cold.

I lifted the latch on the bar door and went inside. It was near the end of the midday session. In the corner by the door a father, a mother and two children had finished their lunch and were putting on rainproof clothes. A young couple were finishing their drinks; she wore an engagement ring and he had a blue crash helmet beside him on the bench seat.

Gerald was standing at the far end of the bar, listening without interest to the remarks of a spider-veined barfly. Gerald was straightbacked, in a blue suit and polished black shoes, the full vodka and tonic and bucket of ice in front of him. He was impassive. When I walked towards the bar he looked at his watch and nodded at me expressionlessly.

'Serve him,' Gerald instructed the barman, 'and then that's the lot.'

'Time please,' the barman called.

The young motorcyclist brought his empties back to the bar and offered to meet the barman outside in ten minutes. The barman hesitated.

'That's all right; you can be off now,' Gerald dismissed him. 'Be in at six-thirty, all right, son?'

We were left to each other.

He swallowed at his drink, thick-lipped, like a fleshy grouper fish.

'How's your book?' he asked.

'Fine,' I said, as though it was away at school.

'Yes, she told me about it.'

He raised a deep, blank stare, as though he was about to stun a caged rabbit with a brick hammer.

I raised my glass. 'Cheers. Here's to absent relatives.'

If he had brought the ball of his hand up, it would have slammed against the bottom of the beer glass. The lower lip would have shattered against my teeth and the top lip would have sliced along the bridge of my nose and embedded itself in my eyes. 'Absent writers,' he said.

'I want to marry her.'

His expression was shallow; contempt floated on the surface.

'Marry her?' he laughed. 'You'd do better to bloody piss on her. Or didn't she tell you?'

His eyes were misty with alcohol. His menace hung like a stiff, dull fire curtain. 'You won't keep her. She'll be back. She always comes back.'

He coughed, and he wiped his lips with a silk handkerchief which he pulled out of his breast pocket. He drummed the fingers of his left hand on the bar and coughed again. Then he sneezed violently, four or five times.

'Bloody perfume,' he said, straightening up and blinking now, rapidly, wrinkling his nose. 'Bloody thing.'

He packed himself off to the Gents, thick-headed, leaning forward between the tables as though he was mounted on the prow of an icebreaker. He groaned and sneezed on the other side of the door.

I took the stairs quickly and silently, two at a time. There was no one in the office; there was only N's coat, her leather handbag and a carrier bag from a men's outfitters in London. I left the door open and went on upstairs.

I opened the studio door. The curtains were not very efficient in shutting out the daylight, but in any case the bedside lamp was on. She lay, a clothed still-life, with her legs drawn up, her buttocks presented on the edge of the duvet.

'Get out.'

Her voice commanded in tone but the words were misshapen and slobbered.

'Get out, Gerald. No more.'

'It's not Gerald,' I said.

She made to roll over but moaned and fell back. I went round to her side of the bed. She was disfigured. Her top lip was split, the blood caked and glutinous. It formed, with her hair, a maroon clot which sucked her into the bedsheet. Her left eye was swollen.

'I'll get the police.'

'No!' Her voice rasped. 'No. He's finished. He knows that now.'

'He's still here.'

Some swollen smile floundered across the surface of her lips. 'It's not as bad as it looks. Trust me. If you go to the police he's got nothing to lose. He'll find you and kill you. Wait at home.'

'Come with me.'

'Leave the car outside.' Her eyes begged me to leave. She sighed. 'I'm sorry. I didn't want you to see.'

At the foot of the stairs was the one-armed bandit. I was in front of it when Gerald came out of the Gents. I wrenched the arm down. Gerald smiled dully.

'New perfume she's got,' he said, clutching a packet of Kleenex. 'I'm surprised you can stick it.'

'It's shit,' I said, 'smarmy, vicious shit. Shit sticking to shit, that's the feeling, isn't it? Like an endless stream of shit dribbling out of your brain and sticking in your throat. From your throat to the top of your head, nothing but shit. I'll turn you in.'

He blinked, and he laughed. 'No you won't,' he said. 'She never signed the deposition. She'll tell you why not. Then see if you want to marry her.'

When she returned to 15B, after dark, I was in the middle of packing. I wanted to stay, but the atmosphere was too overwhelming. I wasn't scared of Gerald, I wasn't even angry with him after my outburst in the bar – I was simply defeated. I didn't understand.

I could have packed and left before she came home, but I stayed.

She had cleaned herself up. There was, in her walk from the door through the sitting-room, a sadness and a pride which moved me in spite of myself. I couldn't think of anything to ask her. She walked on into the kitchen and stood with her hands on either side of the sink. I didn't know what to do.

She came back behind me and passed on into the hallway. She picked up the phone and dialled, and listened for a moment before replacing the receiver. When she returned to the sitting-room, she said: 'I can't think where to go.'

I said that I would go back to London and leave her.

She made no comment. I went into the kitchen. I wanted to keep her at a distance.

She seemed to find something to do in the sitting-room. I picked up the electric kettle and filled it from the tap. I put the lid back on and set the kettle down on the light blue surface, near the socket. All the while, the thoughts in my mind were swept around by my emotion. Despair, love and fear canoned back and forth.

Eventually I asked her: 'Will it go on with Gerald?'

She was standing with her back to the grey, cold bars of the electric fire.

'No.'

'How can you say that!' I raged at her. 'You don't know! You don't know that it won't go on! Why did you let him bring you back from London? Why? Look how hurt you are; I . . . '

I saw the swollen eye, and the thin plaster across the top of her lip; and I saw that I would never understand her. I reached and touched her cheek above the plaster. 'Look at the hurt . . . '

'It will go away,' she said.

'But he'll be there, won't he? You'll always go to him. He said that.'

'I will never go back to him.'

'You're lying.'

'No, I'm telling you the truth. I might well have used Gerald before, but not any more.'

'Used him for *what*?'

'It's finished.'

'I don't believe you! How can you say that it's finished?'

'I can.'

'How? You can't answer for yourself. Tell me.'

She looked away.

'I love you,' I pleaded with her.

'I know.'

'Then tell me.'

She came downstairs. She had bathed and had changed her clothes. I watched her walk towards me. She had that uncertain smile, and the beauty hung about her like a discarded gesture.

I will always remember that moment; and I will always remember her words before she had gone upstairs to bath.

'I needed him, before; after George. But it's gone. I had to prove it to myself. This time he tried to force me and I knew then that it was finished. Nothing in me responded.'

'But it might do, some time. You'll go back.'

'Never!'

'Then *sign* the papers,' I urged her.

'I have. The signed copy is in my safe. I'll use it if I have to; if he comes after me again. I will. I promise you. I can understand why you don't trust me. I've told you that sometimes I don't trust myself. But this time it isn't only me. You see, I'm pregnant. I've been carrying your baby for two and a half months.'

Nineteen

Slowly and stealthily, the English spring made an appearance. When, from the window of our bedroom, I watched N leave the house, I saw a woman who had anticipated spring, a woman in full sap walking across a pale, watery lawn.

She drove herself away along the avenue, under trees whose gaunt fingers struck freshly painted dark green claws above her car. She bore only one small scar, on the top edge of her lip.

She was going to see George, for the last time as his wife. And the next day I took the train to London to meet Deborah.

When N and I met up, outside Victoria Station, after her appointment with the Harley Street gynaecologist, she told me that the divorce would go through without any difficulty. George, it seemed, held no grudge whatsoever. She had not told him about being pregnant.

She was as generous in her loving as she had ever been, but there was now a sealed resolution about her which brooked no interference from me.

She laughed when I asked her if the conception had been an accident, and I could only strike back at her by suggesting that Gerald was the father.

'Gerald,' she snapped, 'can't have children.'

When I asked her if she loved me, she said yes, she loved me.

At the end of May, we went for a week to Cornwall. We stayed with a friend of hers called Pat, who ran a dilapidated pub–hotel on the northern coast. She was a former police sergeant, tall and formidable. She and N laughed their way through dinner with stories about the criminal fraternity. I went to bed early. When N joined me, she was happy that the two of them were still close friends.

'The last time I came down here,' she mused, 'Pat had just broken the jaw of a biker who thought that he had the right to stay for a late drink. She was assigned to keep an eye on me when George was arrested. I once made the mistake of thinking she was stupid. She's the only person I've ever met who doesn't see any difference between hitting a man and hitting a woman. She's rather beautiful, don't you think?'

'Someone you would trust.'

'Yes.'

On the northern coast of Cornwall, very quiet although we were only five hundred yards from the sea, in our bedroom, I knelt and watched my penis pucker the thin scarlet lips of her vagina. They received me rather like the flaps of a security-screening machine at an airport. N, biting the side of one hand, watched on the screen of her closed eyelids the passage of the contents.

I knelt and serviced her apparatus with the most delicate attention; until she was peeled back from herself into emptiness, her limbs bewildered, her eyes full of the strange panic of stampede. 'How well you know me!' A high priestess, with a vision of cataclysm, farting and crying, beside herself with the glorious humiliation of pleasure.

I felt that I was becoming increasingly unreal.

She agreed to let me photograph her. She said that she would have the films developed, she would keep the negatives and send me a copy of the prints.

Each morning it was foggy. I went down to the bar and ordered our breakfast from Pat, while N bathed and dressed. She wore large sweaters and a healthy flush to her skin. The breakfasts were English and gigantic. Between us we cleared the board and then we sat with coffee and newspapers. Each time my mind stirred I found myself placing my hand on N's thigh, and her own hand would come across and lie on mine, like a consolation. Near noon, the first visitor having just come into the pub, the day stretched and sighed, the last of the fog parted company from the land and we would feel the blank blue vault of sky looking for a sign of life along the cliff tops.

We went across the road, down the farm track to the cliff, each day at noon. We found ourselves a ruin, forty minutes' stroll from the pub. Undisturbed by any tourists we lay and read, or sat and looked at the Atlantic.

Across watermarks of the red froth which was discharged out at sea by the tin mine, the breeze chased cloud shadows – across waves which scrambled over the reefs, across the face of the cliffs and over and past us, leaving us with a sense of slow erosion.

I asked her if she wanted to walk further down the cliff.

'No,' she said. 'You go. I'll finish this book and wait for you here. I wouldn't like the climb back.'

After I had walked for a hundred yards I stopped and waved. She waved back.

I plunged on downwards, dimly aware of the false exuberance which was evaporating off the surface of my melancholy. The path didn't reach the ocean. It took me within thirty or forty feet, which was enough. On my left there was a beautiful magenta smudge of cloud. Waves smashed headlong against the cliff with a noise like crumpling metal in a car crash; the spray jumped desperately at the rocks and failed to get a hold. It reminded me only of a Hollywood Western, when the brawler lurches forward into a solid fist and reels punch drunk back into the arms of his followers. For a time I sat in shadow, exasperated at the strength of my feelings for her.

I climbed back and lay beside N in the sun. I listened to the vapid ring of the sea's challenge and the rustle as she turned the pages of her book. Late in the afternoon, as the last acknowledge-ment of our endurance, a boiling light of sunset ricocheted across the goosepimpled surface of the ocean, soldering it to the jagged edge of the land.

'It's strange,' I said. 'I've always thought of you as having something to do with the sea. Something in the way you move around people, your hard-nosed people. I took it as your gift, something you were aware of.'

'I am aware of it.'

'But you're not like that, are you? You know exactly how much to give of yourself.'

'So do you.'

'Please then, please marry me.'

'No.' She closed the book and sat up, with her chin on her knees, gazing at the ocean. 'Ask me in five years.'

'But why?'

'Because from the beginning, from when I first met you, I planned to have this baby on my own.'

'I won't threaten you.'

'Who can say?'

'I can.'

She took a long time to answer, and then she said: 'It's getting cold.' She stood up.

'Why did you go to Gerald? Were you sick of my love?'

She murmured, 'I am a lot better off on my own. I had something to prove to myself. I wanted you to father a child. It wasn't a light decision.'

'You were never in love.'

'Yes. Oh yes. I care very much about you. I've cared about other people. I've trusted you more than almost anyone.' She smiled quickly. 'And I was right to trust you.'

She dusted off her skirt and took my arm.

'More right than I was.'

'No. I know that you trust me. That's why you're not going to make a scene. You're not a weak person. You're not stupid. I admire you for that.'

She held out her hand for me to take. 'Come on, let's walk back.'

We started along the cliff path. She shielded her eyes from the showers of brilliance which bounced up towards us off the water.

'You know,' she said, 'when I wasn't pregnant by Christmas, I had decided not to go on with you. I thought that it was unfair, and my feelings for you were getting in the way. Fiona talked me out of my decision.'

'She knew that you wanted to have a child?'

'Oh yes. But she's good at compromises, I'm not so good at them.'

'Would marrying me be a compromise?'

'Yes. For both of us. We would destroy each other, I promise you.'

When we lay in bed, late at night, we were uncomfortable with each other. There was nothing really to say. She was calmly detached and I felt the pressure of isolation. I got out of bed and went down the corridor to the bathroom. When I came back she had switched on the light and was reading.

'Is it a good book?' I demanded.

'Yes.'

'Better than mine?'

She closed the book and looked at me sadly. I was being foolish, I knew that. I walked towards the window. Her voice reached out to me.

'Just because I've said that I don't want to be married, it doesn't mean that I'm rejecting you.'

I hated her.

I turned and I said: 'George killed the wrong man, didn't he?'

She picked up the book and her glance fell across its printed pages.

'George killed the wrong man because it was Gerald you were having the affair with. Wasn't it? George noticed that you liked the rough.' I sat down beside her. I watched her. 'What was Emerson like in bed?'

She held my stare. In her eyes there was only a kindness and a dismay. She whispered: 'Nobody's threatening you. I'm not threatening you. Come to bed. Don't worry, I love you. Don't be scared. Come to bed.'

For a moment I felt that she was right. I really only wanted to lose myself in her, to feel her love. There was a beseeching acquiescence in her eyes, a concern. She said: 'It's just that I'm not sure about being married again. It's so soon. Perhaps . . . '

And, with the beginning of the compromise, I knew that she was lying.

'Perhaps you never saw Emerson. Did they make you see him when he was dead? Or was he too badly disfigured for you to identify him?'

She threw off the bedclothes and ran to the basin in the corner of the room. I watched the cellulite shudder on her bottom as she retched. I looked away, down at the bed and the creased sheet on which she had been lying. When I turned back, she was shivering and looking at herself in the mirror over the basin.

I handed her a sweater. 'I'll make you a cup of tea.'

She nodded.

When I came back from the pub kitchen, she was curled up protectively on her side of the bed. Her frightened eyes followed the cup as I rested it on the bedside table. Some time later, when she had not moved, I came to bed. I switched off the light and lay against her cold skin.

In our ruin, the next afternoon, she picked at her skirt and told me.

'I was stupid, unforgivably stupid. Gerald was in love with me. He always had been. It was such a tight family. And Sylvie was a stupid bitch. She set herself up to challenge it, and when that didn't work she crucified Gerald. She made him suffer for it. She never forgave him for the fact that he couldn't give her a child, and of course George and I had David. Gerald was as much of a father as George, which Sylvie couldn't forgive. Their marriage was a nightmare.

'God knows why they didn't get a divorce. She was obviously only staying for the money. Gerald felt guilty and inadequate, and he drank. I don't excuse myself, although there are excuses. Gerald was better when he was with us. Anything would have been better for him than staying around Sylvie.

'George was very sorry for him. George saw himself as head of the family, he was proud that I worried about Gerald. There weren't any boundaries. There was no end to the love. I had a new baby, two grown men, and Paul, who was as happy as I was with this new family. There weren't any limits.

'You must think that I am pathetically naïve. It seemed to be completely harmless. It just didn't occur to me until later, when Gerald and I became involved. And at first even that seemed natural.

'I don't know why I didn't tell George. I should have told him straight away, and I'm sure that nothing would have come of it. Gerald would have straightened himself out and I would have accepted that I had made a silly mistake. I don't know if it could have lasted; or I suppose I thought that sooner or later Gerald would find somebody else. We were always setting him up with women, but he didn't make a move. I realised that he was in love with me.

'From that time, everything changed. Everything became partitioned. I tried to manipulate everyone, including myself; trying to simplify things. George adored me – you were right – I provoked that. And with Gerald I got over the guilt.

'If Gerald turned nasty, it was because of me. I was responsible. I know that. In spite of everything, I still care for him. He is the most misused.

'I felt completely safe. There was just the right amount of danger. George and I didn't have sex very often. I was in control. Both of us liked a lot of privacy. But he caught me by surprise one day, not long after I had been with Gerald.

'He went mad.

'He would have killed me at first, but I came out with some sob story. I had trained him very well.

'He called Gerald over and they spent half the night deciding what to do. God knows how Gerald handled it, that first night, but he did. He couldn't have handled it much longer than that. Nothing worked. We even had a doctor in to give George a shot. He wouldn't sleep. He was mad. We couldn't hang on to him. Years of frustration came out – things that I had never realised about his relationship with his father and his fear of the world.

'I refused to tell George anything and he respected me for that. But he tried to trace back every movement I had made in the last months. In the daytimes he and Gerald would go out driving around London, looking for this phantom lover.

'I couldn't stand it any longer. I moved in with Jean and Charlie. George understood that. He wanted the children out of the way. But it didn't stop him from coming round and punching Charlie when Charlie told him that he was being a bloody stupid child. It broke Charlie. He died just before the trial.

'I didn't know what to do. Neither did Gerald. George exhausted him. Gerald said that we would have to come up with somebody. I told George that he should take it out on me, but I had set him up too well; he would never harm me.

'Gerald found Emerson. I never met Robert Emerson. I was shown photographs of him at the trial – before, and after, George had killed him.

'I don't know where Gerald found Emerson but he did. And he gave him thirty thousand pounds to leave the country. Gerald told him some story about a divorce trick. Emerson agreed with the plan. He was broke.

'He had a flat in Knightsbridge. Gerald took some of my clothes and photographs and put them in the flat. He told George that he had found out where I went. They were to go round there together – but at the last moment George wanted to go in on his own. Gerald dropped him off in Knightsbridge and he thought that George would find out that Emerson had left the country. Even the night porter had been tipped and left with a forwarding address in Australia, if George should enquire.

'Gerald waited on the other side of the square for two hours. When he saw George came out, he knew that something was wrong. When George got into the car, he opened his overcoat and his clothes were covered in blood. He had a suitcase with my belongings in it. Gerald drove him home. George drank half a bottle of whiskey and went to sleep on the sofa.

'He killed Emerson as soon as he broke into the flat. Emerson was in there. He hadn't gone. He must have thought that it was all a bit of a game. George stayed with the body for two hours.

'I didn't go to the trial on the day of the pathologist's report.

'The thing between Gerald and I should have ended after that. It did, for a while. I moved to Portsmouth. It became incidental. Gerald has suffered more than I have. It became nasty and perverse

213

and loveless. It was like a ritual. It was something to hang on to. We couldn't untangle ourselves. Do you see?'

'You never told George?'

She stared at me. 'What good would it do him? What possible good would it do him to know that he killed the wrong man?' She plucked a piece of grass and dropped it on to her skirt. 'What man is there to kill? No one is guilty, are they? Are they?'

'Yes,' I said.

She picked the piece of grass off her skirt, holding it between her fingernails for a moment before letting it fall to the ground beside her.

'It will be nice having something new and innocent. I think so. And knowing that it's a love child. We don't want to hurt each other.'

She stood up. She shook out her skirt. She walked away, balancing on the rocks, occasionally reaching a hand behind her to steady herself.

In the evening she came downstairs into the bar wearing her rings, the sapphires and the diamonds. She invited Pat to eat with us on our last night in Cornwall.

When I asked her upstairs why she had worn the rings, she said that she had just wanted to see how they felt. She invited me to make love. In the morning, she drove us back to Portsmouth, happy and with a sparkle in her eye. She had never looked lovelier.

I was to go to London to help with the editing of my stories. She handed me a small case at the station.

'It's a present.'

I asked her again, there at the end of the platform, to marry me. She smiled. 'Go back to the flat and think about it seriously.'

'I will. Will you?'

'Yes. I promise you. I love you.'

My rooms were effectively destroyed. The furniture was in pieces and the upholstery was slashed. My clothes were piled in a corner of the bedroom with an open suitcase on top of them. The carpets and the bed were damp and stained – a gallon-container of bleach had been emptied over the walls and carpet in the sitting-room; someone had soaked the bed in cheap, pine-scented disinfectant.

I opened the window and sat in the middle of the wreckage. There was nothing worth saving. It had only been a makeshift room at the best of times. By the window, my desk and my papers lay unmolested. On the mantelpiece was an envelope.

I stood up and took it into the kitchen. I opened the case she had handed me at the station. Inside was the small collection of items which I had taken to N's when we had first decided to live together: my sentimental belongings, newspaper cuttings, and an undeveloped film.

I opened the envelope. There was a cheque for three thousand pounds, a credit note from British Airways, and a sealed letter from N. It was written on cheap notepaper, and the letter was dated from Cornwall.

'My darling,
    'I have hurt you, sharply and suddenly. There will be a shock which will slowly go away, and which will take you away from me. I don't feel that there are any questions to be answered, or that I need to explain. I think that you understand. No? I'm sure that you do.
    'With all my love,

N.'

Twenty

I went away. I never did write about N. I travelled. There were only tangled simplicities, many of them within myself, and from them I could only contrive an artificial complexity.

I couldn't have stayed in England. I went first to Paris and then, through contacts, to Turkey. I ended up on a small agricultural commune that survived the political repression only because it kept its sympathies and antipathies securely hidden. There, amongst people with whom I could hardly talk, I worked manually until at the end of the day I was exhausted.

It was a long way from N. I remembered her frequently, and with the slow assumption of my loneliness I admired her solitude. I had no clear sense of what pain she made dealings with, nor what love she felt.

It grew cold, and so I returned to England. I heard from my publisher that N had given birth to a baby girl. I sent them some red roses.

There have been moments when I would have loved to hear her talk again, to have her voice slip from her lips across to me. To watch her in the wingbacked chair, with one leg folded under her, the other stretched nonchalantly towards the floor. Feeling the night age against her perfume, the rise and fall of her hesitancy.

It was dawn.

I awoke my wife with a cup of coffee. I had watched her for several minutes, sleeping peacefully. I wondered how much she knew and what exactly I had told her at odd moments about N. I couldn't remember if I had told her the truth.

She awoke quickly and clearly. She once told me that she had the ability to do this only since the birth of her first child. She could react instantly and surely for about ten minutes, and then she could go back to bed and fall immediately asleep again. Unless she really had to get up.

I asked her whether she minded if we stayed in England a little longer.

'You want to go down to Portsmouth?' she asked.

'Yes.'

'All right.'`

'Are you sure?'

'Yes. I think you should go. She'd like to see you.'

'I'm sorry to wake you.'

'That's all right, I'll go back to sleep.'

'I'll call British Airways.'

'Okay, darling.'

She rolled over.

I telephoned N. She was surprised and pleased. She asked me to meet her at the restaurant.

It was the same old train. I fought my way through the crowds of commuters arriving at Waterloo, and I had a carriage to myself on the journey south. As the carriage rocked gently from side to side, I felt childish. I felt a surge of expectation.

The train stopped. The electric engines ticked plaintively and shut themselves off. Both sides of the track were lined with trees; the remnants of last year's undergrowth formed a sparse and docile barrier behind the rusted fencing. We had perhaps stopped at a countryside halt.

I dreamed of N – the years ticking away.

Impatiently, I punched the metal lip with the ball of my hand and leaned out of the window. I looked towards the front of the train, three carriages ahead of me.

The patch of woodland conceded to open fields. A small boy had climbed the fence and was standing near the railway line, looking up at a signal post on which his kite string was snagged.

His companion stood in the field, watching. The driver of my train was at the tip of the post, hanging on with one arm while with the other he tried to free the kite. It was a bright, red, diamond-shaped kite with a ribboned tail.

He freed the string and the kite dropped to the ground. The small boy watched it solemnly, not daring to move. The driver climbed down the signal gantry, gathered the kite and walked back to the boy, who made no move to accept it. The driver lectured the boy, and when the lecture was done he waved the boy away up the bank and shouted at his companion before climbing back into the cab. The train moved off. When my carriage passed the boy he was sitting on the bank, the kite at his side, watching the train go past, very seriously guarding the open mind which belonged to him.

I wanted to know what he would do next; I leaned far out of the window but the last picture I had of him was of that same calm pondering as he sat on the bank while his companion rewound the kite string on a piece of wood.

I telephoned her again from Portsmouth Station.

'Where are you?' she asked.

'I can't see you.'

She paused.

'I understand,' she said.

Richard Thornley, born in the Midlands in 1950, grew up in the South of France. He has written plays, films and books, including a collection of stories, *Zig-Zag*, and a first novel, *Attempts to Join Society*. In 1986 he received the George Orwell Award for Literature. He is married, and lives in California, the South of France and Worcestershire.

A NOTE ON THE TYPE

This book was typeset using Ehrhardt, a typeface based on a design by the Hungarian Nicholas Kis (1650–1702) who worked as a punchcutter in Amsterdam from 1680 to 1689 at the height of the Dutch Republic. A set of his matrices was acquired by the Ehrhardt foundry in Leipzig, hence the name adopted when the modern face was cut.
The type has all the sturdy Dutch character of the *Goût Hollandais*, the characteristic type-style of the latter part of the seventeenth century. The relatively narrow, densely black letters also show the influence of German Black Letter type.